Desert War

Desert War

Book 4 in the
Soldier of the Queen Series

By

Griff Hosker

Desert War

Published by Sword Books Ltd 2024

Copyright ©Griff Hosker First Edition 2024

The author has asserted their moral right under the Copyright, Designs and Patents Act, 1988, to be identified as the author of this work.
All Rights reserved. No part of this publication may be reproduced, copied, stored in a retrieval system, or transmitted, in any form or by any means, without the prior written consent of the copyright holder, nor be otherwise circulated in any form of binding or cover other than that in which it is published and without a similar condition being imposed on the subsequent purchaser.
A CIP catalogue record for this title is available from the British Library.

Dedication

To all my readers. To me, you are all friends. We have journeyed far already who knows where it will end?

Desert War

Contents

Contents 1
Prologue 3
Chapter 1 8
Chapter 2 17
Chapter 3 26
Chapter 4 35
Chapter 5 48
Chapter 6 59
Chapter 7 72
Chapter 8 82
Chapter 9 92
Chapter 10 102
Chapter 11 111
Chapter 12 122
Chapter 13 132
Chapter 14 143
Chapter 15 154
Chapter 16 170
Chapter 17 180
Chapter 18 194
Chapter 19 206
Chapter 20 216
Chapter 21 225
Chapter 22 234
Epilogue 243
Glossary 245
Historical Background 246
Other books by Griff Hosker 248

Desert War

Some of the characters in the book

The soldiers in Persia
Lieutenant Jack Roberts
Sergeant Major Syd Richardson
Sergeant Jake Johnson
Corporal Bill Brown
Trooper Eric Wise
Trooper Ralph Hunt
Trooper Fred Emerson
Trooper John Jones
Trooper Bill Bates
Trooper Dick Wilshaw
Trooper Bob Larriby

The Drillers
George Bernard Reynolds (Engineer)
Ken Collins (Driller)
Bert Willis (Driller)
Bill Ellis (Driller)
Wally Carmichael (Labourer)
Tommy Garstang (Labourer)
Erik Smith (Labourer)
George Law

Desert War

Jack

Prologue

    I am Jack Roberts. I began my career with the army fighting against the Zulus and it ended when I lost my left arm at the battle of Omdurman. My journey back from the Sudan was one where I came to terms with the loss of my limb. The despair I had felt when I had woken and seen the raw stump was replaced by relief. The nurses and doctors at the hospital had been kind but they had also pointed out how lucky I was. I was alive and I could still use my right arm. The long journey back to England helped me to learn to live with my disability. I even managed, by the time we passed Gibraltar, how to fill and light my pipe one handed. The sense of achievement was overwhelming. As a wounded hero of Omdurman, I was treated well on the voyage back to England. The gratitude of ordinary people humbled me but I disliked sympathy. Everyone who met me on the way back, seeing my uniform and my injury assumed that I was some kind of hero. I didn't feel that way. I had just done my duty.
    I determined to make something of myself but I did not know what. I had a pension and, as I had been an officer when I retired, it was better than it would have been as a sergeant major. For that, I was grateful to General Kitchener. The transformation from a man filled with self-pity to one who saw hope was complete by the time I reached London. I was in a better frame of mind than I had been in the Egyptian hospital. I reached the city too late to take a train to Liverpool and so I took a room in a hotel. I chose one that was close to Whitehall. I liked the sight of the uniforms. I had lived in the world of soldiers for a long time and it was comforting to see them.
    I walked up the Tottenham Court Road. The receptionist at the hotel had told me they had some good bookshops there. I had not bought any presents for my niece and nephew. I guessed that they were too old for toys and books would do. After buying a couple of nice books I found a pub just along from Trafalgar Square. I entered as I saw a couple of off-duty soldiers leaving with smiles on their faces. That was a good enough

recommendation for me. It had the smell of English food wafting through the door too and that enticed me. The food on the ship had been excellent but the smell of the roasting meat was irresistible. When I looked at the hand pumps on the bar and saw that they also served porter then I settled myself down to enjoy a couple of pints and savour the roast pork with apple sauce and roast potatoes. I had finished it and was on my second pint when I heard a voice I had not heard for some time.

"Jack, is that you?"

I looked up and saw my first officer from my days with the ESEG. It was Colonel Dickenson and he was now, not just a colonel, but he had the red tabs of the general staff. He was moving up the greasy ladder. I stood, "Congratulations on the promotion, sir."

He took in my civilian clothes and then my stump, "Sit, for goodness sake." I sat. "I can see that you have a tale to tell. Do you mind if I join you?"

"Of course not."

"What'll you have?"

"A pint of the porter, sir, if you don't mind."

I had filled my pipe and had it going by the time he returned. He sat and raised his glass to toast me, "Here's to old friends and those who never came back."

"Amen to that, sir. Cheers." I drank and then after placing the glass on the table took my pipe. It was still burning and I sucked on it. When it was drawing easily and I was aware that I was being studied I said, "I lost the lower arm at Omdurman. Private Adams, Ged, died there."

"Adams?" I saw him struggling to recall the name, "Oh, the batman. That is a shame. Tell me all." By the time I had finished, he said, "I know I should miss the life of an active soldier, Jack, but I don't. I am married now and have three children. I drink here most days and the biggest threat in my life is a paper cut."

"Well, sir, my life will change so perhaps I will enjoy a life of peace."

"Are you in London for long? I would love my wife to meet you."

I shook my head, "I want to see my son as soon as I can. I will get the first train I can in the morning."

Desert War

"How old is, what is his name, Griff?"

"Seventeen coming up to eighteen."

"Working?"

"Do you know, sir, I don't know. When I left for Sudan he was still at school, and you know how letters are often late."

"If I can do anything for him. I mean if he wants to join the army like his father...There are places at the Military College and we can put forward the names of sons of the men who have served their country. You, more than anyone, have served your country and served it well. Just let me know,"

"I will, sir, but first I need to speak to him. I have missed most of his childhood." I shrugged, "It is another reason I want to get home as fast as I can, sir."

He shook his head, "I am such a fool. Where are you staying?" I told him. "One of my duties is the issuing of travel warrants. I think a hero of Omdurman deserves to travel 1st Class. I shall send over a travel warrant to your hotel."

"There's no need, sir."

"Jack, there is every need. I may no longer be a proper soldier, but I respect those, like you, who were. Britain needs to honour its heroes and that is what you are, a hero." I nodded, "One thing though, as it is a military pass you will have to wear your uniform."

The messenger arrived just an hour after I had bid farewell to my old commanding officer. He must have gone back to his office to do it. I was touched by the gesture. He had gone out of his way to help me. The train ticket meant I would travel in comfort. One thing my loss of a limb had done was make everyone solicitous. The hotel had two porters carry my chest to the hansom cab and, at the station, the cab driver ensured that railway porters assisted me in carrying my luggage to the train. He even wished to refuse the tip.

I shook my head, "I don't need charity, my friend. You have been more than helpful and I am just rewarding that good service."

The train was at the platform as this was a terminus and they loaded my chest in the luggage van They both saluted me and I stood to attention when they did so. I went to find a seat. I saw the pipe smoke and chose that compartment. There was another occupant already there. Wearing glasses and smoking a pipe he was reading a book. He smiled, "A hero's farewell, my friend, and I can see that you have had adventures. The medals, the tanned skin and the lost limb all speak of a life well lived. If you too are travelling to Liverpool, we have a long journey ahead of us and it will wile away the hours. I am Rudyard Kipling, writer and poet, formerly of India and latterly of Charing Cross Road."

"I am Lieutenant Jack Roberts, sir, and I doubt that my story would interest you."

"Your tanned skin, the campaign medals and the lost arm tell something different."

I sighed and took out my pipe, I began to fill it.

He chuckled, "Better and better. I am guessing the lost arm is recent and yet you have mastered something which I thought impossible." He settled back into his seat, took out a pencil and notepad and said, "Go on, Jack. Tell your tale."

I had told the story many times. Over the years people had been interested in the story of Rorke's Drift. On the voyage home the civilian passengers had dragged the story from me. The result was that the words seemed to flow and I was able to speak without too many halts. Omdurman was still a raw wound and my account of that was a little less detailed. By the time we had reached Crewe, Rudyard Kipling had filled many pages of his little notepad.

He closed his notebook and said, "God, but you have lived." He leaned over and shook my hand, "I admire men like you more than you can know, Jack. The Kitcheners of this world will reap all the glory but it is the boots of men like you that have made the empire what it is. And now what?"

I held up the stump of an arm, "With this what can I do? I am a cripple and suited to nothing. I have my pension and I shall live but I have to say, Mr. Kipling, that I will not rest easy sitting on my rear and doing nothing. I began work when I was barely a youth and I have worked ever since. I am not a lazy man."

He had his pipe going and he nodded, "Without causing offence, Jack, can you write? I mean I know many ordinary soldiers who cannot write. It does not make them lesser men but is a sad inditement of the way we educate our young."

Desert War

"I can write but I cannot see myself working as a clerk, can you?"

He laughed, "I never thought that for a moment. If you can write, then write stories. Jack, you have kept me enthralled all the way from London. You are a natural storyteller. You have given me inspiration for a dozen stories. Just write down your experiences in the way you spoke them to me. There are many writers who are far too literary, I am not one, I am more of a writer like Mark Twain or Mr Dickens. I like to entertain."

The idea appealed but I shook my head, "I am a working-class boy, Mr. Kipling, a publisher would reject me out of hand."

He shook his head and handed me a card, "Here are my contact details. I have a publisher and when you are ready then send your work to me and I promise that I will get it published. You will not make a fortune. Publishers take the lion's share of the money earned. I am a case in point. To make money I have to tour America and speak to audiences. The publishers will earn more from the books that I sell as a result but at least I will have expenses and be paid for the audiences who sit and listen to me. One day writers will be rewarded for their work but not in our lifetimes. That is not the point though, is it? This will occupy your mind, as well as your time. You will also be passing on to the next generation the true stories of what it was like to be a soldier of the queen." I nodded, "One piece of advice I had from Mark Twain the American writer was, '*Get your facts first and then you can distort 'em as much as you please.*' It is good advice."

We chatted for the last few miles about his tour of America. The Americans, it seemed, loved his stories and his British accent. He made sure that I had the first cab as he only had to go to a hotel. He would board his ship the next day. As the cab took me to the home I would now share with my aunt, son and sister-in-law, niece and nephew, I had the stirrings of an idea and a way that I could keep myself occupied. Mr Kipling had not given me any false illusions. I would not make a fortune from my writing, but I had never been interested in money. That had been my brother Billy's Achilles heel, he had sought money and power. It had cost him his life. I would choose an easier life but one filled with work.

Desert War

Griff

Chapter 1

I missed my father. That was strange as he had rarely been at home when I had been growing up yet when he was there I felt closer to him than any other human being. I loved Aunt Sarah who was as close to a mother as I had known. My father's sisters did not feel like family but Uncle Billy's widow, Aunt Bet did. The mother of my two cousins was like a friend and I was happy in their home but I needed my father. It was strange really as I had now left school and was a man. Most of those with whom I had studied were now working. Some had even left home yet I missed my father.

I had completed my education and all that I wanted to do was to go to university. I loved studying and I had applied for a place at the new Manchester University. I was not arrogant enough to think that I would be accepted at Oxford, Cambridge or Durham but I hoped I could gain a scholarship to Manchester. It was a young university and I thought I might just win a place. I had failed. The rejection letter, when it arrived, made me feel as though my life was worthless. Aunt Sarah told me that there were many jobs that I could do and I would find them rewarding. I don't think that Aunt Sarah understood the idea of university. It did not seem, to her, as though it would lead anywhere. She ran through a whole list of what she termed, '*proper jobs*', but none appealed. Whatever job I took would only be second or third best. I needed the advice of my father for I wanted to join the army. I knew that Aunt Sarah and Aunt Bet both disapproved of the army life. I could understand that. It had kept my father away from us through my formative years yet when he spoke of his time in the army and his comrades he made it sound like a warm and cosy place. If I could not continue to study then I would like a life of action. While my father was in Sudan I had enjoyed shooting with old Joe and I found that I was a good shot. I liked to be out in the woods hunting with the old gamekeeper. He had often told me that I could do his job easily but that I was too clever for that. There lay my dilemma. What to do with the skills

Desert War

that I had acquired? I had learned Arabic with my father and kept it up for there were Arabic speakers who lived in Liverpool. I could also speak French. That was thanks to my Grammar School education and the fearsome Mr Morley. I would be eighteen soon and I had to make a decision. I could not live off my family forever- it was not our way. I acted as a sort of tutor to little Jack and Victoria. Jack was a bright boy but a little lazy and he was not doing as well at the Grammar School I had attended as I had. Victoria was a sponge who soaked everything up but girls at her school were trained to be good housewives. She would be leaving school soon enough and then would have the prospect of finding a job like Aunt Sarah or her mother had. Both would be a waste of her talents. Life was not fair.

When we received the telegram informing us that my father had been wounded at the Battle of Omdurman and was discharged from the army, I was both elated and deflated at the same moment. Elated that he was coming home but concerned about the injury. What kind of wound? The telegram did not tell us and we knew that he would get home as soon as he could. How would a wound have changed him? When he sent a telegram from the ship he was travelling on he did not offer any more information, other than he would be home within the next weeks and he was looking forward to seeing his family. I would be able to sit and talk with him but I feared him returning with some horrible wound.

The horse-drawn cab clip-clopping down the suburban street told us that my father was back. No one used a cab in our street and we raced out to greet him. I saw, first, his tanned face, his uniform and his medals. He stepped down and it was then I saw the stump. He was a cripple. My first thoughts were selfish. He would not be able to do all the things with me that I wanted to. As Aunt Sarah rushed up to him to embrace him, I helped the driver take down the chest and carry it into the house. I felt like a fraud. I had wanted my father home and yet it was Aunt Sarah who had greeted him. Even Jack and Victoria gave him a better welcome than I did. They saw the man and not the wound. The chest was heavy and we had to drag it into the hall. The driver went outside and my father paid him. I stood looking at the chest. It was undamaged but my father was not. The giggling Victoria led him in holding his good hand.

"Good to see you, Griff."

"And you, Dad. A good journey?"

"A long one but it feels good to be home." He shivered and laughed, "This weather will take some getting used to."

Aunt Sarah said, "Griff, nip down to the butchers and buy a pound and a half of chuck. Ask him to dice it for you. That way it will cook quicker. There is money in my purse."

I could not refuse and so I smiled and said, "Righto."

The nearest butcher was almost a mile away. I ran there and back. Aunt Sarah beamed when I made it in the back door. She and Aunt Bet were chopping onions and vegetables. "Tea might be a bit late tonight but your dad likes his lob scouse. Go and talk to him, Griff."

"And if my two are pestering him too much send them in here."

When I walked into the front room it was silent. My father was smoking his pipe and Jack and Victoria were engrossed in the books he had bought them. They both lay on the floor much as I had done in Nan's house, their heads resting on their arms and their legs in the air. I sat in the armchair next to the fire and opposite my father. He smiled.

"Do you want a beer I can…" I began to rise.

"Sit. I can wait for a beer. I am not rushing off anywhere and I want to know all about my son." I glanced down at Jack and Victoria. He understood and nodded, "Very well then, I will tell you about this." He held up the stump. I tried to hide my horror at the injury, but I could not. "Griff, this will not rule my life. I may have to learn to adapt but I have done that all my life. I can light a pipe one handed and I am learning to dress myself too. It takes a little longer but I have all the time in the world now. I have left friends all over Africa, and your uncle, too. Life is precious to me and I am not going to waste it."

I sighed, "You are right, and I am sorry. Do you mind if we wait until we are alone until I tell you my plans?"

He smiled, and pushed himself up, "I am guessing that Aunt Sarah is making a stew."

"Lob scouse."

Desert War

"Good, we have an hour. Let's have a little walk, eh?"

"Good idea."

We went to the hallway. Dad opened his chest and took out a civilian jacket. He laid his uniform on the chest. He was struggling to don the jacket and I went to help him. He said, gently, "I have to learn, Son. Now how did I do it before?" He slipped his right hand in and then raised it so that his jacket slipped to the left. He hunched his shoulders over and was able to slide his stump in. He beamed, "There, not pretty but all my own work, eh Griff?" I was proud of my father. He was indomitable. I nodded and put my own jacket on. As we left he shouted towards the kitchen, "Griff and I are off for a pint. We won't be long."

The pub wasn't far but there would be people in there and as soon as we reached the footpath I began to talk. It came out in a torrent. I was afraid that if I stopped I would not be able to start again. "Dad, I tried to get into university and failed the exam. I was not good enough. I thought I was because I did so well at school but that didn't help me with the interview and the scholarship exam. I don't want to work in an office. I waited until you came back but I want to join the army. I want to be a soldier."

He said nothing at first and I wondered if he had heard me. Then he sighed, "Firstly, you are not a failure. No man who tries anything is a failure. The ones who never try are the failures. As for not wanting to work in an office…" he laughed, "you sound like me when my dad sent me to work in a factory. I didn't like working in a factory and I understand what you are saying but… the army…it is a commitment, Griff. Are you sure?"

The pub was just ahead and I said, "I meet Joe regularly. He says I am a good shot. I can track in the woods and move silently."

"There's more to being a soldier than that but I am pleased that you have those skills." He put his right arm around my shoulder and squeezed, "I will support you in this. We will have to get our tactics right with Aunt Sarah though. She will not like it."

I laughed, "I know."

Desert War

When we entered there was a pleasant fug of smoke and the smell of beer in the bar side. "What do you drink these days?"

"When I meet Joe in here, I normally have a pint of mild. That is the only time I drink."

"Good. A pint of mild and a pint of best bitter."

The pints pulled and paid for, he nodded towards a corner table. We sat and he lifted his glass, "Cheers. It is good to be home, Son."

"Cheers and I am glad that you are back."

He took out his pipe and I watched as he deftly filled it with one hand and then put it in his mouth. He took out the matches and put the box between his stump and his body. He struck the match and soon had the pipe going. He put the used match in the ashtray and then placed the matchbox on the table. I realised that he was not handicapped. He would work around the stump that was his arm. I saw that he smoked for a while and then put the pipe down so that he could drink. The pipe was still going when he replaced it. I had drunk half a pint of the dark mild before he spoke again.

"I think I can help you join the army."

"You mean the Loyal Lancashires?"

He shook his head, "You are too clever to join as a private. I have a couple of connections. It might take some time but I think I can get you into the Royal Military Academy. You could become an officer."

"An officer?"

He laughed, "I finished my career as an officer and I have to tell you, Griff, that you would make a good one."

"I like the idea but what would I do until we had an answer?"

He put his pipe down and took a long drink of the bitter. He picked up the pipe but did not replace it at first, "I met Rudyard Kipling on the train this morning. He said I should become a writer. I know that I have the stories in my head but not necessarily the writing skills. You are a good writer. While we wait how about you and I work on the writing and we can also work on your Arabic. Language skills are always useful."

"I have been working on my Arabic when I go into town."

"Good. Well, what do you say? Shall we help each other?"

"That sounds like a plan."

Desert War

He put his pipe down and raised his glass, "Here's to a father and son partnership."

"Cheers."

"Just one thing, let's keep this between ourselves, eh?"

"Of course."

We had two pints and I told him all that I had done while he gave me a grittier version of the Battle of Omdurman than the one he would tell at home. It brought us closer together. He trusted me and that was important. When we walked through the back door we were assaulted by the wonderful smell of Aunt Sarah's stew. The recipe had been Nan's and her mother's. It was something we ate every week and we all loved it.

"Just in time. Take off your coats and we will eat in the dining room."

The house that Uncle Billy had bought was a palace compared to the tiny house in which I had grown up. The table was laid and I saw thickly sliced buttered bread, pickled beetroot and cabbage as well as piccalilli. The beer and the walk had given me an appetite not to mention the conversation. As we ate I said little. Aunt Bet and Aunt Sarah asked all the questions of my dad.

When it was all finished and we sat to enjoy a cup of tea, still seated around the table Dad said, "I will pay my way, Bet. I have a pension and I have plans. You let me know how much."

"Don't be daft, Jack, you did enough for us before. The money you got from Billy's company keeps our heads well above water."

"I pay my way!" I smiled. That was the Sergeant Major I remembered. Bet nodded.

The next day was a school day for Jack and Victoria. While the two women went shopping to fill the larder I sat with my dad and he wrote the two letters. He told me who they were going to. "One will go to Colonel Dickenson. He works at Whitehall but I shall include a letter for him to forward to General Kitchener. Both of them offered the chance to get you a place at the Military College."

I nodded, "What will I do there?"

He smiled, "I am not completely sure but I think that you spend a lot of time studying. Regard it as a university for officers. Apparently, some start there as young as fourteen while others come after university."

He could not have given me a better answer to my question. The letters written and the envelope addressed I took the letter down to the post office. Within a day or so it would be in London. I was excited beyond words.

When I returned, I found some lined paper and we sat while my father began to write his story. It was slow going at first because he was so nervous. I was not sure that my presence was helping so I suggested that I go into town to buy more notebooks and pens. The relief on his face told me that I was right. I came back on the same bus as Aunt Sarah and Aunt Bet. Aunt Sarah looked at the paper and asked, "I thought you had finished studying."

I was aware that Dad had said to keep silent about his project. I just said, "You never know. You don't mind do you?"

She sighed, "Griff, you are almost eighteen and have never done a day's work in your life. You should be looking for a job."

I smiled, "Would it surprise you to know, Aunt Sarah, that this morning I posted a letter and I hope that a career will come from it?"

"Yes, it would surprise me. What career?"

I tapped my nose, "Dad knows, and he is happy about it."

Aunt Sarah did not like the answer. She had been as a mother to me since Nan had died and now my father was back. She frowned. Lovely Aunt Bet beamed, "That is good. Our little Jack might be starting work as soon as he leaves school. There is an opening at the White Star line for a shipping clerk. Sarah knows the manager there. The money is not the best but there are prospects."

I used the opportunity to talk about Jack but I saw Aunt Sarah's hawk-like gaze fixed upon me. She would worry at it like a cat with a ball of wool.

When we entered the house I shouted, "We're home, Dad."

I wanted him to be able to hide the evidence of his writing until he had the chance to tell Aunt Sarah of his decision.

As the two ladies disappeared into the kitchen, I went into the dining room. He had cleaned up the detritus of writing. "You will need to tell Aunt Sarah sooner rather than later, Dad. She is used to running this house."

"And she can still run the house but I am back now and that means she no longer has to worry about you."

"But she will. Since Nan died she has been the one to steer my course."

He sighed, "You are right. This afternoon then I will tell her."

"The writing?"

"And the letter to Whitehall. Best to get the storm over with in one fell swoop and then you can cast your eye over my writing."

"You have finished?"

He laughed, "No, but I have made a start."

We had sandwiches for lunch and I offered to do the washing up with Bet. We got on well and chattered on about Dad, Jack and Victoria. We had just finished the drying when Aunt Sarah came into the kitchen. Her face was filled with sadness and she shook her head. It was clear that my father had told his aunt of my decision, "The army? What are you thinking?"

I put my arms out and hugged her. I remembered when her arms had enveloped me. Now her head just came to my chest. "I may not even be accepted. Dad is confident but…"

She pulled back and said, "You are just like your father. If you don't get into the college then you will just join up. They will send you to South Africa to fight the Boers. Just like your father!" A thin smile creased her face, "You could have a worse model to follow." She turned to Aunt Bet, "And my nephew fancies turning his hand to writing."

Aunt Bet smiled, "I still have my typewriter in the loft. I could type up his stories."

The fact that none of us had thought of that idea made all of us smile, especially my dad who was less than happy with his penmanship. Surprisingly, it made Aunt Bet happier than anyone. She could still be a mother but do something in which she had a real skill. The future looked bright. I went into the loft and brought the typewriter down. I spent the afternoon, under Aunt Bet's supervision, cleaning the worst of the dust from it. There were a couple of faults and I would need to repair them before Aunt Bet could begin.

Desert War

While we waited for a reply I had lessons in Arabic from my father and I gave him lessons in French. He wrote and asked for my advice on words. We worked out that he need not worry about spelling too much as, when he had finished, I would be able to correct it before Aunt Bet typed it out. I cleaned up the old machine properly. Joe had taught me how to strip down a gun and clean it. A typewriter was easier and I enjoyed the satisfaction of taking something that needed minor repairs and making it as good as new. I went with Aunt Sarah and we bought paper for the typewriter as well as the ribbons.

It was during this time of adjustment that Jack and Victoria left school. Jack had no time to enjoy, as I did, free time after leaving school. Aunt Sarah had secured him his job at the White Star line and he began to work there. Aunt Bet also decided that Victoria could learn a skill and whilst waiting for the first draft of my father's tome to be finished, Victoria had typing lessons from her mother. Time passed as we lived our new lives.

Griff

Chapter 2

The letter came quicker than we anticipated. Two months after I had posted the letter we had a reply. Rather like the letters we had sent there were two. One was from Colonel Dickenson and the other from General Kitchener. They arrived within a day of each other. My father read them and said that they both gave the same news. I had a place at the college and the college would let me know my starting date. It seemed that while they normally had their main cohort start in September, they allowed others to join in the New Year. For me, that was both exciting and fearful. For Aunt Sarah it ended the hope that I might not join the army. The letter from the general was a long one. My father did not read the whole of both letters to me but told me what I needed to know. He looked serious when he had finished it, but I did not press him about the rest of its contents. The letter from the college came a week later. It confirmed what the other two had said. I was given a list of things that I would need. Aunt Sarah's eyes rolled but my father was happy. Whatever expense was needed he would bear. He owed it to me, he said, for the years he had not been there.

A fortnight after the letter there was a knock at the door and when I opened it I saw, to my amazement, that it was two soldiers. The corporal said, "Does Lieutenant Roberts live here?"

"Yes, I will get him." I suppose I should have asked what it was all about, but I was so shocked at seeing soldiers that I just went for my father.

When I returned with him, he said, "I was Lieutenant Roberts but I have retired."

They both stood to attention and the corporal pointed to the road where I saw a wagon and horses, "We are here to deliver a chest to you, sir."

They went back to the wagon and I said, "Curiouser and curiouser."

They carried a metal trunk between them. We stood away from the door so that they could bring it in. After putting it down in the hall the corporal took a letter from his tunic. "This should explain it all, sir."

"Would you like a cup of tea before you get back?"

The corporal shook his head, "We have to get back, sir, but thanks for the offer."

The letter was from General Hunter.

Lieutenant Roberts,

I hope that you have recovered from your wound. Events moved so swiftly and that meant I was not able to bid you the proper farewell for you deserved more praise than you have received.

The chest belonged to Private Adams. He left a will and named you as his heir. All of his belongings are in the chest. I can assure you that no one touched them. He was a brave soldier and died well.

Enjoy your retirement, Lieutenant, you deserve it.

Archibald Hunter

General

My father had a profoundly sad look on his face. "It belonged to my batman. He died at Omdurman."

"I will take it into the kitchen and set it on the table. Aunt Sarah is in the back place doing the washing." The washing was a whole day's job and with Aunt Bet teaching Victoria my father's aunt would be busy.

"I can take one handle, Griff, I am not helpless."

Desert War

I smiled, "I was just going to impress you with how strong I am, Dad, but if you insist."

We manhandled it into the kitchen and lifted it onto the table. When we opened it, I saw that it was a lifetime of memories. Everything was neatly packed and organised. On the top was an envelope and it was addressed in a neat hand: Lieutenant Roberts.

"I will put the kettle on." I could see that this was upsetting for him. It would be like being visited by a ghost.

"Thanks, Griff."

By the time the kettle had boiled he had read the letter. I poured the water on the leaves and then put the tea cosy on the teapot.

I saw that my father was weeping. They were silent tears. I said nothing. He coughed and handed me the letter, "Here, you might as well read it. Part of it concerns you."

I took the letter but before I read it, I said, "But I never knew the man…how…"

"Just read and perhaps it might help you when you become an officer because people like Ged Adams are the reason the Empress has her empire."

Sudan 1898

Dear Lieutenant Roberts,

If you are reading this letter then I am dead. I did leave a will but this is for you to read.

I hope I died well. Some of the chaps I served with died when they fell off their horses and I have lost count of the number of comrades who died of disease.

As you know I have no family but in the short time I have served with you, I have come to regard you as the son I never had but always wanted. You are a proper soldier and it has been my honour to serve you. The chest has my life in it. Feel free to dispose of it as you wish but I hope that your son, Griff, might like some of the things in here. As I recall he likes soldiers and reading. There are books in there too. If the uniforms are any good to you then please have them with my blessing. There is also a little money box. It is not much after a lifetime of service, but I have been frugal with the money I have earned. I would like you and your son to use it. If your boy grows up to be anything like you then Britain will have another hero.

If you think of me now and then I hope it is with fondness.

Your batman and your friend,

Ged Adams

"He sounds like a nice man. I bet he and Joe would have got on like a house on fire."

My father smiled, "I know that they would."

He had placed the uniforms and belts on the back of a chair. There was a Webley service pistol in a holster and some ammunition as well as a cleaning kit. The books and toy soldiers he placed on the table. The figures were beautifully painted and well looked after. He took out the caps, hats and the single helmet and placed those on the table. I saw a cavalry sabre too. It looked unused. Finally, he took out the little money box. It was not so little. When he opened it, I saw that there was gold inside, guineas.

My father sat down and shook his head, "Who would have thought."

I went to the teapot and poured us two mugs. We didn't bother with the fancy china that Aunt Sarah liked. I knew how he took his tea and I handed him the mug. He just nodded and drank. I was learning that there were times when no words were needed. This was one such occasion. It took the whole mug for him to compose himself.

He pushed over the books, toy soldiers, pistol and holster, "These are for you. I have my own Sam Browne and Webley. Keep the gun safe and out of Jack's reach. He is a good lad but…" I nodded. "If you want any of the uniforms or equipment they are yours."

I shook my head, "Until I have finished college, I don't know what I shall need."

"Then I will store it." He patted the metal chest, "This, however, you will need. It is sturdy and all we need to do is stencil your name on it."

Desert War

Just then the kitchen door opened and Aunt Sarah, a scarf tied around her head, came in. She took in the laden table and frowned, "What on earth...?"

My father said nothing but handed her the letter.

She read it and slumped into a chair. She said, "I am sorry..." She put her hand on my father's.

He shook his head, "It is like he died again. It was the same when I came back after burying Billy. This house, Bet, the children, all of it reminded me of him."

It took some time to bring order to the house but in that time I saw a change in my father. When everything was as it should be he took me into the dining room. "Now I know what to write, Griff. I had been trying to write about me and I couldn't do it. I need to write about the lads I served with, the Geds, Syds and Jamies. I will tell my story through their eyes and I will start with Rorke's Drift. I will write the real story of that incident." He smiled, "It is a good job that your Auntie Bet hadn't started typing, eh?"

From then on he was up every morning at the crack of dawn. I knew he was up early as by the time I came down there would be four or five pages for me to check and edit. There would be an empty pot of tea and a plate with the crumbs of his toast. We developed a routine. When I came down he would get up and go to make our porridge while I read what he had written and using red ink, for he insisted, I corrected his mistakes. Over the weeks the mistakes became fewer and by the time Christmas approached and with it my imminent departure to college, we had almost a hundred pages written.

It was then that we involved Aunt Bet. The story was getting close to being finished and she would soon be able to type it up and send it to Rudyard Kipling's publisher. My father had no confidence in himself and was not certain that it would be published. As we sat in the pub, having a quiet drink before Sunday lunch he said, "But it doesn't matter if no one reads it. I enjoy the activity and, if nothing else you and the family can read it."

I had read it and I shook my head, "It is a good story Dad and I enjoyed reading it. It is fiction but I know from the things you have told me that all the incidents that happened are real. You can tell that when you read it."

He smiled, "Perhaps. Anyway, once you go to college, I won't have anyone to read it and correct it."

"Aunt Bet and Aunt Sarah could do that, I am sure, but let's get this one sent off, eh?"

That Christmas was the best one I could remember, well, ever. Dad was home and we had a goose. Normally we made do with a large chicken but Aunt Sarah used some of the money my father contributed to the household and bought a goose. Little Jack was no longer little, he had turned fifteen, and having been at work for some time felt himself to be a man. He had inherited his father's dress sense. While my father and I just wore clothes that were comfortable, Jack bought stylish clothes and on that Christmas Day, he dressed like a young man about town. He had used some of his pay to buy a fancy waistcoat and his mother had tailored one of his father's old jackets to fit. That he was still barely a boy didn't seem to matter. I was like my dad and clothes were just something to wear. I knew from the correspondence with the college that I would be wearing a military uniform at the college; not that of a soldier but a cadet. It was as I saw Jack with his new jacket and waistcoat that I realised I had soldier's blood in me. Even had I gone to university I would still have been at sea in terms of a career.

When we had been in Liverpool buying presents my father had gone into Dewar's, the tobacconists. I had always liked the shop as there was a wooden Highlander soldier outside and I had passed and admired it each time when we had gone to Liverpool. It always made me think of my father. Inside he bought five cigars. I didn't smoke and I didn't think that Jack did either. After Christmas dinner, when the pudding had been eaten, he opened the bottle of port he had bought.

Aunt Sarah smiled, "Ah, now it is time for the men to enjoy port and cigars. Let us do the dishes."

"I can go outside, Aunt Sarah."

She shook her head and placed an ashtray on the table, "No, the smell of cigars is the smell of Christmas. When your mother and I were little children, our dad would always have a cigar after dinner. He said it made him feel like a gentleman."

Desert War

Left alone he said to us, "You don't have to smoke. I shall have one and I will toast my dead comrades with the first glass of port and then savour the cigar with the second." He poured three glasses. Neither Jack nor I had ever drunk port, but I could smell the drink as it glugged into the glass.

Jack shook his head, "If you don't mind, Uncle Jack, I will decline the offer of a cigar. I am not certain that I would retain the contents of my dinner. The port, however, is something I would like to try."

He nodded and pushed the glass over to my cousin. "Griff?"

"I suspect that if I ever do become an officer and we have mess dinners then I might well be expected to smoke. I shall try one now, Father, but if I don't finish it, I hope you will not think any the less of me."

"Of course not." He pushed the glass over to me. Taking out the snipper he had also bought in Dewars he snipped off the end of the cigar he had in his mouth. He handed the tool to me. Then he took the cigar and put it between his stump and his side. He took out the ubiquitous tool he used to clean out his pipe. There was a long spike attachment. He made a hole in the opposite end of the cigar to where he had snipped it. Putting the cigar in his mouth he went to the fire and taking a taper warmed the end of the cigar while drawing on the end. I saw it glow and he nodded with satisfaction. He waved the taper to put it out and then nodded to me.

I found it much easier to do than my father because he only had one hand. He had adapted well. As I lit the taper he warned, "Don't inhale. Take the smoke in your mouth and then blow it out."

Already the dining room was filled with the smoke of cigars. I smiled, Aunt Sarah was right, even though I had never smelled cigars at Christmas it smelled like Christmas. When mine was going he put his cigar on the ashtray and he raised his glass, "To Ged and the other soldiers of the Queen. Rest in peace."

Jack and I solemnly repeated the toast.

I was enjoying the cigar, but I began to feel lightheaded. I had only smoked an inch or so but I put the cigar on the ashtray. The port I savoured and when it was gone my father said, "It is Christmas, pour me another one and one for yourself. Jack?"

"Yes, please, Uncle. I like the taste. It sort of warms when it goes down. Wait until I tell the fellows in the office that I had two glasses of port. They will be so envious."

"How is work?"

"Not as dull as I expected, Uncle Jack. It is easy work but the other clerks are about my age and when Mr Fotheringhay is not in the office we can joke and banter. He is a very serious gentleman."

I asked, "What is it that you do?"

"Our office makes sure that our ships have the right provisions. We are sent the names of ships arriving in port and write out the orders for supplies. Some of the larger ships…you would not believe how much food and drink they need for a voyage across the Atlantic."

"I would, Jack. When I used to sail to Africa the ship was laden and we ate well, even on a troopship."

"If and when I ever become a soldier, where might I be stationed?"

"The days of serving in Canada and Australia are long gone, Griff, but if you are sent abroad it could be to India or Egypt. This war in South Africa also means that soldiers will need to be sent there. I am not sure that the war with the Boers will still be ongoing when you become an officer. As a soldier of the queen, you could be sent anywhere or just stationed in a barracks in England."

My cousin said, "That sounds dull."

"Aye, dull but necessary. The skills you learn there and the camaraderie you build up in your men is vital should you be called into action."

"Uncle Jack, what is a battle like? I mean you have fought in lots. Were you afraid?"

"Afraid is the wrong word. You know, every time you draw your weapon, that you could be killed or," he held up his stump, "wounded. The fear is that you will let down your mates. When I was in Zululand I was given orders but I trusted men like Colour Sergeant Bourne to do the right thing. When I became an NCO I tried to be like him. It is not as easy as I had thought. For a start not all officers are good ones." He looked at me, "Griff, always remember that. No matter how good your sergeants are they obey your orders." I nodded. "When I was an officer, well, it was only for a short time, but things changed. I was the one making the decisions and I often had to think fast. We nearly lost at Omdurman. When the Dervish came at us and were hidden by the land they nearly caught us out. So, Jack, to answer your question, a battle is often confused and always dangerous. You need eyes in the back of your head. You have to trust the men that you lead and hope that someone you have trained with or have given orders to, is watching your back."

My cigar had long gone out and my father had just a stump left. He tossed it into the fire and drained his port. The three ladies re-entered with a pot of tea and some Christmas cake. Aunt Sarah had drunk a couple of glasses of sherry and had a happy smile on her face. "And now, a cup of tea, some cake and then how about a game of charades?"

The best Christmas!

Desert War

Griff

Chapter 3

I was due to start the college at the beginning of January. My cadet uniform and the rest of my equipment would have to be purchased at the college and I had been given some of what we termed Ged's money. My father was insistent that I take plenty. "There will be men from rich families there and I don't want my son to be the pauper at the feast. Don't be profligate but don't be mean either." We packed Ged's pistol and belt and I was given Ged's cavalry sword. "Fencing is on the curriculum as is equitation. I could have taught you that but I am sure you will cope. I began life as an infantryman and ended up riding camels."

The college was in Surrey and we had been to the station a week before I travelled to buy the ticket. I would have to change trains in London to travel to Surrey. As well as Ged's gold I had plenty of change for the porters I would need to tip. I was now a young gentleman and my father had taught me as much as he could about how to act as one.

The night before we left was in direct contrast to Christmas. There was little jollity. Only my father appeared to be at peace with my departure. I suspected that inside he was as upset as Aunt Sarah and Aunt Bet but he had told me that you had to hide your feelings. I tried to put on a brave face too but it was intimidating. I was leaving a warm and cosy world to go to a place that would be filled by my betters. I would be learning new skills and challenged. Grammar School had been easy. As Dad had said I had been a big fish in a little pond. Now I would be a small fish in an ocean. Aunt Sarah and my father came with me in the cab to the station. We arrived early. They would return by more mundane transport. My father insisted on helping me to carry my chest. We had painted over Ged's name. It was reassuring to think the old soldier's name would still be on the chest but we had stencilled my name over it.

"Ged would like this. His chest, his pistol and his sword being an officer's." My father pointed heavenward, "I bet he is smiling up there now."

As we waited, I thought about Ged. How many other soldiers were there like him? Men who had dedicated their lives to serving the Queen and her Empire and had neither family nor home of their own. Would that be me or would I emulate my father and come home from time to time, each visit changed by my experience? Would I meet someone, well into the future, who might become my wife? Perhaps I might be doomed to be a Ged or like my Aunt Sarah, single. As we watched the porters load my chest onto the train, I had serious misgivings. Was this what I really wanted?

Aunt Sarah burst into tears when the guard shouted, "All aboard."

"My poor bairn. You always have a home with us, Griff, if it does not work out. I shall miss you." She hugged me so hard that I thought my ribs would break.

Dad held out his hand, "Good luck, Son. I am proud of you. Do the right thing," he tapped his heart with his stump, "what feels right in here and you won't go far wrong. If you need more money then write to me. Don't go short."

The guard came along, "Hurry along, sir. The train must depart."

I climbed up and the guard shut the door. I lowered the window, "Thank you both for all that you have done for me. I won't let you down."

As the train hissed and steamed its way out of the station my father shouted, "You never will." The two of them, still waving, disappeared in the smoke from the engine and I waited until the train had turned and I had lost sight of them before I went to take my seat. I felt initially sad but then brightened. This was the start of an adventure. When I had corrected my father's work, I had felt that sense of adventure in his words. He had survived and I would too but I missed them both already.

The journey passed and any doubts and misgivings ended when I had to race to make my connection for the train to Sandhurst. It was on that train that I met some of my fellow cadets. I made the station before my train arrived and I waited with my chest. The other cadets were easily marked by their chests. A few seemed to know each other and their laughter drifted down the platform to me. There were about a dozen of us, all with chests. When the train came in I looked for the second-class compartment. The porters loaded our chests in the luggage compartment and we tipped them. When I entered, I saw that only four others were in 2nd class. The rest were in 1st class. The five of us sat in the same compartment but four of us took a corner and sat in silence as the train chugged out of the station. What was clear to me was that at least four of us wished to speak. I could tell that from the half smiles and the looks we all gave each other. The fifth just stared out of the window.

I took the plunge, "Good afternoon, I am Griff Roberts, and I am heading for the military college."

It was as though I had unleashed a dam. "I am Peter McKay, and I am a new cadet too." We shook hands.

"Geoffrey Fairbrother." We shook hands.

"Robert Fuller, call me Bob."

We all looked at the last youth. Aware of our looks and the fact that we were standing he said, without either rising or offering his hand, "James Quigley and I have been sentenced to this punishment too." He turned back to the window.

We sat down but the ice had been broken. Peter McKay said, "My grandfather fought in the Zulu wars. He died at Isandlwana, and it was because of him I won my place at the college."

My face broke into a smile, "My father fought at Rorke's Drift."

Geoffrey Fairbrother frowned, "The officers who fought there were Lieutenants Chard and Bromhead. You said your name was Roberts."

The disdain in his voice and his superior attitude ensured that I did not like Geoffrey Fairbrother from that first moment. I smiled, "He was not an officer then he ended his career as a Lieutenant and fought at the Battle of Omdurman."

Peter grinned, "I say, how splendid."

I asked Geoffrey Fairbrother, "And your family?"

He coloured, "I shall be the first soldier in my family." Enigmatically that was all that he said.

Desert War

Robert Fuller said, "Like you, Roberts, I have a father who was a soldier. Mine died fighting in the Sudan." He glared at Fairbrother, "He was a sergeant and died at Alt Klea."

"My dad fought there."

In that instant the three of us, Peter, Robert and I all became instant friends. Fairbrother slid down to sit opposite the silent and enigmatic James Quigley. We exchanged stories from our family history and as the train pulled into Sandhurst station, I felt happier than I had when I had left Liverpool.

Bob Fuller said, "What say we share a cab? I have a feeling that if we do not we may have to wait."

We agreed and he was proved right. The ones in 1st Class took most of the ones that were waiting. We three crammed into the next one and that left one for Quigley and Fairbrother to share. The three of us were buzzing with excitement but, when we reached the college, we were brought down to earth. The 1st class cadets were greeted by the officer at the gates with smiles as the sergeant checked off their names. They were taken away by a waiting cadet. We waited patiently and I expected the same smiles. The officer's face darkened as we gave our names, "Ah scholarship cadets, eh? I am Lieutenant Simpson. Let us hope that you obey all our rules or your time here will be a short one."

I am not sure that the others noticed it, but I did. The sergeant's eyes narrowed. He had not liked the officer's words either.

The officer snapped, "Watson, take these three cadets to their dormitory."

The cadet looked to be four or five years older than we were. As we hefted our chests he said, "Follow me." When we were out of earshot of the officer he said, "Don't mind Lieutenant Simpson. He is new here. The other officers and sergeant instructors are all decent chaps. Travelled far?"

"Liverpool."

"Norwich."

"Shrewsbury."

"You have had a long journey. There will be food at seven. You will have to look sharpish."

Peter asked, "Do we dress?"

"If you have it then yes but you will be given your uniforms tomorrow. Just be as smart as you can, eh?"

There were eight beds in the dormitory. As we three were the first ones to arrive we had the first choice, and we chose three next to each other. We placed our chests at the foot of our beds. I saw that next to the bed was a sort of wardrobe. I guessed that would be for our uniforms. There was a clock on the wall and I saw that we had just thirty minutes to dress. There was no bathroom but there was a bowl of water. It was cold but it would have to do. I took off my shirt and vest and used my bar of soap to make a thin lather.

"You are going to shave?"

I nodded and took out my razor, "He said to be as smart as possible. I am guessing they might notice this peach fuzz."

I began to shave. The other two saw the wisdom of my words and shaved too. The door opened and Fairbrother and Quigley stood there. The clock showed that they had just fifteen minutes to dress. I had scraped my chin and dried it on the towel that was there. Fairbrother was unpacking but Quigley just sat there. "Better get a move on, chaps, dinner is at seven."

I dressed as quickly as I could. I was lucky that I had been taught how to tie a bow tie, not by my father, but by Aunt Sarah. She believed that gentlemen should know such things. My suit was a good one but I doubted it would be of the same quality as those who had travelled 1st Class. My time at the Grammar School had introduced me to snobs. There were those at the Grammar School whose parents were solicitors and bank managers. They could not afford the fees charged by Public School but they did have tailored blazers and trousers. I had learned to deal with them. I was dressed first and it was eight minutes to seven. Peter and Bob soon followed but Geoffrey Fairbrother was struggling. The first to leave was James Quigley who did not bother to change and just wore the same clothes he had travelled in. Fairbrother made a half-hearted attempt to tie his bow tie but failed and it looked a mess. He raced out of the door behind Quigley.

We followed and I regretted my chivalrous attempt to help Fairbrother and Quigley. We made it to the refectory but only by a minute and we were given places at the lower end of the table.

Desert War

The eight who had travelled 1st Class were conspicuous by their absence but I saw that places had been left for them at the top of our table. Everyone else was in uniform. It was a sea of dark blue. I was pleased that my father had insisted on a haircut. The hair of everyone, the ones not in uniform excepted, was short. We were scrutinised. I saw that the officers were seated at the top table and, from the uniform one was a lieutenant general. That did not intimidate me. Dad had letters from General Hunter and General Kitchener. I was here because of a recommendation from the hero of Omdurman, Kitchener.

I saw the officers look at their watches and then a sergeant major appeared at the door and whispered something to the lieutenant general. He nodded and then rose, "Due to transport delays some of our new cohort of cadets will be late. We will say Grace and begin our meal. I will save my comments for after dinner."

We bowed our heads and said grace. Mess orderlies suddenly appeared with tureens of soup while others brought baskets of bread. As hungry as I was, I knew that I had to eat with decorum. I would be judged on my manners. We had just finished the soup when there was noise from behind me and the eight 1st Class passengers entered. They all wore white tie and tails. I now knew the reason for their late arrival. It was nothing to do with transport delays, after all, we had arrived on the same train and they had reached the college before us. They were making an entrance and it marked them from their first appearance. They acted as though they had a God-given right to be there. They bowed a sort of apology and took their seats as though they owned the place.

Peter said, sotto voce, "I can see that we are well down the pecking order. They are setting the bar high, eh?"

I shook my head, "We are here to be soldiers. Let us wait until we begin the training and then make our judgement."

The food was excellent and I enjoyed it all. After we had eaten the lieutenant general stood. He looked at the ones who were not in uniform yet, "I am the Governor and Commandant of this college. My name is Lieutenant-General Sir Edwin Markham. I always like to come to greet the new intake of cadets. You are joining an establishment that predates the Battle

Desert War

of Waterloo. The alumni who preceded you have all enjoyed glorious careers. I hope for nothing less from you. For forty-four weeks we will teach you to be soldiers and then officers. At the end of that time, if you have been successful, then you will become a second lieutenant and be assigned to regiments. I wish you all well."

There was spontaneous applause.

The major next to the general stood, "Gentlemen you may smoke but ties must remain fastened. For those newly arrived, breakfast is at seven and you will be taken at eight to collect your uniforms and equipment. I would suggest you retire early. Tomorrow promises to be a long and arduous day for you all."

James Quigley rose and without a bow or a salute, simply left. I heard murmurings from the uniformed cadets and from the 1st Class cadets, who had all lit cigars, there was outright laughter. While James Quigley had not endeared himself to me I did not like the attitude of those at the head of our table.

Bob clearly felt the same, "Come on, there is no reason to stay here." The three of us stood and bowed to the head of the table.

I looked down at Geoffrey, "Are you staying?"

"I think so."

When we reached our dormitory James was sitting on the edge of his bed. I sat on the end of mine for it faced him. "It is none of our business, but we are going to be sharing a dormitory for the next forty-four weeks. If we can help…"

He looked across at me, "You all seem like nice chaps but you want to be here. I do not." He shook his head, "I most definitely do not." He sighed and looked thoughtful. It was as though he was deciding something. Eventually, he looked at me, "Tell me, Griff, how old are you?"

"Eighteen."

"I am twenty and I wished to marry a young girl from the village where I live…lived. Both sets of parents objected. She has been sent to India to stay with a widowed aunt and I was sent here to forget her. My father was a soldier and has retired."

"I am sorry. Does the life of a soldier not appeal to you?"

"It matters not for I see it as a punishment. I cannot see Dorothea who, even now, is sailing to India. She will forget me and while the life of a soldier may suit some, for me it will always be a prison sentence."

Peter sat next to James, "But what is the alternative?"

Bob said, "You could always follow her there."

He shook his head, "And how would I pay my way? I have never earned a penny in my life."

I thought of Ged's gold and felt guilty. "I have a few pounds if it would help."

The three of them stared at me and for the first time since I had known him James gave a sad smile, "But you barely know me."

Bob said, "Are you rich, Griff?"

I shook my head, "No, my father retired as a lieutenant, and we are not rich but I have a couple of guineas and if it would help…"

James shook his head, "That is more than kind, but it would take more than a couple of guineas to pay for the passage. No, my only hope is that when I graduate, I can gain a commission in a regiment that is based in India. She is a pretty young thing and I hope that another does not steal her heart away."

Peter nodded, "If there is anything we can do then you rely on us. We should swear an oath to be brothers, eh? You know, like the musketeers."

Bob shook his head, "We can help each other but oaths and the like, let us leave those for romantics. I am under no illusions, gentlemen this will be hard. Those chaps in their dinner suits are already treated differently from us. I cannot see that changing."

Peter nodded, "And if the officers are like that Lieutenant Simpson, then it will be almost a year of hell."

Peter shook his head, "My father said that most of the instructors are sergeants and warrant officers. They are all chosen for their skills. If the lieutenant was any good he would be a captain. Each platoon is commanded by a captain."

"Thanks, Peter, that is good to know."

The ice being broken James became one of us. The one who did not was Geoffrey Fairbrother. None of the four of us had drunk at the table but the 1st Class had opened wine. When Geoffrey staggered through the dormitory door we could see and smell that he was drunk. We were all wearing pyjamas but had not retired. He almost fell into the room and he giggled.

"You chaps missed the most fantastic time. Those chaps at the other end of the table are all blue bloods but terribly nice…"

I saw from his face and his movements what was going to happen and I grabbed his bowl and had it under his chin even as he began to vomit. I held it there even though the smell made me nauseous.

Bob shook his head, "What a bloody fool. I bet they are all laughing at him now. Take your puke and get rid of it, Mr Fairbrother. I do not want to sleep with that smell in my nose all night."

I was learning much about my new bunkmates. Bob did not suffer fools gladly. Fairbrother obeyed him and disappeared down to the latrines. He must have been there some time for I was asleep when he returned.

Desert War

Griff

Chapter 4

Since my father had begun writing from the crack of dawn I had started to rise earlier. That, allied to the new bed and surroundings, meant I was awake while it was still pitch black. In a way that was not surprising. It was the time of year when the nights were interminable. I also needed to make water and so I slipped from the dormitory and, taking my toilet bag with me, made my way to the latrines. They stank of vomit but at least Fairbrother had hit the target. I made water and then washed and shaved. There was hot water and this shave was much closer than the cold one the night before. Other cadets entered the latrine while I was shaving. None of them was from our cohort. They came in pairs and chatted to each other assiduously avoiding me. I understood and appreciated that. We were outsiders and until we had been inculcated into the ways of the college were to be treated warily. I finished and headed back to our dormitory. The others slept on but I could hear movements from other dorms. I left the door ajar and a shaft of light entered the room. I put my toilet bag down noisily and I coughed.

Bob growled, "What on earth is the time, Griff?"

"I have no idea, I can't see the clock in the dark but as the cadets are up and about I thought it prudent to wake you."

"Bugger!" He leapt out of bed and shouted, "Wakey, wakey boys, up and at 'em. The sun is cracking the flags."

I took a match and lit a candle. Fairbrother apart, the others rose quickly and, grabbing their toilet bags, hurried to prepare themselves for the day. James rose more slowly than the others but he would be dressed before Fairbrother who slept on. I went to the curtains and pulled them back. It was still dark. I had no watch but now I could hear footsteps moving to the latrines in greater numbers.

As I started to dress, I said, "Fairbrother, you had better get up, you don't want to be late on your first day."

He groaned from beneath the sheets, "Go away! I feel sick."

Desert War

I was half dressed by the time the rest returned and with more candles lit it was easier to see. Peter had a pocket watch, an enormous thing and he took it out. Before he could tell us the time we heard the bugle sound. Peter said, "Six o'clock. At least we know what time the alarm call is."

Bob nodded, "And the reason why people go down to wash early. The washroom is full already. Fairbrother, hurry up. An hour is not as long a time as you think."

I winked at Peter, "I think I just saw some of those blue blood friends of yours going down."

"Algernon?" He leapt out of bed and, grabbing his wash bag, raced off.

James shook his head, "He is so desperate to be one of them and he can't see that they will be mocking him."

"Do you know them, James?"

"Just the type. They probably all went to Oxford or Cambridge and this is just a waypoint on their route to their future life. You could smell the money on them. I am guessing that they already have places secured in either the Guards or Cavalry regiments. If we all succeed here we will end up in some little unfashionable regiment stationed on the far side of the world."

I was dressed and I sat on my bed as the others dressed, "How do you know this?" My father had never really spoken about the officers. I knew that Colonel Dickenson and General Kitchener were not the normal officers. The 24th Foot, the Loyal Lancashires and the ESEG were most definitely not fashionable.

"Although my father was not in the army, my grandfather was and he was bitter about being passed over. He served before the Cardwell reforms when commissions could be bought. It was one reason why my father never joined the army." He stood and donned his jacket, "As I said, I am being punished by my father. If my grandfather was still alive then this would not be happening."

It was 6.45 and Fairbrother had not returned. Bob shook his head, "We did all we could for him last night. I do not wish to risk the wrath of Simpson or the other officers. Let's go to the refectory."

Desert War

As sorry as I felt for Fairbrother I agreed with Bob and we left. We joined the line of blue heading to the refectory. I had already worked out that there would be some order to the seating and as we neared the refectory and the noise grew, I said, "We had better sit in the same seats we did last night until we know their systems."

"Good idea."

We reached the entrance at seven but I saw that the blue line was already queuing for food. We joined it. Thanks to our early arrival we were close to the front. I saw that the food was basic but plentiful. There was porridge, toast, butter and conserve. An urn at the end of the row of serving tables obviously held tea and there were mugs close by. We sat at our table and I saw that there was a bowl of sugar as well as salt and a milk jug. Everyone eats porridge differently. I was fond of porridge with either honey or golden syrup. My father always added salt; it had something to do with the desert. I made do with sugar and a little milk to cool it. I drank some of my tea while it was still hot. The butter was plentiful and I smeared a healthy amount on the toast and then the conserve. It was while I was eating my second piece that the 1st Class cadets entered. They were noisy.

Peter looked at his watch, "Seven forty, they are late and where is Fairbrother?"

As if he had been summoned our companion hurried after them like a lap dog. I could not hear their words for the refectory was a hubbub of noise but the condescending looks they gave Geoffrey and sneering laughter accompanying them, told me that they did not like him.

When he sat, we had all finished and were about to take our dishes to be washed. "Those chaps I was drinking with last night told me to stick close to them today. They know how this place works."

Bob said, "And yet you are not sitting with them."

He put his head down to eat his porridge and mumbled, "We were assigned the seats and…"

We deposited the dishes and then headed outside. Bob said, "I reckon that we will be collected. Let us wait in the corridor. I mean they can't miss us, can they? Everyone else is in blue and we stand out like sore thumbs."

Desert War

There was a clock on the wall and at precisely one minute to eight and with the refectory almost empty, the sergeant who had checked us in the previous night arrived with a clipboard.

He said our name and when we said, 'Here sergeant,' he ticked off, "Fairbrother, Fuller, McKay, Quigley, Roberts." He frowned at his list, "Where is Fairbrother?"

Bob was the confident one, "Still eating, Sergeant...as are the others."

I wondered why he had not called out their names but said nothing. He sighed, "I am Sergeant Windridge and one of your instructors. You are number eight platoon and your officer is Captain Collins." He smiled, "He is a good chap and served in India." He looked at the clock. It was now five past eight. He put the clipboard under his arm and strode into the almost empty refectory. He shouted, "You shower, move yourselves. You are all five minutes late. All of you are on pash bash tonight."

Geoffrey quickly deposited his dishes and raced out like a frightened rabbit but the other eight moved more laconically. I noticed, as they emerged, that at least four of them sported moustaches. I was not sure that was allowed and they all had an arrogant sneer across their faces.

Sergeant Windridge read out their names and I could hear the blood blue cascading through their veins, "St John-Wilson, Cartright-Jones, Willoughby, Danvers-Walker, FitzWilliam, de Warenne, Granville-Smythe and Garnet."

Their 'yes sergeants' were imbued with as much contempt as they could muster.

"And you are, Fairbrother?"

Geoffrey still looked a little green, He had not eaten much breakfast. "Yes, Sergeant. What is pan bash, Sergeant?"

"A little punishment we keep for those who do not follow the rules. Tonight, after we have eaten, you nine will be taken to the kitchens and have to clean out the pans used to cook our food."

While Geoffrey nodded the others looked horrified. St John-Wilson said, "Surely you can't expect future officers to scrub pans."

The sergeant grinned, "Oh yes, we can, Cadet, and another little punishment is cleaning out the latrines. Lucky for you some other defaulters are doing that and as someone was sick there last night it is a more unpleasant punishment."

Geoffrey blushed but no one else saw it.

We were whisked off to be kitted out. I knew what to expect having been taken through the procedure by my father. Laden, we returned to our dormitory. The dress uniforms were hung up and we wore the overalls we would wear each day. The sergeant had given us until nine o'clock and this time even the blue bloods were early when we gathered at the designated area.

We found ourselves taken to a classroom, where our officer awaited us. He had a tanned face like my father and that somehow reassured me. He gave us an outline of our days and duties. He explained how we would have lessons in mathematics, as well as fencing, riding and shooting. He also told us that we were the first cohort to be trained in navigation and an officer had been seconded in for six months just to train us. Nothing that was said upset me in any way.

The first day, however, was not spent in learning but in marching. Sergeant Windridge took us to the parade ground and with a newly issued rifle, we marched up and down. We learned to present arms, slope arms and generally learn all the manoeuvres and orders that an officer might issue.

As we trooped to the refectory for lunch Willoughby complained, "I can't see why we need to do all of this. After all, we will be giving orders to men and they will have to obey them."

He foolishly said it while we were close to the Sergeant Instructor, "Cadet Willoughby, that is precisely the reason you need to become proficient in these skills. You have to know what it is like and understand your men." It was clear to me, from his tone and the look he gave them, that Sergeant Windridge did not have much time for these arrogant, pampered young men.

Garnet snorted, "Understand them? Surely, they are just those dragged from the gutter who know no better."

His eyes narrowed and his voice became even more threatening, "Cadet Garnet, I hope you are not referring to me. I joined the army when I was eighteen and I have served my country."

Desert War

The cadet heard the tone and backed down immediately, "Sorry, Sergeant Windridge, a slip of the tongue."

I noticed that the blue bloods tended to drawl and the end of their words drifted on past the end of the sentence. It was almost like an echo.

By the end of the day, we were exhausted and ready for food. There was no Commandant Governor this time and the officers were not dressed in their best. This was clearly the way we normally dined. The food was also a little more basic. I deduced that they were preparing us for the diet we might endure on the campaign. If so, it was a good idea.

If the ones on pan bash thought that they had got away with it they were wrong. As soon as the tables were cleared they were whisked away by the duty senior cadet to scrub pans. I had done it at home on Sunday when the roast potatoes stuck to the roasting tin and I would have to use wire wool to clean it. I suspected that the blue bloods had never even seen a kitchen let alone toiled away with a dishcloth.

There was a lounge and we retired to it. Watson, one of the senior cadets came over to join us. I saw that he was smoking a long, thin cheroot. "Well, boys, how was your first day?"

Confident Bob was the one who answered for us, "Not as bad as I expected." None of us knew what to call the senior cadets so Bob added, "sir."

Watson smiled, "Cadet Watson will do. The sergeants are all called Sergeant Instructors and the officers, well, just sir. That will save you from having to worry about the rank although most of the officers are Captains, we have two lieutenants. You have met one and the other is an instructor." He seemed a genuinely considerate man and I thought he would make a good officer. "Tomorrow is your introduction to equitation. The day after that will be fencing and the day after that shooting. We finish the week in the classroom. I think you will find that tougher than the other activities. Anyway, well done for surviving your first day." I liked the senior cadet who appeared kind.

Fairbrother came into the dormitory with a face as black as thunder. I got the impression he blamed us for his punishment. The four of us got on and when he came in we were playing whist. I liked the game, which my nan had taught me. It seemed to me a little like chess in that you had more chance of winning if you tried to think a few moves, or cards ahead. Whist was played by four people and so Geoffrey was excluded although not deliberately. He rolled on his side on the bed and sulked.

I was not looking forward to horse riding although my father's advice had helped. He had told me not to grip the reins too tightly and to use my knees and body weight to guide the animal. James had ridden before and of the five of us in our dormitory, he proved to be the best rider. I watched the others and heeded every word of instruction. I managed to sit on the horse and I hoped I did not look like a bag of potatoes on its back. The blue bloods looked as though they had been riding since before they could walk. The instructor, who had been in the Dragoon Guards, was mightily impressed by them and the ignominy of pan bash was forgotten. Geoffrey was the worst of us. He was the only one who could not keep his saddle. He fell and fell badly. The instructor had little sympathy and sent him alone and having to lead his horse, to the sick bay. We later learned he had broken ribs. As there was little that could be done he had to endure the pain. The one concession that was made was that he would not have to participate in the fencing and the shooting until he had recovered. In many ways that was a punishment. He came with us but just watched and while we learned and showed improvement he was a mere spectator.

The fencing was another area in which the blue bloods excelled. This time the instructor was less impressed. Sergeant Hargreaves had also been in the Guards, but the Footguards. He did not like the way the blue bloods stood.

"Cadets, you may know how to fence in a gymnasium, your instructor at public school was probably a very skilled fencer. However, when you get to use your sword for real then your opponent will use every trick in the book to defeat you. Fencing in war is not a sport. It is a matter of life or death. Now let us try again."

I was faced with James and he had used a sword before but, somehow, and I don't know why, I seemed to have natural reactions. I did not think about what I did. I just flicked his sword away, Sergeant Instructor Hargreaves came over, "Good defence work, Roberts, but you can afford to be more aggressive, God knows a wild Afghan will be."

I took him at his word and when I parried his next blow I swept my blunted sword at James' side.

"That's better and Quigley, you were seduced by Robert's lack of aggression and paid the price. Again."

By the end of the day, I felt no fear. I had not, by any means, mastered the sword but I did not feel like it was something to dread.

What none of us enjoyed as we marched back to the dormitories was the gloating and crowing from the blue bloods. The first two days of what one might call military training had shown that they were already skilled. They rammed it down our throats. They did not just imply, they actually said that we would be better placed enlisting as ordinary soldiers as none of us was officer material. It hurt Fairbrother the most. I knew it wasn't true, Quigley did not care and Bob and Peter were supremely confident cadets. It was Fairbrother who took it to heart. Since he had fallen from his horse he had been shunned as well as ridiculed by those he had hoped would be his friends. The worst of the comments were always directed at him and as he tended to walk close to the elite little club he aspired to join, he suffered more than we did.

The next day, as we left the refectory to head to the firing range, Cadet Watson said, "Today you are in for a treat. Sergeant Instructor Snoxall is the instructor and he holds the speed record for the Lee Enfield. He put 38 rounds into a 12-inch-wide target at 300 yards in one minute. It is regarded as a record. He is a proper soldier."

I could not help but think of my father's batman's letter. Before I met him I knew that I would like the man, no matter how gruff he was. We had been issued with the Lee Enfield when drilling but they had been returned to the armoury. We were now issued with one that we would use until the end of our training. We had to sign for it. I had used its predecessor, the Lee-Metford. My father owned one and so I had a basic idea of the weapon and knew the action. I would be ready for the kick and the smell. I could not help but smile at the distaste on the

Desert War

faces of the blue bloods. The rifle was the weapon of a common soldier.

Sergeant Instructor Snoxall gathered us around him and we sat. It was like being in kindergarten once more. He spoke to us as though we knew nothing and that was probably a good thing. "This, gentlemen, is the Magazine Lee-Enfield or MLE." He smiled, "The men you lead will probably call it Emily. It is a fine weapon. I liked the Lee-Metford but this has more stopping power and a ten-round magazine. It weighs almost ten pounds and the barrel is thirty inches long. It takes a bayonet but I am here to teach you how to shoot. You will be taught the bayonet by others." He demonstrated, "The magazine goes in here. It will click into place. No click, no firing, no firing and...well a rifleman who cannot fire may well be a dead man. You pull the bolt back and when you hear that click then the rifle is ready to be fired." He looked at the blue bloods, "I know that some of you gentlemen have fired a shotgun before and so you will be aware of the kick from the gun. The difference with this weapon is that, if you have quick hands, you can fire more than twenty rounds in less than a minute." He waited for any comments but there were none. "At all times you will wait for my command. Today you will lie down. Support the barrel with your left hand and when you fire squeeze the trigger. For the first magazine, I want speed. If you hit the target then I will be delighted. Later we will work on your accuracy. I want you to get used to using the gun as quickly as you can."

Cadet FitzWilliam snorted, "Surely that twenty shots in a minute is impossible, Sergeant Instructor. I mean you could do it with a pistol but..."

His face never altered as he answered, "I can assure you, Cadet FitzWilliam that such a feat can be easily attained. Especially, if you are being charged by Dervishes. Now you gentlemen are lucky. You are the only ones using the range today. You can spread out. The targets are ahead of you. Take the prone position and when I say fire then fire at the target until I say stop."

As luck would have it, I was between FitzWilliam and James. I placed the rifle on the ground and then lay down. I was handed a magazine and, remembering how it had been demonstrated to me, I loaded it and heard the click as it locked.

"Chamber a round."

I chambered a round and the first thing I noticed was how much smoother the action was compared with the Lee-Metford. I saw that the sergeant instructor was being kind on our first day. The targets were just one hundred and fifty yards away. I tested the wind, there was virtually none and sighted the rifle. Until I had the paper target in my hand I would not know the idiosyncrasies of my weapon.

"Right, cadets, as fast you can. When you have finished lay down your weapon, raise your right hand and shout, 'Done!' Ten rounds rapid fire, fire!"

I squeezed, chambered and fired again in a smooth action. There was smoke from the guns and I was not sure how accurate my bullets were. I laid down the rifle and shouted, "Done."

"Well done that man, Roberts isn't it?"

"Yes, Sergeant Instructor."

The others followed with a shouted, 'Done.' The last to do so was FitzWilliam. He was a good thirty seconds after the last cry of 'Done!'

"You may stand while the targets are brought here."

FitzWilliam complained, "My bolt stuck."

"Hand it here." The sergeant instructor lifted the weapon and after putting in a fresh magazine he aimed it in the air and fired ten shots so fast that it sounded like a machine gun. "I think it works fine. Perhaps it is the arm that needs work, Cadet." The corporal instructor collected the targets and he showed each one to the sergeant instructor. "Not bad McKay, two hits. Cadet Fuller, you managed to hit the target, well done. Cadet Quigley, a real Annie Oakley here, three hit the target." He looked at mine and said nothing. He moved on to Cadet FitzWilliam, "Not a one, Cadet." The rest of the blue had managed to hit the target but James had the most hits. I wondered what vitriol was coming my way. He smiled as he held up the target, "Not only was Roberts here the fastest to fire he was also the most accurate. Eight hits. Well done."

My three friends cheered. Willougby sneered, "Beginner's luck."

Desert War

The sergeant instructor frowned and then said to me, "Would you like another go, Roberts, but let us make it interesting. Let us say three hundred yards. This time you can take your time."

"Yes, Sergeant Instructor." The rest all stood. I took the proffered magazine and lay down. I loaded it into the gun and breathed more slowly as I waited for the target to be moved. I did not chamber a round until the corporal instructor had returned and Sergeant Instructor Snoxall said, quietly, "Whenever you are ready, son." His kind words helped me and I aimed and fired. This time there was less smoke and I saw the strike of each bullet. The gun pulled a little bit to the right. After the first round, I adjusted my aim and fired. Every bullet hit the target. "Done!"

I stood and we waited for the results. Sergeant Instructor Snoxall positively beamed as he held up the target. "All ten in the target and three in the centre. Well done." He turned to the corporal instructor, "Jennings give them another magazine and let them take their time. I want a word with Roberts here."

He led me away from the firing. We had to move some way so that we could hear each other. "That was not just luck, Cadet. You have fired a rifle before."

"Yes, Sergeant Instructor Snoxall, my father served in Zululand and Sudan. He was invalided out and he brought home his Lee-Metford. I have used that."

He nodded, "That explains a great deal but the College is for university graduates or the sons of officers. The Lee-Metford is not an officer's weapon."

"He was promoted from sergeant major by General Kitchener himself."

His face broke into a grin, "You are Jack Roberts' boy?"

"Yes, Instructor Sergeant, did you know him?"

"No, but I heard of him. Your father was a legend amongst the sergeants. I was sorry to hear about his arm."

"He copes. Er, Sergeant Instructor, I would be grateful if you kept that to yourself."

"Why, are you not proud of him?"

"Inordinately and he is my hero but there are some cadets who…well…"

He looked over to the blue bloods and his eyes narrowed, "Aye, I know exactly what you mean. I will respect your wishes."

As we tramped back to the dormitory we were tired. We had spent the afternoon stripping down the Lee-Enfield and then fitting it back together. To me, it had been simplicity itself, as I had done it with the Lee-Metford. The blue bloods found it hard. As we had walked back the sergeant instructor and the corporal instructor had chatted to me making me the last to reach the block. When we entered the dormitory block I found FitzWilliam and Willoughby waiting for me. "Proper little teacher's pet aren't you? We have our eye on you. It would be a mistake to try to show us up."

"I have done nothing except my best. You are clearly better horsemen and swordsmen but I am the better shot."

"I think the oik needs a lesson, Algernon."

I stepped back and braced myself as they launched themselves at me. I heard James say, from behind the two of them, "Need a hand, Griff."

I blocked the haymaker from FitzWilliam and rammed my right hand into his solar plexus. "I think I can manage these two." With his friend writhing on the ground Willoughby launched himself at me. I stepped aside and he tripped over FitzWilliam's feet. He cracked his head on the wall as he tumbled.

The fight, if that is what it could be called, ended for Senior Cadet Watson came out of his room which was at the end of our corridor. He saw the two cadets on the ground and nodded, "What is going on here?" He took it all in and as the two cadets pulled themselves to their feet said, "You want to be careful running around the corridors you could get hurt. Do you need to go to the sickbay?"

The two stood and glared at me. Willoughby said, "No, Senior Cadet Watson, and thank you for the advice."

The three of us were left alone and Watson said, "You handled yourself well there but watch out. Those types are treacherous."

Desert War

James smiled, "Don't worry, Senior Cadet Watson, he has the rest of the musketeers to watch his back. We take care of our own."

As we headed to the dormitory, I realised that lines had been drawn and we had taken sides. Life would be more interesting.

Desert War

Jack

Chapter 5

The house felt empty without Griff. The sadness was compounded within a short time of his leaving when we heard the sad news that Queen Victoria, the Empress of India, had died. It was, truly the end of an era. I had been a soldier of the queen, and no matter how good a king her son Edward was, I would still always feel like a soldier of the queen. It affected the whole country. Shops were draped in black. Men wore black armbands and women wore black on Sundays. She had been the longest reigning British monarch and as Empress ruled a land that went all around the world. Canada lay to the west, India and Australia to the east. The maps of Africa showed a long pink blob that went from Egypt all the way to South Africa. Never had there been a more powerful monarch.

It was early March and we had finished the first draft of my story and Bet was typing the last chapter. I wrote a letter to the address given to me by Mr Kipling and said what I had done. I did not want to start a new story and I took to taking long walks. I often met Joe and we would speak of Griff. I did not expect letters but each time the postman arrived my heart raced.

The letter from Major Dickenson gave me pause for thought as it was on War Office stationery. When I opened it then I remembered the long letter from General Kitchener. I had told no one of the contents but now I had no choice. When I had been pensioned off, I was kept on the officer's reserve and Colonel Dickenson confirmed what the general had told me. I was being recalled to the army.

That evening, I told Sarah and Bet my news. That they were appalled was an understatement.

"Recalled! You have one arm, Jack. Have they not had enough of your flesh?"

I sighed, "Sarah, they have every right to recall me." I tapped the letter, "Anyway this does not seem like I will be in much danger. I am to command a small section of men and protect a drilling crew prospecting for oil in Persia. I have been chosen

Desert War

because I speak Arabic and I can cope with the land. It is just a six-month contract. I am available and I will be paid more than I would as a lieutenant. Mr William Knox D'Arcy is funding the exploration and he is a millionaire. I may not be wearing a uniform and I doubt that I will even have to draw a weapon. We are there to keep the surveyor safe from snakes and the like."

My words fooled Bet but not Aunt Sarah who knew me too well. "Kitchener has asked for you."

"He has always looked after me and he did get Griff a place at the College."

Her face became angry, "You knew about this when the place was offered to Griff?" I said nothing but my aunt knew how to read a lie in my eyes. "That is awful. You are being coerced."

I sighed, "It is what I did best, Aunt Sarah. I have enjoyed writing the story but I can't make a living from writing. Mr Kipling told me that. For six months I will be doing something useful and as Griff is away for a year…"

"So, you will happily leave us."

"Of course not. I shall miss you but you do not need me here."

Bet put her hand on mine, "We do not need but we do want you here, Jack."

I sighed, "Six months, Bet, the time will fly and it will not be as though I have to face the Dervishes again will it? I am merely providing protection for a surveyor and his engineers."

The letter asked me to go to Liverpool where the Australian millionaire had an office. I went alone. The letter told me that Augustus Milner ran the British end of the millionaire's empire. He kept a suite of offices close to the docks. When I arrived at the swanky offices, there was a liveried porter there. He looked to be ex-army and more suited to working at a hotel as many such men did. They liked the chance to still wear a uniform.

"Jack Roberts, I have an appointment with Mr Milner at ten o'clock."

The man smiled and nodded to the clock, "Mr Milner keeps a tight timetable, sir. If you would wait here in the lobby with me."

I nodded, "Which regiment?"

"Royal Artillery. And you, sir?"

Desert War

Few people had heard of the ESEG and I gave my usual answer, "The Loyal Lancashires."

"If you don't mind me asking, sir, where did you lose the arm?"

"Omdurman."

He frowned, "The Loyals weren't at Omdurman."

"No, they weren't. I was seconded."

"Did you meet Lord Kitchener, sir?"

"I did. A great general."

"Did you hear he has been given command of the army in South Africa? Those Boer rebels won't know what hit them."

I said nothing. I knew that the Boers were not rebels in the true sense of the word. They had tamed vast areas of South Africa. I had been a soldier there when we had defeated the Zulu and gained a toe hold in that country. I had great respect for those Dutchmen who had fought the Zulus. It looked as though the Empire would be enlarged but men would die. There was always a cost.

The clock ticked over to ten and the porter led me through a door to the outer office. There a secretary nodded and said, "You must be Lieutenant Roberts." I nodded. "Thank you, Jenkins."

The porter saluted and left.

Rising, the secretary took me to a huge mahogany door, knocked and entered. It was an opulently furnished room. The desk behind which Augustus Milner sat was as big as a dining table and eight people could have sat around it.

"Lieutenant Roberts."

Augustus stood and held out a hand, "Delighted to meet a hero, a soldier of the queen. I am Augustus Milner and I represent Mr D'Arcy's interests here in England."

The man was older than I was and he looked to be a rugged type. His handshake was firm and he had the tanned skin of one who has spent a great deal of time out of doors in the tropics. He waved an arm, "Take a seat."

There was just one empty seat as the other was occupied by another man who also looked like he spent most of his life outside. I sat and nodded at the man who nodded back.

"This is Mr. George Reynolds, and he is our surveyor. Your job, when you go to Persia, will be to guard him and his men."

Desert War

I shook my head, "Mr Milner, there must be a misunderstanding, I was asked to come here to discuss a commission. Hitherto this has been dealt with by letter. Before I commit six months to this venture I will need to know more."

He frowned. I had clearly upset his plans, "But I was told by the War Office," he opened a manilla file and read, "by a Colonel Dickenson, that you were the perfect man for the job and I should employ you."

"That is very kind of the Colonel but as you can see, I am no longer on active duty." I held up my stump.

He leaned back and lit a cigar, "Would you like one?"

"No thank you, Mr Milner."

"You have given me a problem. Are you saying that you do not want to take the post we are offering? It is a lucrative one."

"What I am saying is that I need to know more about it. I promise that I will give you an answer today, either yeah or nay, when I have heard what it is that you wish."

He looked relieved, "Then I hope that I can convince you." He stood and went to a map of the world behind his desk. He jabbed a finger at Persia, "This is Persia and Mr Reynolds and our owner, Mr D'Arcy, believe that there are vast reserves of oil beneath the desert there."

"Oil? Oil for lamps?"

He sat and smiled, "Oil for ships. It is the future, Lieutenant Roberts. Admiral Fisher believes that the ships we build in the next ten years will be fired not by coal but by oil. If the Royal Navy had oil-fired ships they would have a greater range and not need to seek coal to replenish their stocks. Now America has oil but there is none here in Great Britain. Before the Admiralty commits to building oil-fired ships, we need to have our own supplies. Mr D'Arcy has managed to gain drilling rights in Persia. Mozaffar ad-Din Shah Qajar is the ruler of that land. The Qajar dynasty has ruled Persia for more than a hundred years but they need money and Mr D'Arcy has provided that money. So, as you can see, we have friends in that land."

"And yet you need soldiers."

He nodded and relit the cigar which had gone out, "Sadly, yes. There are bandits and warlords. The Persians do not have a standing army. In addition, there are the Russians."

Desert War

"The Russians?"

"The Russian Bear seeks to make his own empire bigger. They want to increase their sphere of influence. So, you can see that you will be serving Britain as well as yourself. You were a soldier who served his country well and you have the opportunity to continue to do so."

I was not convinced about that and as I doubted that he had served in the army I would disregard his jingoism. I turned to Mr Reynolds, "Do you know the area?"

He shook his head, "I have been working in Indonesia, but I am confident that we will find oil in this land." He smiled, "Lieutenant, I have been told of your military career. My men and I would be much safer if you were in command of our escort."

"And who would they be?" The last thing I wanted was a bunch of mercenaries who were just in it for the money. I wanted real soldiers.

Mr Milner smiled, "I think you will appreciate the men we have procured. Thanks to the good offices of the War Office we have ten men waiting at Suez for you to take command. They were part of a unit raised to fight against the Dervishes. That unit is now disbanded and they were given the opportunity to either join other units or serve under you for six months before being honourably discharged."

"They are being paid too?"

"They are and paid much more than they earned serving Great Britain but as you are retired, from the army, so to speak, your pay is considerably higher." He held up a green file. "Their service records are here." I nodded. "Time is pressing, Lieutenant, the SS Carnic needs to sail within the next three days. If you do not take up the commission then it will be the unit's senior non-commissioned officer who will have to lead."

"Non-commissioned officer?"

"Yes," he opened the file and read the name, "Sergeant Major Richardson."

"Is his first name Syd?"

He looked down and nodded, "Sydney. Do you know him?"

Desert War

Knowing that Syd was leading the men made all the difference and the decision was an easy one. "I do. I will accept the commission."

Excellent." He looked relieved and he stood handing me the file. Glancing at the clock he said, "I have another meeting so if you two would continue this discussion in the outer office…. If you need anything then just ask my secretary. She is most efficient." I tucked the green folder under my stump.

Once outside we sat on the leather settee I had seen on the way in. The secretary came over, "I am Miss Williams. Would you like tea or coffee?"

I said, "Tea would be nice."

"And me."

She went to a small door, opened it and said, "Two teas and biscuits." She turned back to me. She handed me a sheet of paper. On it was my address and the names of Aunt Sarah, Bet and Griff as well as the address of my bank. "If you would just ensure that all the details are correct."

"Why do you need all this information?"

She gave me a smile but it was a cold one without any warmth, "If anything should happen to you on active service then your dependents would need to be informed and compensated for your loss, of course." She turned and left.

George smiled and shook his head, "That one is a cold fish. Not like my Lavinia."

"Lavinia?"

"My wife. Are you married?"

"Widower."

"Sorry. Look we do not have much time. William Knox D'Arcy, as you heard, is a rich and powerful man. He is gambling that the huge sums he has paid Mozaffar ad-Din Shah Qajar will result in an oil field that will make him one of the richest men in the world. Your pay is a drop in the ocean as is mine. Whatever you need for the expedition will be paid for by the company. He has hired a steamship. My crew is aboard already and we are just waiting for the drilling equipment to arrive. When you were told three days that was the outside figure. The ship will be ready to sail the day after tomorrow. Will you be ready?"

Desert War

It was short notice but the sooner my six months began the sooner I would get home. I nodded, "What happens if you do not strike oil in the first six months?"

He shook his head, "I am not sure but you and the others would be free to leave at the end of your contract."

"I haven't signed anything yet."

I was not sure if she had been listening but the ice maiden approached with a clipboard and a document, "Lieutenant Roberts, if you would read and sign the contract then it will all be legal."

I nodded. The tea and biscuits arrived and I read and drank at the same time. It was clear that I was still a British soldier, but my pay would come from the Anglo-Persian Oil Company. The pay, by army standards, was an enormous sum. Miss Williams stood watching me and I said, "Anglo-Persian Oil Company? You haven't found oil yet, isn't the name a little premature?"

"But we will. It is a working title."

I saw that at the end of the contract, I could leave and the company would fund my return to England. The pay for one month was greater than my annual pension from the army. In six months I would make six years of pension. I had to check my details and add the bank information for my pay. I would be a fool not to sign so I did. She looked relieved. "When you have finished here then you should visit Turnbull and Proctor. They are in the next building. They specialise in providing clothing and equipment for the tropics. Whatever you need you are to order and the company will pay. Your pay will be paid at the end of each month into the bank account you identified as yours."

I had finished the tea and I turned to Mr Reynolds. "So, we sail on the SS Carnic."

"Yes, she is a White Star vessel. She is not one of their larger ships. You will meet your men at Suez where they will be boarded."

"They have camels?"

He shook his head, "We will be buying animals when we land at Bandar-e Deylam. It is a small port in the Persian Gulf. It is little more than a fishing port. The thing is, Lieutenant..."

"Call me Jack."

Desert War

He smiled, "Jack, is that we have to keep a low profile. The Russians will do anything to stop British influence. The men you lead were chosen because they do not look like British soldiers. They all wear the keffiyeh and ride camels. We want to slip ashore and then make our way the one hundred miles to Shardin, hopefully unseen."

"With drilling equipment?"

"It is not as bulky as you might think."

"And your men, are they prepared?"

He laughed, "You will find that the eight men I have can handle themselves. They will all be armed."

I shook my head, "I want no loose cannons, Mr Reynolds…"

"George."

"I will give the orders and your men will obey me."

"Of course."

"We have done all that we can here. Show me the ship and then we will visit Turnbull and Proctor."

"When I have shown you the ship, Jack, I shall be busy. I will be spending as much time with Lavinia as I can. I have already been fitted out."

The ship was smaller than the ones I had sailed in before but, then again, they were huge liners or troopships. This one was a small liner with cabins for passengers but also carried cargo. Captain Hall seemed to know his business and he assured me that his ship was fast. Until my men joined me we would have the whole ship to ourselves. Satisfied that I knew where the ship was berthed and having learned when we sailed, I headed to Turnbull and Proctor. I knew what I needed before I entered. I would use my old helmet from Sudan and my cloak, but I would not be wearing my uniform. A very accommodating young man efficiently took me through all that they could provide.

"Our contract with Mr Milner is a good one, sir, and whatever you want you shall have."

I was furnished with two pairs of boots, one for riding and one for walking. There were also two light jackets and four pairs of trousers, I was even supplied with jodhpurs. With a reinforced seat they would be perfect for riding. The young man supplied a pair of expensive-looking leather valises. I realised that if I was travelling on a camel I would want an easy way to carry my clothes. The two leather cases were very well made and looked like they would cope with the rugged ride I anticipated. He also produced a pair of binoculars. They would, of course, be very useful. With shirts, underwear and socks all suitable for the climate, as well as the mosquito net, I was ready although it had taken two hours and it was now approaching lunchtime. The young man promised all would be waiting for me at home. He had also provided some lemon-scented candles as well as creams for the sun and the insects in addition to the first aid kit. I had not thought of any of them but they would all be useful. I headed for a pub lunch to reflect on what I had taken on. The last stop before I caught the omnibus home was to my tobacconists where I bought enough tobacco to keep me going, at least until we reached Persia. The tobacconist placed it in an airtight humidor that would keep it moist for longer. I had some tricks to maintain the moisture. If there were oranges to be had I would use the peel. I could also use a few drops of whisky or rum. There was bound to be some aboard the ship.

I reached my home just when the horse-drawn van from Turnbull and Proctor arrived. I was impressed. They did run an efficient service. I knew that Aunt Sarah would not be happy on many levels. The house would be a mess and it was a sign that I was going. Neither could be helped. I had them put the equipment in the hall. I would use the dining room to pack. With Griff away we ate in the kitchen more than in the grand dining room.

Bet looked bemused while Aunt Sarah looked cross. As the door closed, I said, "I will be out of your hair within a day and a half. There will be money paid into my account each month and I have already been to the bank to arrange for you to be able to access my account." We had got to know Mr Critchley well when we had dealt with Billy's estate. "As far as I am concerned you can spend it all."

Slightly mollified Aunt Sarah said, "You know we will not do that. You must understand, Jack, that we care for you and neither of us like this. If Griff was here I am sure he would be against it too."

I sighed, "Despite my one arm I still feel fit. I can do this. Who knows if I will still be able to five years down the road?"

Desert War

They could see that I had made up my mind and it was not mentioned again.

When young Jack came home from work I asked him about the Carnic as the ship bore the flag of the White Star line. He nodded, "I wondered about that when I ordered the supplies she would need. It is one of our smaller ships. The directors have decided to concentrate on the Atlantic market. The Carnic was a ship that did the eastern run. The Peninsular and Oriental Steam Navigation Company is the line that serves India and Australia now. She is a good ship and the captain knows those waters well." He frowned, "She leaves in two days."

I nodded, "Tomorrow is my last day." I smiled, "You can have a lift to work in my cab when I leave."

His face brightened, "The other clerks will be so envious."

I ignored the packing until the next day. I was used to packing for sea voyages and I had a system. I chose the time when Sarah was at the shops. She would only want to interfere. I packed my weapons too. I debated about taking or leaving the sword. As it fitted into the bag, I took it. The pistol, holster and ammunition went into the bag along with my bayonet and daggers. I hoped I would not need them but I knew that if I didn't take them then I would. The keffiyeh and puggaree were like old friends and I knew that I would need both of them as well as my helmet. When I was quite happy with the balance of the bags I chose the clothes I would wear to the ship and my old army boots. The boots I had been given were expensive but only time would tell if they were comfortable.

Aunt Sarah and Bet had made a good dinner for my last night and she had bought a bottle of wine. I could take or leave wine but for Aunt Sarah, and I think Bet, it was a sophisticated thing to do. When I had told Aunt Sarah my pay her eyes had widened.

When I left, at the crack of dawn, there were few words and all three ladies held back their tears but the squeeze that Aunt Sarah gave to me spoke volumes. Jack helped me to unload the cab and came aboard to view my cabin. He was impressed as I had been given what was considered a 1st Class one. He enjoyed walking about the ship he had read of but never seen and was disappointed when he had to hurry off to work.

Desert War

Captain Hall and George Reynolds were more than delighted with my early arrival. It meant that we could catch the noontide and leave a few hours earlier than they expected. I was off again but this time there was no train and third-class ticket, and there was no crowded troopship but, until we reached Suez I would be amongst strangers. No matter who the soldiers were with Syd, I knew that they would be brothers in arms and I would no longer be alone.

Liverpool was a bustling port. As we made our way along the busy river to the sea, George told me that Bristol had once been the pre-eminent port on the west coast of England but that prize had now been taken by Liverpool. It was the first time I had left from the west coast and I looked forward to the views of Wales.

Desert War

Jack

Chapter 6

Unlike a voyage from Southampton, we had land to our left, the larboard side, all the way to the tip of England, Land's End, and it was good to watch Britain slip by. When I had first trained as a soldier it had been in Wales and now I saw it from the best vantage point of all, the sea. I passed the mighty mountains and impressive castles. I was almost sorry to leave the deck when the gong sounded for dinner. The last rays of the setting sun were painting the mountains with a palette that an artist would envy. I would never see them as beautifully coloured again.

The ship's dining room had been built to accommodate more than the ten of us. Captain Hall had already arranged for his officers to join us. It was a sensible arrangement. The alternative was to have his mess orderlies serve two dining rooms. The company was comfortable. Not all the officers dined with us at any one time as there had to be one group on watch. It meant that it took a couple of days for us to meet all of them. They were surprisingly happy to have such a rough set of passengers. The first mate sat at the head of the table on the first night as the captain had the watch and he said, "When we take passengers normally they are all especially fussy. *'The ship is moving too much. My bed is uncomfortable. This isn't the tea I normally drink. Why does the ship go up and down so much?*'" I had to laugh for he was an excellent mimic and the falsetto, affected voice he adopted gave me an accurate picture of the passengers who must have made the crew's life a misery on the long voyage to India.

George laughed too but he said, "How do you know my men won't be like that?"

The first mate shook his head, "Mr Reynolds we have just spent five days with your men loading the equipment. They are like us, working men doing a job."

George nodded, "And this seems a good time to introduce you to them, Jack." He smiled and said, "Jack is to command the men assigned to protect us. You will have noticed his stump. It is still, I believe, a little red for it was incurred at the Battle of Omdurman." George and I had spoken about the stump and I had assured him that I was not in the least self-conscious about the arm. I had seen the men studying it while the first mate had been speaking. "His rank is Lieutenant but he has told me that he does not mind us calling him Jack. As well as being a soldier he speaks fluent Arabic and we all know that skill with languages is as valuable as a rifle in the places where we shall work."

He paused to allow me to speak and I said, "I know some of the men we will be picking up at Suez, the sergeant major and I served together for some years. They are all good men."

George continued, "This is Ken Collins. He is my foreman and what he doesn't know about drilling is not worth knowing."

"Pleased to meet you, Jack. With your permission, Mr Reynolds I will take it from here. I hate eating cold food."

I liked Ken from the off. He looked to be about the same age as me and had the tanned skin of one who has seen the Tropics first hand. He was blunt and honest. He did not waste words.

"My number two is Bert Willis." Bert looked to be older and had thinning hair and the yellow nicotine-stained fingers of one addicted to cigarettes. "Bert has more wives than a Mormon and if they ever find out about each other then he is in trouble."

Bert grinned and the others laughed, "Technically, Ken, only three of them are actually married to me and only one lives in England."

I leaned forward, "Have you ever worked in an Arab country, Bert?"

"No, Jack.".

"They are very protective of their women there. I would hate to hear you singing like a soprano." They all laughed at the joke, understanding the allusion only too well.

"Thank you for the advice."

"Bill Ellis here is the chief driller." I nodded to the young man who looked to be in his twenties and was not as tanned as the others.

"Harry, Wally, Tommy and Erik are the muscle of the crew. If there is anything to be lifted or hauled, then they do it."

The four men were well-muscled and like Ken had the mahogany-coloured skin of one who has seen a great deal of the

Desert War

sun. I smiled, "Before I joined the army I worked in an iron gang in a foundry. I know how hard you lads work."

The smiles I received told me I had said the right thing.

"Lastly, this is George. He is our token Geordie. His skill is as a toolmaker but he does a bit of everything including cooking and putting plasters on scratches."

"Pleased to meet you, Jack." His accent marked his origins even without my being told.

"You will get on well with my sergeant major, Syd Richardson is also from Newcastle."

His face lit up, "I know some Richardsons. I might know him." Ken shook his head. "Well, at least I will be able to converse with someone who talks proper, like me."

They all laughed at that. We did get on and get on well. The one who proved the most distant was George Reynolds. That had nothing to do with anything other than a need to do as much research as he could on the voyage. He spent much of the time in his cabin poring over maps and studying reports. He told me on one occasion that Mr D'Arcy had unrealistic expectations. "He seems to think, Jack, that we can just walk into the desert, sink a hole and up will come black gold. It doesn't work that way. I fear we may have to travel all over Persia before we find what we are looking for."

"Then we will need good animals. Can your men ride?"

"I can but my crew? Ask Ken."

I found myself in conversation with Ken every day and we grew close. That first morning, as we slipped beyond Land's End and skirted the Scilly Isles, we stood at the stern. He was a pipe smoker and we both had our pipes going.

"Can they ride?" I nodded. "If you are asking if they can ride as well as your lads will then no but they can stay on the back of a horse. They can stop them and make them go. Is that good enough?"

"It is. Mr Reynolds has said that we have the funds to buy as many animals as we need. I will buy horses for you and your lads but camels for my men and your equipment. They can carry more and it is what we are used to."

"My lads can look after themselves. They all carry handguns but we are more than happy that you and your men will be there.

We have worked in some hairy places where you had to keep one eye on the locals and that is not conducive to good drilling."

I nodded, "And I am unsure of the reception from the locals. The officer who commissioned me sent a report. The King of Iran, the one who gave us permission to drill, is not popular. He has little control over his own country and there are warlords aplenty. At the very least they may try extortion and blackmail but at worst they may try to take your equipment, our animals and our lives."

My sombre words ended the conversation but over the next weeks, as we made our way from the cooler north towards the Pillars of Hercules, I got to know the man and found we had much in common. He had been married but his wife had died in childbirth. The youngest in his crew, Bill Ellis, was his nephew and Ken regarded him as a sort of foster son. They were close. Ken was training Bill to take over the crew.

"The thing is, Jack, I have made a tidy pot. This will be my last commission. When I am done here, I will retire to England. I am not too old to take a wife." He chuckled, "Bert can't keep it in his pants and that is why he has so many women. I am not like that. Nancy was the love of my life but I know she wouldn't want me to be alone for my whole life. I am coming up to forty-one years of age. This job will take a year and then I can go home."

"Mr Reynolds thought six months."

He shook his head, "Mr D'Arcy thought it would take six months. Drilling is one thing but finding oil needs more than skill, it needs luck."

As I wrote the letter that I would post at Gibraltar I wondered if they would expect me to stay longer than six months. Would Griff become an officer before I returned to England? Would I miss his passing out parade?

The ship was a faster one than the troopships I had previously used and the voyage to Suez passed quickly. It was pleasant. We enjoyed the sun, the food and, at night, we played cards. Some enjoyed poker but I found that George Reynolds, Ken and Bill preferred whist. We played each night. The ship had a bar and a bartender who soon knew what we liked. Mr D'Arcy had hired the whole ship and the alcohol was free. I was impressed that

Desert War

none of the men abused the privilege. As we neared Alexandria and the canal, memories came flooding back. I could not help but be haunted by those who had died: Harry Fielding, Tommy Eliot and Danny Kemp had all died out here. I wondered about men like Middy Dunn who had been promoted from sergeant to officer in the Egyptian Army. Sam Smith, who had managed to retire, whole, and return to England. Was I a fool to voluntarily enter the world I had managed to escape?

I spent the whole of the trip down the canal on deck. I stared, not at Arabia, to the larboard, but at Africa and Egypt. I had spent more of my life as a soldier there than anywhere. I felt proud that I had been part of the army that had avenged Gordon but wondered if Britain could continue to be Africa's policeman. As the war in South Africa was demonstrating, our soldiers were spread too thinly. When we neared Suez I stared, not to see the land, but to see the men I would command. I was disappointed when I did not see them waiting for me.

Captain Hall smiled when I asked him where they would be, "Lieutenant Roberts, you of all people should know that communication in this part of the world is not always what it should be. I sent a telegraph message to say when we would reach here but I could not give a specific time. We will spend the day taking on coal and supplies. You go ashore and find your men."

I donned my helmet and puggaree for protection from the sun. I also put my Sam Browne on and my pistol. I had long ago left England. This was still a place of war. I found the port official and he directed me to an area just away from the port on a piece of open ground. I saw the tents and smelled the wood smoke. It was Syd and the camp. I did not approach directly but edged my way around so that I could appear unseen. I heard some familiar voices and I chose my moment well. There was a lull in the conversation and I roared, in my best sergeant major's voice, "Attention!"

I stepped out from the shadows of the building I had used for concealment and saw that they were all at attention. It was Bugler Brown who recognised me first, "Lieutenant Roberts! You are here!"

I nodded, "I am indeed. So, Sergeant Major Richardson, these are my motley crew."

He grinned, "They are indeed, sir, and we are glad that you are here. We have had enough of Suez."

"Get the tents packed away. For the next couple of weeks, you will enjoy the pleasures of a steamship and you will each have your own cabin."

Syd clapped his hands together, "You heard the officer. Sergeant Johnson, take charge and have the equipment taken to the port."

Jake grinned, "Righto, Sergeant Major."

We marched together to the port. As with all old comrades we marched in step. "So, Syd, tell me about the men. I recognised half of them."

He nodded, "It was straight after Omdurman that we were disbanded. General Kitchener was away in London and the other generals decided that we were surplus to requirements. I think they disliked the freedom we had enjoyed. They used the argument that we had no officer." He shook his head, "All bullshit, sir. Sorry, sir."

I shook my head, "No I agree with you."

"Anyway, we were offered a choice, join a regular regiment or an honourable discharge. The lads you see here are the ones who didn't want a transfer. In the case of Jake and me we are getting too old for this game and the others didn't fancy serving any other officer but you."

"That's daft, Syd."

"No, it's not, sir. There are some ropey officers out there and you know it. Anyway, before we were paid off General Kitchener returned." He chuckled, "He was not a happy man, sir. Apparently, he gave the generals a right good tongue lashing but the deed was done. He sought me out and said that he could offer me a six-month contract as a sort of thank you. He told me the pay and I jumped at it. When he told me that you would be the officer in charge, well…"

"When was this, Syd?"

"A month ago, why?"

"That was about the time that I was asked to take it on. General Kitchener was obviously confident about my answer."

Desert War

I must be honest, sir, glad as I am that you are in command I wondered why you came back, with the arm and all."

I sighed, "I don't know but when I was told, on the ship, that you were leading the men then I saw it as a vindication of my decision."

"How is Griff?"

"At the Military College, my son will be an officer, a proper one."

"Don't do yourself down, sir. You have more right to be an officer than most of the ones sent to command us."

We had reached the ship and I said, "The SS Carnic. A good ship and plenty of room."

"Travelling first class, eh sir? Perhaps we should have tried this mercenary malarkey years ago. I shall be able to use the money to get a lease on a place back home."

"Speaking of home, there is a Geordie with the drilling crew. His name is George."

He rubbed his hands, "Better and better."

The second mate was supervising the loading of the supplies in the hold. I waved him over, "This is Sergeant Major Richardson. He is in command of the men. They have tents and the like. Where do you want them stored?"

He pointed, "The hold."

"I will wait here, sir until the tents are loaded."

I said, "I will meet you aft of the funnel. Your quarters are there. We are not sailing until tomorrow so if you need to buy anything…"

He shook his head, "This place has changed, sir. They charge twice what they used to for everything. It is a seller's market. We have all that we need."

"Don't forget, Syd, we are going to a Muslim country, no pubs."

"We have a few bottles stashed away, sir, but you know the lads. They know there is a time and place for drink. Six months and then back home and they can drink as much as they like with plenty of money to do so."

"I should warn you, Syd, that the drillers reckon it might be nearer to a year."

"Even better. Twice as much money!"

The drilling crew were all about to go ashore. I said, "My sergeant major has just told me that the traders here have doubled their prices."

Ken nodded, "Thanks for the heads up, Jack. We are not desperate for anything but it will be good to walk on solid land for a bit."

George was in his cabin, as usual, working on his maps and reading the scanty information he had brought. The captain, his pipe stuck in the corner of his mouth, came to join me. He used the pipe to point, "Are those your men?"

I turned and saw them as they approached, laden with tents, rifles and their bags. "That's them."

He chuckled, "I wondered if the War Office had sent some biscuit tin soldiers, these look more like bandits than soldiers. No offence, Jack."

"None taken. I regard that as a compliment. They know how to survive in the desert and having handled Dervishes they are more than ready to take on anything else that the desert throws against us. They are used to fighting enemies both human and natural."

The purser appeared, "The new passengers are here, Captain Hall?"

He pointed, "Just stowing their equipment."

"Good. Atkins, Walters, come and join me if you please." The two senior stewards, immaculate in their whites appeared. "We have our last ten passengers. You can show them to their cabins when I have checked off their names."

Syd and the others soon had the tents stored and they strode up the gangplank. I saw that they had their rifles slung over their shoulders. All wore their helmets but their keffiyeh were around their necks. Their bags bulged. They were leaving Africa and the army as they knew it. These were veterans and knew not to discard anything. They might not have looked like biscuit tin soldiers but they knew how to obey orders.

"Attention."

The captain smiled and the purser read out their names and their ranks. Colonel Dickenson had been efficient. They were taken away in two groups, the NCOs, Syd, Jake and Bill and then the other ranks. As Syd left, I said, "I will see you in the bar

Desert War

when you are done." I did not need to give him directions. Syd would find it.

He smiled, "No Sergeant's Mess then, sir?"

"No, Syd, you will have to slum it and drink with the officers."

When they had gone Captain Hall said, "You have a good relationship with your men, Lieutenant."

"War does that, Captain. It shows you the best and worst in men. I am lucky. Those men are all the best."

The bar steward, Peters, was refilling his shelves. With the hold open he had taken the opportunity to replenish spirits and beers that had been consumed. We all knew that once we reached Persia such luxuries would be rare.

"When my sergeant comes could we have two beers, preferably ice cold?"

He smiled, "I have just brought up some from the hold. They are chilled before I put them in the cooler. Will you sit in your usual seat, sir?"

I had taken to sitting in the same seat when alone. It was at a small table and there were just two chairs there. It was a good place to read and to reflect. I shook my head, "No, I will sit at the larger table. Mr Collins and his men will be ashore for a while."

Syd entered and stood, hands on hips to admire the beautiful 1st Class lounge. "I could get used to this, sir."

Even as he moved towards me Peters had the beers and a small bowl of pistachio nuts. To him, it did not matter that we were soldiers. We were passengers on his ship and he had standards.

"Cheers."

"Cheers. Now tell me everything that happened to you, sir, after you left us. I confess we all feared for you when you were wounded and even though you seemed fine when you left us we all know that wounds can be funny things."

I told him all including my meeting with Kipling as well as Griff's application and successful entry to Sandhurst.

"A writer, eh? I am lucky if I can write my name properly."

Desert War

"Just because I have written the book does not mean that I will be published. It wiled away the hours and I enjoyed putting down our story."

"Our story?"

"Of course. I was part of a team and a proud one at that. Now, before the men come is there anything I need to know about them? I know half of them but the others…"

"Good lads. The ones who you wouldn't have wanted to join other battalions. Some took the chance to join the Egyptian and Sudanese armies for the promotion and the pay. You got the best of the rest."

"Tell me about them." I had the file and a pencil on the table.

"Jake and Bill Brown you know. They are the last of the ones from Omdurman. Ralph Hunt, he transferred to the ESEG from a cavalry regiment. He had a falling out with a sergeant. I think a woman was involved. A good bloke. Fred Emerson is a whizz with guns. He is as good an armourer as Jake. If he can take something apart and put it together again he is a happy chappie. John Jones is our Welshman. Happy go lucky, he is the one looking forward to this expedition more than most. The rest of us see it as a last payday but Jones sees the adventure."

I shook my head, "I want as little adventure as possible."

"Bill Bates' family have always been horsemen. He couldn't get into the cavalry but joined the Camel Corps. He will look after the camels. Dick Wilshaw is the youngest in the troop. I think he wants to emigrate to Canada. This is his chance to have the money to do so. Bob Larriby is the oldest. He is my age. His trouble is every time he got promoted he did something daft. He is ready to retire."

I looked down the list, "And Eric Wise?"

"Ah, the quiet man: he is probably the best soldier in the troop. Does everything right and the first time but we call him the quiet man as he doesn't say much. He is not miserable just, well, quiet. He would make a good sergeant."

"But?"

"But he has a widowed mother and he wants to go home to look after her. His brother was killed in India and he feels responsible."

Desert War

I looked down my list and the pencilled comments. I had a better picture of them now. "And what equipment do you have?"

He grinned, "The quartermaster was new and, freshly promoted, green as grass. Not long after the battle we were issued with the new MLE, Magazine Lee Enfield. It is a lovely piece of kit, sir. The lads all call them Emily, you know, MLE?" I smiled. That was soldiers all over. "When we were ready to leave he asked for our guns back. We still had our Lee-Metford rifles and we gave them back. We said we had yet to be issued with new ones. General Kitchener made sure we kept the rest of our equipment and he personally ordered us new tents. Top bloke is Kitchener. Scary but good."

"Ammo?"

Syd tapped his nose, "Jake managed to acquire a couple of boxes of .303 and some spare magazines. We spread them out. What about animals, sir?"

"When it is just us two, it is still Jack." He nodded. "Mr Reynolds has gold to buy them when we reach our destination. I daresay that we will be fleeced but beggars can't be choosers. I was going to buy camels for us to ride and to carry the tents, and horses for the engineers."

"Good idea. We were sad to lose ours. That last long ride we made through Sudan to Suez showed us what good animals we had." I nodded. I understood the relationship. "What about a local guide, Jack? We need a Saeed."

I had already thought of that. "There is an agent of Mr D'Arcy in the port, we will ask for a recommendation."

"These engineers sir, what are they like?"

"Tough as nails. They all have a sidearm and I get the impression that they know how to use them. I have told them that they obey our orders."

The troop, that was how I viewed them, entered and did what Syd had done. They went to the bar. I shouted over, "The drinks are all paid for. I recommend the beer." They cheered. I tried to identify them from Syd's description.

"Before the lads join us, Jack, what about the opposition?"

"Ah, there you have me. All I know is that there are local warlords who command their own warbands, bandits and, finally, Russians, who do not want us to find oil."

"So basically anything that we meet in the desert that walks on two legs or rides on four will be out to kill us."

"A fair assessment, Syd."

"Well, that is good to know." He raised his glass as the others joined us, "First Class and working with Lieutenant Roberts, have we landed on our feet or what?"

They all gave a cheer and I saw the smile on Peters' face. He did not get this reaction from his normal passengers.

Desert War

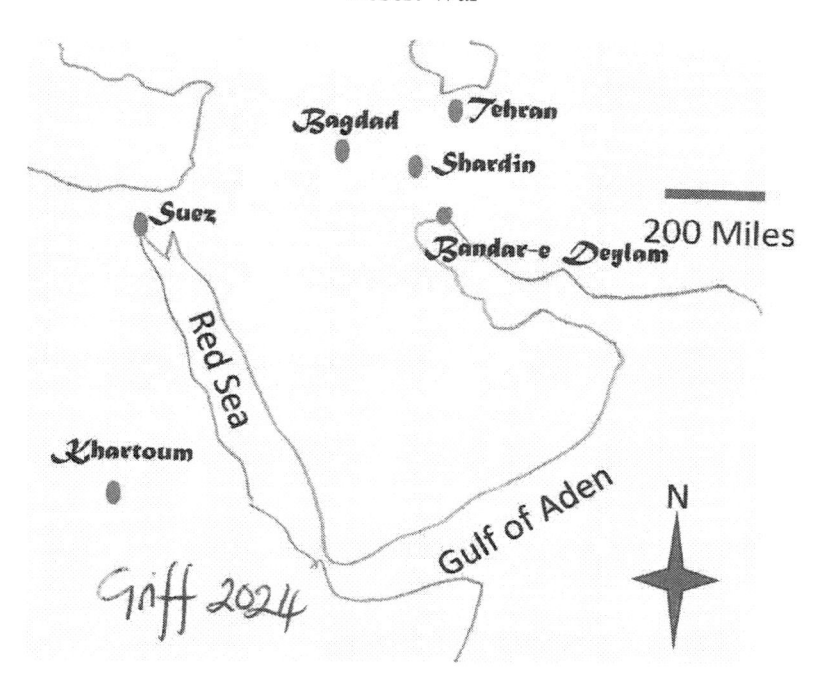

Jack

Chapter 7

I would not be using the new rifles but I was interested to see them in action. The troopers were happy to show them to me and the next day, as we headed into the Red Sea, I was given a demonstration and I realised what a superior weapon the men had been issued. If we had been given such guns at Rorke's Drift then the battle would have lasted less than an hour and a regiment would have been saved at Isandlwana. After they had fired them for me I told them they could leave their guns in their cabins and dress casually. It was too hot for even the new lightweight khaki uniforms. The ship had shades rigged and I did not mind them going bare-chested. The engineers did so. I was delighted when both groups melded. They were all cut from the same working-class cloth and got on. Syd and George did not know each other but they had plenty of people and places in common. When they discovered that they had both enjoyed beer in the same pub, the Crown Posada, it was as though they were brothers separated at birth. They both spoke yearningly about the beer and how you could not get a pint anywhere else in Britain that was as good. That, of course, initiated a lively debate with the others. Each man championed his own area. There was banter and humour in their arguments, and it was all harmless fun.

Ken and I kept apart from the debate. He waved his glass of beer at the discussion, "This bodes well for Persia, Jack. Long after there is no beer to drink, and we are all being baked alive they will still keep up the argument about whose beer is best."

I agreed. Team spirit was not something you could buy. You could try to foster it but if it came naturally, as this had, then it was like gold.

The captain sought me out on the same day the men had fired their weapons. I thought he was going to chastise me for their use but I could not have been more wrong. He took me into the bridge and pointed to the horizon, "What do you see, Lieutenant Roberts?"

Desert War

"The sea." We had left sight of land but I knew that it was just below the horizon on both larboard and starboard.

"Empty?"

I looked and saw neither sail nor sign of smoke, "Aye, empty."

"And that is where you are wrong. There are ships just below the horizon and they are heading for the canal but there are also pirates. The lands to both the east and west teem with them. The Royal Navy keeps patrols, but the pirates are most elusive. They sail small fast dhows, more like nautical greyhounds than ships. I am pleased that your men have their weapons. If you hear me sound the ship's whistle three times then you know it is pirates about to attack us. I want your men on the deck armed and ready to fight for their lives and, I might add, my crew. When we were on the India run, we always had a Royal Navy vessel to escort us. We have no such protection this time." He went on to tell me some tales of the results of piracy and it made my blood run cold.

"Thank you for taking me into your confidence, Captain, we shall endeavour to protect you and your ship."

The men were all in the lounge and there were games of cards and dominoes taking place. This was not the time for being close-mouthed and I clapped my hands, "Could I have your attention?" Silence dropped like a hammer. The tone of my voice must have given them some sort of warning. "I have just spoken with the captain and he warns me that these waters teem with pirates."

Bill Ellis said, "You mean like Blackbeard, Captain Kydd and the like?"

"Worse, apparently, these pirates take any ship. They come in huge numbers and if they make the deck then we would be overwhelmed. Troopers, if you hear the ship's whistle sound three times then grab your gun and ammunition. Our job will be to repel boarders." I looked at Ken, "And I assume your men would not be averse to fetching their pistols and joining us."

"We never shy away from a fight, Jack. We will back you up."

"Then I suggest we all get an early night and check our weapons. Once we reach the Gulf of Aden then the captain can make sea room but while we are between Africa and Arabia, we are in danger."

It was once I was in my cabin that I realised the problem I would have. Reloading my Webley, which had been such a simple act with two hands, now involved holding the gun between my stump and my body while I filled each chamber. It could not be done quickly. If the pirates made our deck I might not have the luxury of time. I would not be able to waste a single bullet. I had worked out that to fit my Sam Browne belt, the easiest way was to slip it over my head. I had my sword but I had not planned on using it. When I had the use of two hands, I was able to wield both weapons at the same time. Now I could not. I might need the sword so I fitted it to the belt. It made it both heavier and more awkward to fit. I tried it and it took some minutes to do so. Perhaps it had been a mistake to take this commission. This potential attack was just a trial run for the dangers we would face in the desert. I took off the sword and holster and hung them from the hook behind the door. I undressed. As I lay beneath the freshly laundered sheets, another Carnic luxury, I ran through my decision-making. I was finally able to sleep when I realised that had I not taken the commission then Syd and the others would be without my leadership. Syd was a good NCO but I knew that I was the leader. I had to be here. I might not return but I was needed.

There was no screeching whistle that woke us and I was pleased. The mood at breakfast was sombre. Syd ate with me and he pointed out of the starboard window towards Africa. "The thing is, sir, that we have sailed these waters before and saw neither hide nor hair of a pirate."

Jake and Bill were eating with us which is why he called me, sir. I shook my head, "You are forgetting, Syd, that when we sailed these waters, we normally travelled in a Royal Navy gunboat or in a convoy. These pirates are not rebels. They don't want a war with the Navy. They want to rob unarmed vessels like this one. Look around, this is a luxury that can normally only be afforded by the rich. Do you think that the pirates will think that there are less than thirty passengers on board? They will see a liner that they believe will have a couple of hundred rich passengers. That means wallets, jewels and the like.

Desert War

Normally a ship like this would have no guns that could keep them at a distance or defend the ship in numbers."

"Then, sir, why not have the lads bring their weapons on deck? The MLE can send a bullet five thousand yards. It can't do much damage at that range but at five hundred yards we can hit a ship or a man. While we waited for you in Suez, we practised and the lads are good."

"You make sense. Make it so." I also realised that I would be able to dress with my sword and pistol. I would not have the problem of having to struggle with my Sam Browne.

When Ken and the engineers saw what we were doing they went to fetch their guns. Corporal Bill Brown laughed, "It looks like we have Billy the Kid and Wild Bill Hickock." Some of the men had bought books and magazines with the stories of the Wild West and he was right, they had holsters without flaps and as many of them had a Colt, they did, indeed, look like cowboys.

Jake, who was our weapons expert said, "And at close range, those Colts have a better stopping power than Lieutenant Robert's Webley."

What did surprise me was when Mr Reynolds brought out a Purdey double barrel shotgun. He smiled at me, "I thought to use this to do a little hunting. If they get close enough, then I can give them a shock."

We lounged beneath the awnings strung up for shade. The chairs we used would normally be occupied by rich passengers who liked their comfort. As with regularly laundered sheets my men were enjoying luxury they had never experienced. When we had travelled from England on the troopships only the most senior of officers might have had what we enjoyed. The rest of us had been crowded into cabins that were meant for two but often had six soldiers.

"You know, sir, if the White Star line bought a couple of machine guns they would be safer."

"I know, Jake, but my nephew told me that the White Star does not sail this route very often. The liner was contracted for this single run. She is smaller than most of their fleet and has a hold. I am not sure that the SS Carnic has much of a future. When she has dropped us off and returns to England she might be decommissioned." I had not mentioned that to the captain but

Desert War

it had been Jack who, once he knew the name of the vessel, had made enquiries and whilst the information was not set in stone it seemed likely that the SS Carnic would be laid off and the crew sent to other vessels.

We had enjoyed another pleasant lunch, and we were lazing on the deck, smoking when the strident blast of the ship's whistle woke us from our reverie.

Syd shouted, "Stand to." I donned my helmet, as did the men. It would afford some protection but I also thought it might deter the pirates. If they thought that there were soldiers aboard they might think again.

"Where away, Captain?"

"Larboard side, they are coming from Arabia. There are four ships."

"Load your weapons." We all went to the larboard side and saw the triangular sails of the four pirate ships.

I slipped the lanyard from my Webley over my head and studied the ships. They had the advantage that we had little sea room. While the Red Sea was almost two hundred miles wide at its widest point it also narrowed to less than seventy. With shoals and rocks close to the coast there were a limited number of options open to the captain. He chose the only one he had. He began to turn to starboard and I heard him order full speed. That was just thirteen knots. We normally sailed at a sedate speed of eight or nine knots to save coal.

The first mate, Mr Seymour, now with a pistol strapped to his waist came to join us, "I see you and your men are prepared, Lieutenant."

Nodding I pointed to the leading pirate, "How fast can they sail?"

"With the wind, they can reach fifteen or twenty knots. They have the wind." He pointed to the funnel and then the pennant, "Those are a magnet for them. The buff-coloured funnel with a black top is a distinguishing feature for our ships, as well as a distinctive house flag, a red broad pennant with two tails bearing a white five-pointed star. The White Star line does not often sail this route. The pirates have spies at Suez. They will have seen us leave and now think to take us here where the sea narrows."

"Can we outrun them?"

Desert War

"It depends on the wind. The captain is doing his best to shake them off. I will go around and ginger up our men. If we are boarded…"

George Reynolds was close to us and said, "Surely it won't come to that."

"We can't guarantee anything." He saluted, "If you will excuse me."

George opened the shotgun and slipped in two shells, "You know I thought to take out some ducks or the like. I never thought that I might be taking a human life."

Syd shook his head, "Sir, these are not humans. They are animals walking on two legs. Kill them and you are doing the world a favour."

He shook his head, "I am an engineer, Sergeant Major, not a killer."

I said, "Syd is right George, if you don't become a killer then there might be no opportunity for you to be an engineer and find the oil that you seek."

He nodded, sadly, "I think I have a little insight into your world, Jack. You choose to do this?"

I shook my head, "We hope that we might not have to kill but we are prepared to do so."

Bill had good eyes and he shouted, "We are losing them, look."

Shading our eyes, I saw that he was right. Just then Mr Seymour shouted, "Ware there! Pirates on the starboard side!"

The men began to move to the other side of the ship and I shouted, "Hold your ground." I ran to the other side and stood with the first mate. There were three pirate ships and they were closer than the others.

Mr Seymour said, "Cunning blighters, Lieutenant. The captain has taken us closer to them. We will have to change course and that means the other four will be able to close with us."

"How far away do you think that they are?"

"A thousand yards."

"Ask the captain to hold this course for a while. We will try to discourage them." He looked dubious. I sighed, "There are just three ships here and four on the other side."

77

Desert War

He nodded, "Very well."

"Sergeant Major, bring the men to this side of the ship."

Ken shouted, "Do you want my lads too?"

Without turning I said, "No, keep your eyes on the other ships. Your handguns don't have the range that we do."

My men arrived. "I know there are only ten of you, but you are the only chance the ship has of surviving. Sergeant Johnson has told me that you can use these new rifles. Today is your opportunity. There is your target. When you think you can hit them then open fire."

Jake asked, "Should we not wait until they are closer and give them a volley?"

"You told me that this was a good gun and accurate, Sergeant."

"Yes sir, but five or six hundred yards is the optimum range."

"Then you give the command."

"Right, sir." He took a breath and then said, "Use the gunwale for stability and mark your target. When I give the command then fire at will."

He and Syd took their positions. I cursed my lack of an arm. I was the best shot here and yet I could not use a rifle. I took out the Webley. It would be useless at this range but holding it I felt as though I was part of the action.

The three ships began to spread out. Their huge sails would have obscured us from the helmsman and they each had two men at the prow. When Jake shouted, "Open fire!" the ten rifles all barked as one. Even though there were just ten rifles, Jake was right, they were accurate and two of the men at the prows of two of them fell. I heard the bolts slide back as another round was chambered and this time, as the three ships were slightly closer and the men had adjusted their aim then the other men at the prows fell. Some of the crew cheered as the bodies fell into the water but the three ships ploughed on. My men were now firing independently. There was no sound of a volley but individual rifles cracked as my men saw a target and took their chance. Still, the three ships came on.

Ken shouted, "Jack, the other four are gaining on us."

"Syd, take half the men and do the same on the other side."

"Emerson, Jones, Bates and Wilshaw, come with me."

Desert War

I said, "Right lads, it is down to you now. Let's see what you can do."

When I heard Syd's section begin to open fire I knew that they were in range on that side too. Luck sometimes plays a part in war. I knew that. One of the pirate ship's prows lifted and a bullet intended for flesh, found the wood of the hull. The bullets we used could punch a hole in a man and the wood of a small ship was easily punctured. The ship began to slow. At first, it was barely noticeable, but as more bullets found their targets it became more obvious. The pirates had been so focused on us that they must not have noticed it and by the time they began to bail it was too late. The other two left their stricken consort.

I shouted, "Forget the one that is sinking, concentrate on the other two." They were now less than two hundred yards from us and I saw that they each held what looked to be twenty or thirty pirates. They were close enough for me to fire at. I took aim at a pirate close to the prow. As I squeezed the trigger I said, "Jake, go for the helmsmen." If I had a rifle then I knew that I could have hit them. Jake was almost as good. I watched the pirate I had wounded with a splinter of wood slump as Jake's bullet took a helmsman. Falling across the tiller he veered into the second pirate. Just as importantly it allowed the rest of my men to fire into the side of the pirate ship. As Jake took out the second helmsman the two ships collided. The prow of the first one Jake had hit became entangled with the rigging of the other. The attack on our starboard side ended.

Syd shouted, "Sir, they are close to boarding." Even as he shouted, I heard the sounds of the pistols and George's shotgun as the four ships on the larboard side closed with us.

"Larboard side!"

My men ran across the deck but even as they reached it I saw that a group of pirates had made the forecastle. There were just a handful but they had gained the deck. I made an instant decision. "Sergeant Major, destroy these ships. Ken, bring your men with me. Mr Reynolds, we need your shotgun."

The first mate was firing his revolver at the pirates. He was keeping them occupied and no more. They took shelter behind the deck fittings. I waited until I was forty paces from the nearest one and then fired. I saw Mr Seymour reloading as three pirates,

Desert War

wielding wicked-looking swords charged at him. I emptied my Webley and managed to hit them. More men were pouring over the foredeck. George's shotgun scythed through four of them as Ken and his men began to fire their revolvers. Letting the Webley hang from its lanyard, I drew my sword. We had to give Syd and my men the opportunity to kill as many of those on the other boats as we could. Even as I neared the first of the pirates I was aware that we were moving to larboard and when I heard the crunch of wood I knew that the captain had damaged the pirate ship that had grappled us.

    I blocked the swinging sword that came at my head. My sword had belonged to an Egyptian officer and was well made but the blade that struck it was heavier. If I had been able to use my left hand then I could have drawn a dagger and stabbed the pirate. I could not do so but he could and I saw the look of triumph on his face as he drew a dagger. I punched with the hilt of my sword and struck him in the mouth. He reeled but not before he had slashed open my stump with his dagger. I brought the sword down and hacked into his neck. I do not know if the man I had slain was important but whatever the reason four men ran at me. I had no chance of defeating four of them. The double boom as George gave them both barrels, saved my life. With Ken and the others, we ran at the last six men on our ship. I did not get a chance to wield my sword again for the drilling crew cleared the decks with their pistols.

    "Back to my men!"

    My men, at the waist of the ship, were fighting three pirate ships and their crews. I saw what Syd had meant about my men. Eric Wise was firing calmly and smoothly. In contrast, John Jones was shouting insults at the pirates. All of them were showing the pirates what well-trained British soldiers could do. Before we had even reached them, I heard a cheer from the members of the crew who had run to the aid of my troop. Syd and the others were still firing but the last two pirates were heading back to Arabia. The other ship was already filling with water.

    Syd said, "Keep firing! Let's take as many of the bastards as we can. It will save some other poor sods from being attacked."

Desert War

When they were five hundred paces from us, I shouted, "Cease fire."

Everyone cheered and the captain began to sound the whistle over and over as a triumphant paean.

Syd turned, grinning and then his grin changed to a look of horror. "Sir, your arm!"

I looked down and saw the blood pooling on the deck. Ken shouted, "George, get your medical kit."

Syd took my sword from my hand and sheathed it, "Lie down, sir, before you fall."

The excitement of battle had made me ignore the wound but the puddle of blood showed that I was weakened and I allowed them to lay me on one of the loungers that would have been the preferred spot for a 1st Class passenger to relax. It now made an improvised hospital cot for me.

I gave George the Geordie a weak smile, "Another skill, George?"

He nodded, "As I said, sir, I can turn my hand to many things. If you like I can give you a haircut too. Now lie back."

He took some brandy and poured it over the stump. The end was still red from the amputation. Being in the sun had not helped it. The blood washed away I saw that the cut was about eight inches long but it had missed anything vital.

George took some catgut and a needle. "Ken, give him a good slug of brandy. This will hurt."

Syd said, "Shift that awning to give him some shade."

The mug of brandy burned as it went down and made me sleepy. It could, of course, have been the loss of blood. I managed to say, before I passed out, "Take command Sarn't Major."

Desert War

Jack

Chapter 8

I was in my cabin when I came to. Geordie George and Syd were sitting on the two chairs and chatting as I opened my eyes. As usual, they were talking about Newcastle and sharing memories. When there was a lull I said, "How long was I out?"

George and Syd rose and came over to me, "Long enough for me to stitch you up. It is about an hour since we saw off the pirates."

Syd nodded, "It was the sharks who finished them off. I hate pirates but that is no way to die."

George nodded at my stump, "You know, sir, I can do something about that."

I gave him a wry smile, "You can grow a hand again?"

He laughed, "No, Syd and I were talking. You can utilise the stump. If we encase it in a metal sleeve then you have protection. I am pretty certain that we might run into trouble in the desert." I nodded, he was right. "We could put some padding around it, and I could tailor-make it so that it was a snug fit."

"You can do that?"

"There is a machinist shop aboard and there is plenty of metal I can use. The chief engineer wants to help. He reckons you and your lads saved our bacon today."

"I am not so sure. If we weren't aboard, then the ship would not have been here and the pirates would not have attacked."

"But we are here, sir. Anyway, I can also make some attachments. If I thread the end we can give you a hook, that is always handy and would enable you to use your left hand for holding the reins. I can make a holder for your pipe. I know you can do it one handed but that would help."

Syd chipped in, "And would enable you to hold the Webley while you reloaded it."

"I don't want to be any trouble."

They exchanged a look and George said, "Look, sir, we have another fifteen days before we reach Bandar-e Deylam. I can't abide being idle. I will enjoy the challenge and, from what Syd

Desert War

has told me, we have more chance of surviving in the desert if you are kept fit."

"Very well, in that case, thank you."

He whipped a tape measure out of his overalls and said, "Syd, write down these measurements, eh?"

When it was measured George left us and I said, "A useful man, that."

"Comes with the blood, you know. Salt of the earth are folk from the Tyne." I made to get up, "Where are you going to, sir?"

"Just up on deck. It is like an oven here. At least there is a breeze up top."

"Just to the deck and then you are on sick leave for a few days. That is an order. You are not a spring chicken anymore."

The men, soldiers and drillers alike, all greeted me warmly. I had been the only casualty. Bill Brown said, "I will go and rustle up some sergeant major tea with plenty of sugars in it. That is what you need."

I felt like an invalid as everyone was so solicitous. I just felt foolish. It was a daft wound to have incurred. The steward brought me some cake to have with the tea and I felt like a real first-class passenger. I could get used to a life where you were waited on hand and foot. I suppose officers like the colonel and the general took such things for granted. For the likes of me, it was a surprise when it happened. It made me think about Griff and his life at college. He would be rubbing shoulders with the very people who normally travelled the way I was travelling. Would it change him? I hoped not. Perhaps I was biased but I thought my son was as close to perfect as a young man could be. Thus far I had not seen any vices. He did not smoke, he drank in moderation and while he was still single he always treated women like ladies.

After the tea and cake, I just fell asleep. When I woke, I saw that someone had found a straw hat and covered my face with it.

One thing the attack had done was to make us as one. We had fought together and no one had performed badly. The voyage to Persia had been pleasant before the attack now, although we were vigilant, it was joyful.

By the time we had passed the island of Socrata the threat of pirates diminished for we were able to travel further from the shore. Geordie George made good progress with the metal hand. One of the stewards proved to be a dab hand with needle and thread and he made a glove that fitted over the stump to stop chafing from the metal. A week after the attack he had made the actual metal sleeve. We tried it on and it needed only minor adjustments. I would have been happy with just that but I was learning that the engineer from Newcastle was a perfectionist. He liked things to be just so. He had made the screw part of the head anyway, so he said, and now it was just what he called the interesting part, where he made the attachments. He went a little overboard with them and by the time we reached Dubai, just four hundred and fifty miles from Bandar-e Deylam, I had a variety of attachments. Some would only be of use when I returned to civilisation but I was able to drink with my left hand and the fork attachment he fashioned was a godsend. Cutting meat had been a nightmare. When I had been at home Aunt Sarah had insisted upon cutting it up for me. On the ship, I had tried to eat only those things that were already small enough to be forked.

As we neared Bandar-e Deylam so we held more meetings to work out what we would be doing. Mr D'Arcy had an agent in the port. He was a local man and George Reynolds was already relying heavily on his skills. I was less certain about how much use he could be.

I said, "If he can direct us to an animal trader, I can happily negotiate."

"It would be easier if he procured them."

"With all due respect, Mr Reynolds, you know machines. I know animals. I want the best that there are. This agent might well be a respectable man but I don't know him. I want good animals. Syd and I will get our animals."

"Very well. I will provide the funds."

"And that is something else, Mr Reynolds, we need to work out how we are going to protect the bullion chest you have with you."

"Protect? From whom? Our men?"

I snorted, "I can guarantee that there is not one among ours who would take a threepenny bit. No, I am more worried about opportunist thieves. I will assign a man to watch the chest. If we run out of money then we will be in real trouble."

Desert War

I don't know what I was expecting when we saw the port in the distance, but it was not this. Bandar-e Deylam was able to accommodate us and that was all. We nudged into the harbour with two lookouts to ensure we did not ground. We filled the quay. I prepared myself for the landing and donned my Sam Browne and pistol as well as my keffiyeh. The new tools George had made changed my life and I felt like less of a cripple.

We were not the largest of ships yet we dwarfed the tiny quay. The locals swarmed around us, trying to board and sell us things. Mr Seymour had two of the biggest stokers on the ship assigned to stop them coming up the gangplank. The pickaxe handles in their hands were deterrent enough.

George Reynolds said, "Would you and the sergeant major like to come ashore with me?"

"Syd."

"I will just get my pistol."

The engineer said, "Ken, you can have the equipment brought out of the hold, but I don't intend to land it until we leave, and we will need draught animals for that."

"Righto, Mr Reynolds."

I said, "And Ken, I think that sidearms will be the order of the day."

Syd dressed like me. I had no insignia on my khaki jacket and Syd's stripes were so faded that they were barely discernible. It was only our pistols and gait, and Syd's swagger stick, that marked us as soldiers. As we crossed the quay we marched in step. It was the soldier's way.

We spied the agent across a sea of imploring hands and strident voices. Syd bellowed, in Arabic, "Out of the way or I shall give you a sharp tap on the head with this." He held the swagger stick threateningly and allied to his voice and use of their language, it made them back off.

George did not speak any Arabic but his agent spoke English; he wore a fez and a grubby jacket that might once have been white, "Effendi, I am Mohammed Ali Teymourtash, I am Mr D'Arcy's agent here in Persia. Whatever you need I shall gladly acquire it for you." He beamed like a child eager to impress a visiting grandparent, "I can get horses for you and porters if you need them."

George Reynolds looked at me and I said, "All I need from you is the name of an animal trader."

He shook his head, "Effendi, they would rob you. I can negotiate a better deal for you."

My tone brooked no argument, "The name?"

His face became sulky, and he pointed, "On the way out of town there is an animal dealer, Fazlollah Ali Taqizadeh. Without me, you will pay more."

Ignoring the man, whom I did not like at all, I said, "Will you be alright, Mr Reynolds?"

He nodded, "We shall return to the ship where I can speak with our agent in slightly more comfortable conditions."

As we headed in the direction of the animal trader Syd said, "He looked like a slimy piece of work."

"To be fair, Syd, I can understand it. He works here alone, and he is merely looking after himself."

Syd waved a hand around the people through whom we were passing, "He looks to have more than these poor sods."

The place did look run down. I spied a couple of new buildings, as we left the port. One of them was a telegraph office. They had links with the outside world, but I knew that the last letter I had sent home, from Suez, would be the only one until we left Persia. There were one or two solid-looking buildings. I guessed that they were from the time of Turkish occupation. This was still, ostensibly, part of the Turkish Empire but there was a great deal of autonomy as the presence of a British drilling crew showed.

The building that looked like it belonged to a horse trader was solidly built. As we approached it a young man emerged, "I am Mohammed Ali Fazlollah, can I help you?"

He spoke in Arabic and I answered him, "We are seeking animals."

He nodded, "To buy or to hire?"

"We may need them for a year or more. What would you suggest?"

He smiled, "I would suggest that we go inside to discuss terms. It is cooler and away from the inquisitive eyes of others."

As we entered the cool building I said, "We were told that the horse trader was Fazlollah Ali Taqizadeh."

Desert War

"My uncle. He is away buying more animals." We had passed through a corridor to a shaded courtyard with a small fountain. Lemon trees shaded it and gave a pleasant smell. "Sit here." He clapped and a servant appeared. "Coffee."

The man bowed and left. I knew that coffee was the preferred drink in these parts. Syd would have preferred tea but as they serve tea here without milk this would be as good a drink as we were likely to get.

The man smiled and pointed to the hookah, "Would you care to enjoy it?"

"No thank you." Syd shook his head too. "We need camels and horses. We would require a large number."

He took a wax tablet and asked, "How many?"

"Twelve horses and sixteen camels."

He raised his eyebrows as he wrote down the number, "That is more than we anticipated."

"Anticipated?"

"Yes, my uncle is away as he is trying to get the animals that you need from those who live in the desert. Mohammed Ali Teymourtash asked us to get them for some foreigners who wished to travel in the desert. We assumed he would give us the details."

"I will be honest with you, Mohammed Ali Fazlollah, my friend and I are soldiers and we know camels and horses. I am not sure that the agent does."

He smiled as the coffee came. It was, as I had expected, in tiny cups and there was a bowl of sugar. It would be incredibly strong. He waved the servant away and said, "Ali Teymourtash does not know one end of a camel from the other but he knows how to extract the last coin. You are wise. When we have finished our coffee we shall go and inspect the animals that we have here."

I put in four lumps of sugar and stirred it. Syd saw what I did and emulated me. I drank and the sugar had made it palatable. Syd wrinkled his nose.

"And where is it that you wish to visit? The ancient tombs?"

I shook my head, "The men we accompany are engineers. They wish to drill beneath the desert."

He frowned, "Why? There is just rock beneath the sand."

Desert War

"There is oil, or so they believe."

"Ah. And where is it that you wish to drill?" He struggled with the word I had used. It was one of the few words of Arabic that Mr Reynolds knew. He had learned it before we had left England as part of our preparation.

"Shardin."

He frowned and shook his head, "That is not a good place to go, my friend. There are bandits and warlords aplenty and the land there…it is hot."

"My friend and I served in Sudan and Egypt. We know heat and we know the desert."

"And the men who seek beneath the sand?"

I nodded, "You may be right. However, our job is to protect the men and keep them safe."

We had finished the coffee and he stood, "If it causes no offence, can you tell me how you lost the arm?"

"It was in battle."

"And yet you still carry a gun and look like a soldier." There was admiration and respect in his voice, "Come."

We passed through more buildings but this time they were less grand and clearly housed the servants. When we left the buildings, the heat hit us as did the smell of animal dung and the noises they made. I saw, immediately, that the camels were outside, each of them squatting while the horses were in stables.

"My uncle is seeking more horses. We did not think that you would need camels."

"What were you told?"

"Mohammed Ali Teymourtash asked us for twenty horses for foreigners."

"How many camels do you have?"

"Thirty. We trade more camels than horses. Merchants like them."

"Then you have enough. May I…"

"Of course."

I walked over to the animal that reminded me of Aisha. She had been the best camel I had ever ridden and I had been sad to let her go. I walked over to the camel and spoke gently as I stroked its head. I was running my eyes over the beast. It looked strong. I took the reins that were around her neck and, still

Desert War

speaking to the camel, sat astride it. I pulled back on the reins and, smacking the rump, gave the command to rise. There was no saddle but I did not intend to be on its back for long. I was really trying to show the trader that I knew camels. I rode a circuit around the yard and then returned to Syd and a bemused Ali Fazlollah. After I made it sit, I dismounted and gave the camel one of the sugar lumps I had taken from the house.

"You know your animals. That was well done."

"A good camel."

"Fatima is the best one we have. You have a good eye."

"We would like others of that quality. The men I lead all rode camels in Sudan. There are eleven of us. The other five would be used to carry the equipment."

He nodded. He had left the wax tablet inside but I saw him calculating a price. He said, "I promise that you shall have the best. And now the horses. I think that we have enough. As I said we did not expect you to use camels."

The horses were perfect. If I had been a cavalry officer I would have been disappointed for they were not chargers. They were working horses. As they were led around the yard I saw that they were sure-footed and broad in the back. They would do.

"Let us retire inside and begin the negotiations."

We haggled. I did so because our host expected it, but I was happy to pay whatever he asked. The animals were good ones and worth all that we paid. When the price was agreed he said, "One more thing."

"Yes?"

"You will be taking away most of our animals. They are an investment and the price we have negotiated is a fair one. We will buy them back from you when you leave. I would come with you, to protect my investment."

We needed a guide and he had already indicated that he knew the land through which we would travel. I shook my head, "You may come with us but you will be employed as a guide."

"You would pay me?"

I smiled, "If I pay you then I can give you orders. This suits us both, my friend, you get to watch your animals and I have a guide that I can trust."

He beamed and held out a hand, "I think that this will be a most interesting time. When do we leave?"

"Tomorrow, bring the animals to the ship."

"It will take me until then to find the saddles that we shall need."

We left and Syd said, "They were good animals, Jack, and I think you made the right decision. He reminded me of Saeed."

"And me too."

When we reached the ship, the crowds had dispersed. It was clear that the crew had discouraged their attempts to sell them anything. I saw that under the awning on the aft deck, a second Arab had joined George and the agent. We boarded the ship and Syd said, "I will go and get the lads to pack. Tomorrow will be all go."

I joined George who said, "Ah, Jack, a successful foray?"

"We have the animals and they will be here in the morning."

The agent shook his head, "Impossible, for they did not have enough horses. They are procuring them for you even as we sit here. You will not be able to leave for at least a week."

"But they have camels." Ignoring the agent I said, "It is all good, George."

The engineer smiled. "And we now have a guide. This is Mohammed's cousin, Ahmed."

The man bowed. I did not like his looks. I spoke in Arabic. "What do you know about Shardin?"

He beamed, "No problem, sir, it is an easy ride and the people there are friendly."

I knew then that we did not want him, "And what of the bandits and warlords?" His face fell. I could see that George was confused and so I explained, "The man says that Shardin is a friendly place. I know it is not. I have a guide already and we do not need this man,"

Mohammed Ali Teymourtash's face lost the mask he had adopted and became angry, "You insult me. My cousin is a good man."

"Mine is better."

He turned to George Reynolds, "Who commands here, Mr Reynolds, you or this one-armed man?"

Desert War

That decided me, "While we are on the road, Mohammed Ali Teymourtash, it is I who commands. Mr Reynolds is the engineer."

George nodded, "The lieutenant is the one who commands until we reach the site, Mohammed."

The agent stood, "Then on your own head be it." He and his cousin stormed off the ship.

"Was that wise, Jack?"

"Trust me, George, the man who will be our guide is worth double any other we might find. He is the nephew of the trader and he knows animals as well as the land."

"Very well. If you are going to hire a guard dog then you had better heed his warnings." I don't think that George meant the insult. "The captain is ashore. I will let him know our plans when he returns."

We had just eaten lunch when the captain and the purser returned. I told him the news and he nodded, "That is perfect. We have another commission. When I telegraphed our office to tell them of our safe arrival, they directed me to sail to Cape Town. There have been British casualties in the war in South Africa. We are directed to pick them up and return them to England."

Sometimes events happen that you cannot predict. The Carnic would not need to travel through the Red Sea. Instead, they would have a safer voyage to South Africa. We later learned that there had been two battles, one at Talana Hill and another at Kraaipan. British citizens were being besieged in Mafeking. As we prepared to leave the port that seemed unimportant. We would be heading into the desert and danger.

Desert War

Griff

Chapter 9

The vendetta began but I was not the one to suffer first. For some reason, the ones who had been on the sharp end of my fists decided that all of those in our dormitory were to blame. For four of us that was not a problem, we all stayed together, but poor Geoffrey still wanted to fit in and he continued to try to ingratiate himself into their favour. It was doomed to failure. He was mocked and humiliated at every turn. By the middle of the week, he looked like a whipped dog. They made the most hateful comments to him and unlike us, when we were insulted, he took them to heart.

The second week of our training saw Geoffrey having to join in again. It was a disaster. We had all enjoyed a week of training and knew how to hold a sword, fire a rifle and at least stay on a horse. Geoffrey did not. Whilst he did not fall off his horse this time, he clung on for dear life and the instructor despaired of him. He had little control over the animal. We supported him and encouraged him but the blue bloods mocked him. It stopped when the sergeant instructors barked out their orders but when we traipsed back to our dormitory block they were relentless. Of course, the four of us rallied around but they sneered evil remarks at him and there were eight of them. In a fistfight, we would lose. They would take me out first. We did not back down but it was a defeat and each night, of that first week, we heard Geoffrey weeping into his pillow.

The next morning as we dressed and while Geoffrey was in the latrine I said, "What are we going to do about this?"

Peter shrugged, "I can't see poor Fairbrother ever becoming a soldier. He is so inept."

James was a quiet one but when he spoke, we tended to listen, "He will never even have the chance if those bullies do not let up on him."

Bob said, "Look, I agree with you but even if we could take them on the odds are that we would be defeated and punished. I can't afford to lose my place here."

Desert War

"Then we have to tell someone."

Peter said, "Peaching?"

I shook my head at the very public-school phrase, "We could mention it to Senior Cadet Watson or Sergeant Windridge. Both seem like decent chaps."

We had all learned that Captain Collins, whilst a good officer, had little interest in us. We had learned, through the gossip, that he was using this as a step to a post at Whitehall.

James said, "It is better than nothing but we will still need to watch our backs."

I said, "Sorry to have embroiled you all in this."

James laughed, "Don't be silly. They would have tried to humiliate us in any way that they could. It is how they were brought up. They are rich and spoiled. I went to public school and I met their type. They use any means they can to get their way. No, the moment we got off the train and I saw them I knew what lay ahead. I just hoped that there would be more chaps like you."

We decided to give it one more day and then tell Senior Cadet Watson. Saturday was an easier day. We just had to march and drill and were given the afternoon off. Geoffrey seemed even worse that day. I suspected that it was lack of sleep that had caused it. Whatever the reason he dropped his rifle. The drill sergeant was good but had a tendency to be a martinet.

"Cadet Fairbrother, you do not drop your rifle. While you are a useless piece of waste, that rifle is valuable. Hold it above your head and run around the outside of the parade ground until I order you to stop."

"Yes, Sergeant Instructor Thomas."

His voice was weary before he even started. While we continued our drill Sergeant Instructor Thomas was clearly keeping an eye on him for he would shout, "Pick your feet up, Fairbrother." At another time he said, "Keep those arms straight."

When it was over Geoffrey was red-faced and sweating; he could barely hold up his rifle. We marched to the armoury to hand them over and then headed back to the refectory. It was lunchtime and we had an afternoon off. Some cadets would go into the village. I knew that the blue bloods would. They would go to the village pub and hold court there. They knew some of the older cadets and it was a place we assiduously avoided. We tended to stay in the dormitory block and play cards in the lounge.

The short walk to the block saw poor Geoffrey subjected to the most horrible comments from the other cadets.

"It seems, Geoffrey," Willoughby drawled the name out so that it became a sentence in itself and was imbued with as much disdain as possible, "it seems you are not even fit to be an ordinary soldier."

"Perhaps there might be some job you can do. I understand that night soil men do not need either intelligence or skill. That would suit you."

I had endured enough, "Stop this now, St John-Wilson."

St John-Wilson was the biggest of the group and he turned threateningly, "Or what? You have no right to be here, Roberts. Your father came from the gutter and was only promoted through luck."

He was trying to goad me and I knew it. I also knew that he was wrong. We were within sight of the officers and if I reacted then I would be the one that was punished. I smiled, knowing that it would rile him, "Well, I could beat you to a pulp. Your two friends who tried to take me on discovered that but, you know, you are not worth it and you do not have the courage to take me on. You may join a fashionable regiment but you will never be a real soldier. Do you think that those ordinary soldiers you are so scathing of would follow you into battle? You would be more likely to be shot in the back although knowing you and your type, you would be as far from danger as it would be possible to get."

The boot was on the other foot and it was he who swung the fist that was seen by Sergeant Instructor Windridge. I had also seen him bunching his fists and knew what was coming. I took a step back and he not only missed me but lost his balance and fell at my feet. As Captain Collins and Sergeant Instructor Windridge hurried over I put my hands under his armpits and said, "You have to be more careful, Cadet St. John-Wilson. You might have hurt yourself."

Desert War

The captain had seen nothing and said, "Are you alright, cadet?"

"Yes sir." St. John-Wilson glared at me.

The blue bloods all went off and Sergeant Instructor Windridge said quietly, "Nicely done, Roberts but watch out for those chaps. They have influence and the senior officers would side with them."

"Thank you, Sergeant Instructor Windridge, I hear what you are saying."

When I looked around, I saw that the object of the ridicule, Geoffrey, had disappeared. I did not blame him. The attention was on me and not him. As we went for lunch the other three were in high spirits. "You are quick on your feet, Griff."

"Before we moved into the suburbs I lived in the centre of Liverpool. There were some tough kids there and my dad was away more than he was at home. I learned to handle myself. My Nan and Aunt never knew. I had grazed knuckles and the odd bloody nose but I gained respect and I learned a skill. I confess that I never expected to have to use that skill here but…"

While we ate we sat as far away from the blue bloods as we could. It was James who noticed the absence of Geoffrey. Peter shrugged and said, "He is probably having a nap in the dorm. He must be shattered after running around the parade ground with a rifle over his head."

I said, "He still needs food. We will take him some bread rolls and biscuits." There were plates of both in the refectory and after we had disposed of our plates and cutlery we secreted some and headed back to the dormitory. When we entered the first thing I noticed was that not only was there no Geoffrey, all his belongings were missing.

Bob nodded, "He has done a runner."

I shook my head, "We have to stop him. He is ruining his chances of a military career."

Bob sighed, "I don't like those toffs but they are right in one respect, Geoffrey will never make a soldier, let alone an officer."

"We have to try. He will head for the station."

"And he has an hour or more start on us."

James shook his head and stood, "Bob, Griff is right. We can try. What else would we be doing? Playing cards? Isn't this a nobler thing to do?"

"You are right. Let's go."

Even though we ran, as we reached the platform we saw the London train heading out of the station and there was no sign of Geoffrey. We had tried and failed.

"What do we do now?"

"What do you mean, James?"

"If we don't tell anybody about this we may well be in trouble. If Sergeant Windridge is right then the toffs would just use it as a way of hurting us."

"James is right. We find Senior Cadet Watson and tell him."

We had done the right thing and Watson quickly informed both the sergeant instructor and the captain of what amounted to desertion. Geoffrey was in trouble. Senior cadets were sent to the station to confirm what we had said and then the four of us were called into the senior officer's office where we were grilled by both the colonel and the captain about what had gone on. If we had not told the truth then we might have been blamed and I knew that our service record had begun the moment we had entered the college.

After we had spoken, I said, "You can ask Sergeant Instructor Windridge if you want confirmation, sir."

The colonel looked appalled, "This is about officers, Cadet Roberts. We do not need to involve Non-Commissioned Officers in this affair."

The captain said, "Senior Cadet Watson might be of some assistance, he has only one term to go and he will soon be an officer."

"Very well, send for him."

We waited in an uncomfortable silence while Watson was summoned. When he arrived, he was grilled as much as we had been. Luckily for us, he confirmed almost all that had happened. He alluded to the fisticuffs without naming names.

At the end of it, the colonel shook his head, "I can't believe this of St John-Wilson. His father and I are members of the same club. Perhaps he was led astray by this Willougby and FitzWilliam. We had better have them in and you four, you

Desert War

should have reported these incidents to your captain. I trust there will be no more such events. You are dismissed. Watson, you had better stay here. We may need your evidence too. These other cadets are not without connections. We must do everything right and by the book."

It felt as though we were the ones who had been found guilty of the crime. We did not speak until we reached our dormitory. Bob said, "If we had said something then it would have gone badly for us. Damn, Fairbrother."

I had to defend Geoffrey, "You cannot castigate Geoffrey. He was not meant to be a soldier but when we become officers, we may well have men under our command like Geoffrey. We have a duty to those too."

Bob shook his head, "You may be right but this will not do our prospects of a decent regiment any good at all. We are not like Willoughby and the like. We have no connections."

"The army is the army, Bob. By decent regiment do you mean one that is fashionable or one that is well-run? I, for one, do not mind where I am sent. If the regiment is not well run then I have the chance to make a difference."

"Yes, but suppose you were sent to a regiment based in India?"

James smiled, "I hope that I am. Dorothea is there. In fact, Bob, you have made me feel better about this whole thing. Griff is right. Instead of bemoaning our fate, we should embrace it. I have been a whingeing Winnie. I shall do my best and ask for a posting to an Indian Regiment. You are right, they are not popular and I will be nearer to my heart's desire." It was one positive thing which came from the whole sorry episode.

It took almost a week for the results of the enquiry to be made public. Willoughby and FitzWilliam were the scapegoats for what had been the collective act of the eight. They had a week of cleaning the latrines followed by a week of pan bash. We became even more isolated. The blue bloods had friends and relatives amongst the other cadets and we were shunned by all and sundry. Our allies became fewer. The sergeant instructors, on the other hand, viewed us with even more respect. Training became even more competitive. It seemed that the eight were determined to prove that they were better than we were.

However, it backfired. While we became better at fencing, they, who had begun with more skills, became so competitive that in their bouts, there were injuries. Similarly with the riding. Our progress was slow and steady. They could ride but they were so keen to show off that they took chances. When we had a ride across fields, Warenne chose to show off and took a hedge. What he did not know was that there was a ditch on the other side. He was thrown and his horse was injured. More of the sergeant instructors viewed them with barely concealed disapproval. In terms of the shooting, they could never equal me. I gave the other three tips and they became more proficient. In the end, the eight gave up with the rifles and were disparaging about those who used them. Sergeant Instructor Snoxall was not happy about it and they had an extra punishment. When we finished at the range they were the ones delegated to the duty of collecting the spent cartridges.

All of this meant even more enmity towards us. Knowing that another open incident might result in a worse punishment they resorted to petty acts. They poured water on our beds. They bumped us when we carried trays. We asked for a lock for our door and Sergeant Instructor Windridge supplied one. Senior Cadet Watson took to positioning himself close to us when we were in the refectory. It began to get poor Peter down.

As we played cards in our room, it was the safest place to be, I said, "Look upon all of this as a good trial for a life in the army. You do not know what problems may befall you. This is good practice for devising strategies to deal with them. I for one am now better at whist than I was."

James had become a positive force in the last weeks, "Griff is right, and I have thought about changing the game. I suggest we play a game which will help us to become better officers."

"For example?"

"Bridge, Bob. It is like whist but a better preparation for the army. It is strategic and you play as a pair. It is a sort of team sport. I know how to play, what say I teach you?" We learned to play Bridge and whilst it was a harder game it was also a better game.

It was the start of February and new instructors had arrived when my life changed once more. We had enjoyed mathematics

Desert War

lessons and now it was time to begin to learn map skills. Once more the four of us had shown in the mathematics and science classes that we were better than our eight better-educated colleagues. They were clearly better with Greek, Latin and Literature but we had more practical skills. I was looking forward to the navigation lessons. The growing empire had shown that officers needed skills to lead men across terrain that was unmapped. As my father had told me, there were more roads within two miles of our home than in the whole of Sudan. The instructor had been at the college for a short while but he had taught the graduating cadets first and we had not come into contact with him.

The eight were bored before they went into the classroom. It was a young officer and he had the tanned face of one who has served in the Tropics. On the table before him, he had compasses, map dividers, slide rules and maps. I was excited to be using these new tools of the trade.

"I am Lieutenant Dunn and I have been seconded here for four months to teach you young gentlemen how to read maps."

Cartwright snorted, "Maps! Who needs 'em? You find the enemy and charge 'em."

St John-Wilson was the leader and always the one with the snide comments. Usually, it was said for the benefit of his cronies and barely discernible. This time he said it a little too loud, "And from a lieutenant. Can't be up to much."

"And what is your name, Cadet?"

"St John-Wilson of the Dorsetshire St John-Wilsons." He said it as though that made him special.

"Never heard of them but if you gave me map coordinates I could find your home easily and tell your parents that they have failed to inculcate manners in one who aspires to be an officer and a gentleman. Now unless you have anything useful to say I suggest that you keep your mouth shut."

The bully reddened and we four smiled.

"I know the name of one of the noisy ones, you, the one who thinks maps are of little use, name."

"Cadet Cartwright." He had learned from the earlier reply and was polite.

Desert War

The officer put one hand under his chin, "Now let me see if the information I have is correct then you eight are the cadets who think that they are better than the rest." Their mouths dropped open. Lieutenant Dunn smiled, "As a good officer, you use as much intelligence as you can gather before going into a strange land. To me, the desert is more like my home and this is unfamiliar. That would make you, Willoughby, you Danvers-Walker, you FitzWilliam, you Granville-Smythe and you Garnet." They all nodded and mumbled, 'Yes sir'. He continued, "It may disappoint you, gentlemen, but you have to pass this class to graduate and the test is fair but hard." He switched his gaze to us and then the list in his hand, "Cadet McKay?"

"Yes sir."

"Cadet Fuller?"

"Yes sir."

"Cadet Quigley?

"Yes sir."

"And that would make you Cadet Roberts?"

"Yes sir."

His eyes narrowed as he studied me, "Would your first name be Griff?"

I knew from the forms I had filled out that the college had my name as Griffith. Only the family called me Griff, "Yes sir, how…"

He smiled, "I served with your father. A great man and I owe my rank to him." I heard a snort from one of the eight. I could not identify which one. Lieutenant Dunn said, "When I knew him, he was a sergeant major but he did what the officers above him could not. Did your father teach you any Arabic, Griff?"

"Why yes, sir."

He then spoke in Arabic, "I hear those eight have made your life hard."

"We cope, sir."

"Well, while I am here, I am your friend. Remember that. Any more problems then come directly to me. I am not, as some of the other officers are, intimidated by these connections. I serve in the Egyptian army."

"Thank you, sir."

"Do you know where your father is now, Griff?"

Desert War

"Liverpool?"

"He is probably boarding a ship. He is going to Persia."

"But how…"

"I met Colonel Dickenson before I came here. Your father is leading Syd and some of the other men with whom we served. We will talk later." He resumed in English. "And now our first lesson. McKay, would you give out the compasses? Quigley the slide rules and Fuller the dividers. Cartwright try to give out the maps, eh?"

I was stunned and the next ten minutes were like a blur. It had not been long since I had parted from my father at the station and now he was on his way back to war once more.

Desert War

Jack

Chapter 10

Loading the camels was not as easy as I had expected. The drilling equipment was not uniform in size and it took Ken and me some time to work out the best balance for the draught animals. The captain had given us as many supplies as he was able. He knew that he could replenish at Cape Town and so we would have, for a couple of weeks, at least, decent food to go along with the tinned meat and vegetables that would constitute our diet. They were easier to pack. We had also brought as much fruit, dried and fresh as we could. I knew the benefits. Our guide brought his own food. While we packed I asked him about supplies on the way.

"We can buy food but it may not be food you are used to. Goat's meat is very popular."

"Don't worry about my men, we can eat whatever there is on offer and George can cook anything, or so he says."

Syd said, "A Geordie never lies, Lieutenant, if he says he can cook then it will be like dining at the Savoy Grill in London."

The agent had arrived but his cousin, Ahmed, was not present. I could tell that my purchase of the animals had caused him a problem. He could not have known that I would be able to speak Arabic. He would have made a profit. I saw him eye up the two money chests as we loaded them on the camel that would be led by Bob Larriby whom I had assigned to protect it. The agent had not managed to acquire any of it, and I was sure that galled him. I gave it no more thought as we loaded the camels. I had intended to leave well before noon but the problems of the eclectic sizes of equipment meant we had to have lunch and wait until two in the afternoon.

As we ate, I spoke with George and Ken, "I intend to push on until after dark. It is cooler travelling at night anyway."

George was dubious, "We will be lucky to find accommodation that way."

"Mr Reynolds, I have no intention of marking our journey with stops at settlements. If we can find a village or town then

Desert War

that is all well and good but I plan on using the tents my men brought. It will be cosy but the nights here in the desert can be cold."

The Carnic pulled out at noon. It was partly the new contract but mainly because a small steamer arrived at the port. The Carnic dwarfed it but I could see how the port worked. Two or three such coasters could have docked instead of the single White Star vessel. They were the workaday vessels that plied their trade around the coasts. The one that arrived was a steamer but there were many ships that still relied on sail. Merchants appeared from nowhere to haggle and buy the contents of the cargo. The attention we had received when we arrived now made sense.

Syd, Jake and I had decided that Dick Wilshaw and John Jones would be the best scouts. Along with our guide, Mohammed Ali Fazlollah, they would find us a good route and give us an early warning of any danger. Although both younger than the others, Syd and Jake had been impressed by them on their journey north to Suez. They would ride two hundred yards ahead with their Lee Enfields ready to be used. The rest would keep their weapons in their scabbards to protect them from the dust and sand. Mohammed Ali Fazlollah had an ancient rifle. It was a single-shot breech loader but I guessed he knew how to use it. One piece of equipment I had brought from Turnbull and Proctor was a pair of goggles for each of us. I had bought the entire stock from them. The young man was happy enough to sell them to me and I knew they would be incredibly useful. They had tinted glass and would stop eye glare as well as protect our eyes from the sand.

The agent gave a perfunctory wave to George as we passed him but glowered at me. I merely smiled back at him.

The crowded dwellings of the port gave way to huddles of houses and then the odd isolated one until we were riding what amounted to a road in this part of the world. It was a sandy, rock-covered track. We each had two waterskins and they had been filled, not with water from the port, but the ship. From now on we would have to ration it. Firstly, we might struggle to find water and any water we did find might not be of the best quality.

Desert War

With only George the Geordie as a doctor, we could not afford any illnesses.

As we rode, I took the opportunity to look behind at the way the engineers rode. My choice of horses for them was vindicated as they were clearly not riders. One or two looked as though they would not fall off and George Reynolds could ride, but the rest looked to be as uncomfortable as it was possible to be. Syd and I rode at the fore of the column with our scouts firmly in view. Jake and Bill had the rest of my men and the draught animals at the rear and the horses were in between. The engineers smoked as they rode but we had military discipline. Smoking, like drinking and eating, was for the times we stopped.

As the sun began to set I realised that we would not have a village for our resting place. There was nothing. Mohammed Ali Fazlollah was a good guide and he pointed, as the moon rose, to a flat piece of ground. There were no trees but there were no rocks either. We could peg out the tents. Had it just been my soldiers we would not have bothered with tents but the engineers were another matter.

I turned, "Head over to that flat ground. We will stay here for the night."

The relieved cheer from the engineers had more than a hint of a groan in it. I was an experienced rider but the short ride from the port had my backside sore, even wearing the jodhpurs.

"Sergeant Major, get the tents erected. Just put up four we will share. As we will have two men on watch all night it won't be that bad." When we reached Shardin we would organise a proper camp and put up all the tents but I wanted to get there as soon as I could.

"Right, sir."

"Ken, I will leave the food to you."

"George, that is your department."

We dismounted. Fatima was a good camel. Mohammed came over to me, "You are happy with the animals?"

"They are good camels. We are treating them well?"

He smiled, "Even your engineers are not damaging our property. All is well."

The first of the tents was already going up and I said, "You can choose your own tent, Mohammed."

Desert War

"I will sleep on the ground, Lieutenant."

"As you wish."

The fire that Bill lit was necessary. It would take away some of the chill and the smoke would deter flying insects. "Syd, I want two men doing a two-hour duty. Just leave Bob Larriby off the rota. He can stay with the gold. Include me."

"You don't need to, sir."

"I know but I want to. The moment I become a passenger then I might make a mistake. There will be danger on this road, Syd, make no mistake about that."

When I was woken to stand a duty with Dick it came as something of a shock but once I stood, cloak draped around my shoulders, it felt better. I was becoming part of the desert. It always took time but the more I was in the desert the more comfortable I felt. I saw the first hint of the new day and I went to put more wood on the fire.

"Dick, get some water on for a brew." We had brought plenty of tea. One thing we had learned in Sudan was that cold tea was healthier to drink than some of the water we found in oases. Boiling the water for the tea made it safer. None of the tea would be wasted. My men would simply fill their spare canteens. The water beginning to boil, I went to wake the others. Mohammed was already awake and he went to check on the animals.

I offered him a mug of tea when he returned. It was Sergeant Major's tea. I put in some of the tinned milk and added three spoonfuls of sugar. He looked at it suspiciously. "Give it a go, Mohammed, you might like it."

He sipped it and smiled, "It is not what I expected. When we drink tea there is no milk."

"This is British Army style."

He nodded back in the direction of Bandar, "That agent, I do not trust him. He works not only for your company but also for others and he is a treacherous snake."

"Yet you do business with him."

He shrugged, "As I said, he is the agent for many Western companies. His family are like a gang of bandits. We have to make a living."

We left within an hour of breakfast. When the last of the tea was distributed and the fire doused we set off. "Mohammed, we will not ride in the heat of the sun. Find us some shade when it is close to noon."

Mohammed knew the road and we stopped at the old town of Behbaben. There was water for the animals and we were able to buy a little bread. It was flatbread but bread was bread. We made a brew and took advantage of the shade afforded by the buildings. It was a good start for our first real day on the road. This was a mountainous country. Defiles and rocks meant that any deviation from the track might end in disaster. For my men, it was not as much of a problem as it was for the engineers. When we left the village, I suggested that we ride in single file. It made our column longer but it was safer for the engineers. One effect was the absence of chatter. All that could be heard was the clip-clopping of hooves and the occasional scrape as a hoof slipped. I now feared that our next stop might be a more hazardous one. The total journey, according to Mohammed, was one hundred and twenty miles. Thanks to our late departure from the port we had lost half a day already and the road now slowed us down.

Mohammed stopped about an hour before sunset. He rode back, "The road is a little dangerous for the next few miles. I would suggest we camp earlier. Better to lose time than risk an animal and a man slipping down a rocky slope."

"You are right. Find us somewhere."

We travelled just another two miles. The road had dropped to a sort of bowl and it was flat. There was even water. It was not good enough for us to drink but the animals could use it. Ken said, "You know you don't need to put the tents up just for us."

"It is no bother, Ken."

"Your lads told us that they are happy sleeping in the open. With a fire and sleeping close to each other, we should be alright. It means we can make an earlier start in the morning. My chaps are a bit worried about riding this road in the dark."

I nodded, "I understand. No problem then. Syd, we don't need the tents. Use them to make a windbreak."

"Righto, sir." I could tell by his tone that he was happy.

We still had some fresh vegetables and some of the flatbreads we had bought at lunchtime. We dined like kings. The engineers had all brought bottles of whisky, rum and brandy. They knew

Desert War

they would have to conserve their precious store but they each had a good mugful at night. It helped them to sleep and warmed them a little. As much as my lads would have wanted to do that they were under orders. It would be teetotal until I ordered otherwise.

I had the middle watch and it was Mohammed whose hand came across my mouth, "There are men in the dark."

I nodded. He needed to say no more. I rose and donned my Sam Browne and sword. I drew my pistol. I went over to the two sentries, Emerson and Hunt. I put my mouth to Trooper Hunt's ear, "Bandits in the dark. Go around and wake the lads but do so silently."

I shook Syd awake. I needed no hand across his mouth. I put my finger to my lips and held my gun up. He nodded. I saw Mohammed slide a bullet into the breech of his gun. In hindsight, it proved to be a mistake. The distinctive click must have given the men hiding in the dark, a warning. The muzzle flash and the crack of the bandit's rifle woke the engineers.

I shouted, "Use the tents for cover and only fire when you see a target you can hit."

I aimed at the muzzle flash that sent a bullet at me. I felt the wind from its flight as it passed close to me. My Webley cracked as did Mohammed's rifle. They were soon augmented by the sound of the Lee Enfields as my men picked out their targets. The heavy handguns of the engineers ensured that the air was filled with smoke and the night riven with the sound of thunder.

"Sergeant Major, take command."

"Sir."

I grabbed Mohammed's arm and pointed to the rocks. He nodded and putting down his rifle, drew his dagger. I slipped my pistol's lanyard around my neck and, masked by the flash of muzzles and the smoke, we headed back along the track we had followed to the last rocks I had seen. I hissed, "Let us get behind them."

"I will lead."

I shook my head, "I have done this before. I shall lead."

We moved over the rocks and through little defiles. The gunfight sounded as though it was far away. It was not. When I rose from behind the rock I saw that we were behind some of the bandits. There were at least eight of them ahead of me and they had a variety of weapons. I waved Mohammed to my right and took aim. They were just twenty yards from me, and the Webley was accurate at that range. I counted on the fact that my gun would sound like one of theirs. I wanted to cause as many casualties as I could. If we could discourage them then we had a better chance of survival. They might be inclined to give up if they thought that they were being outflanked.

I squeezed the trigger. My Webley sounded like a pop gun compared with the Colts of the engineers. The man I hit spread his arms as he fell. I shot another two before they realised that I was behind them. Mohammed had disappeared and I was on my own. Seeing me they rushed at me with swords and daggers. I emptied my gun, hitting two and then I dropped my Webley and drew my sword. The triumphant bandit who thought he had me had a surprised look on his face as my sword ripped across his neck. Another bandit suddenly found a hand around his mouth and then Mohammed slit his throat.

A bandit's voice shouted, "They are behind us. Let us flee, brothers." As they rose from their places of concealment to run towards their animals, they made better targets for my men. Mohammed picked up a sword and the two of us ran after the bandits.

I heard Jake shout, "Watch out for the lieutenant and Mohammed, they are on our right."

If I had reloaded my pistol I might have accounted for a few more but, as it was we caught up with them as they mounted their camels. Syd and my men reached us and three more bandits fell before the others managed to flee. Mohammed ran and secured four of the camels before they could run after the fleeing animals.

"Sir, no more heroics, eh? There are no medals in this."

I laughed and sheathed my sword, "When have I ever been interested in medals, Syd." I reloaded my pistol. I didn't think there would be more danger but one never knew. My men passed through the dead to make sure that none were feigning death.

"Jake, take half of the men and go back to the camp. Get a brew on. I think that sleep has ended for the night."

Desert War

The first light of the new day illuminated the scene. Syd had the men collect all the weapons from the dead. I was the one who identified one of the bandits. "Mohammed, isn't this Ahmed, Mohammed Ali Teymourtash's cousin?"

He came over and nodded, "I have seen four more bodies who work for that agent."

Syd said, "Sly bastard. He wanted the gold Mr Reynolds had."

Mohammed pointed to the west, "There is another road in that direction. They must have raced to get ahead of us and were ready for this ambush."

"And but for your sharp ears, they might have succeeded."

He shook his head, "It was not my ears but my nose. They smelled like five-day-old dead goats. They stink. Could you not smell it?"

I laughed, "No."

We led the camels, laden with weapons, back to the camp. Only Bob Larriby had remained at his post, along with the engineers. I saw the shock on their faces as we neared the camp. George the Geordie was tending to Wally Carmichael. "Are you hurt, Wally?"

George shook his head, "A stone chip but in this climate, if you don't tend to scratches, it can lead to worse."

Syd poured me a mug of tea, "A firefight at night is always a matter of luck." He nodded to the tents, "Some of those have holes in them that might have been bodies. It was lucky we chose to sleep in the open."

George Reynolds looked to be the most shocked of all, "What were they after?"

"Your boss' agent, Mohammed Ali Teymourtash, sent them for your gold, Mr Reynolds. He would have sent a telegram to Mr D'Arcy to tell him of the tragedy."

Syd frowned and asked Mohammed, in Arabic, "Where did they get the camels, Mohammed?"

"Not from us. These are poor specimens. We can use them to carry supplies but I would not like to ride them too far. There are other camels in Bandar-e Deylam but they were not good enough for you."

Syd was satisfied, "When we get back to the port we will have a little score to settle with that man."

We left within an hour of dawn. The carrion birds were already descending to feast on the corpses. We had no time to bury them. None of us could guarantee that they had finished with us although as we had accounted for at least twelve of them I thought it unlikely that they would risk another attack. The attack had one effect, it spurred us on. The engineers realised that falling off a horse was not as bad as having a throat slit in the night.

Our next stop was not in the open but in the handful of houses at Lisak. With water for our animals and dogs to warn us of an attack, we were safer. We still had sentries, three on each watch this time, but none of us felt as exposed. Mohammed said that we could make Shardin in one ride, it was just thirty miles away and none of us minded riding hard.

Shardin proved a disappointment. I think that all of us, George especially, had expected a bigger place. There were just ten houses. Syd asked, "Are you sure this is the right place, Mr Reynolds?"

He smiled, "It is not what is above the ground that we seek but below. Tomorrow, I want to be taken, along with Ken, to find a place to begin the drilling."

Now that we were close he was a much more confident man.

Desert War

Jack

Chapter 11

The first thing I did was to go with Mohammed and meet with the headman of the village. I took three gold pieces from the money box and gave them to the headman as, I called it, a gift for any inconvenience we might cause. It was gold and he was grateful. His wife made us coffee and we drank it. Mohammed was happy to have his favourite drink once more. It was while we were drinking and chatting that the headman, Safi-al Musa, told us of the local warlord. His voice was fearful even as he spoke, and I could feel the terror in the man.

"Halil Rifat Bey was an officer in the Ottoman army. He did something bad. I know not what and he arrived to plague this land. He had others with him, Russians, and they took all that there was to take. As you can see, we have little to take. Still, they took it anyway. Like locusts, once they had taken all of value they headed into the hills where they have a lair. They have not returned but word will spread that there are westerners here and that means gold. I say this for I do not wish my village to be raided again."

I nodded, understanding his viewpoint, "We will not be in the village for long: perhaps a day or two and then we will leave."

He looked relieved, "And go where?"

I smiled, "We know not yet but if we are close then you can expect more gold for your inconvenience."

As we headed back to the camp Mohammed said, "I know of this warlord. They ride horses as well as camels and have modern guns, not as fine a weapon as the ones you use but good ones. If they have Russians as allies…"

"Let us cross the bridge when we come to it."

I explained the problem to George and his face fell, "There appear to be more obstacles in our way, I wonder why Mr D'Arcy bothered to pay the money to the king. He is doing nothing to earn it."

Desert War

"Perhaps he ought to be told. When we have found where you wish to drill perhaps Mohammed and I could find the king and speak to him."

Mohammed shook his head, "It is five hundred miles to Tehran and besides the king likes the West too much. He is more likely to be in Paris or Rome than in his own city."

I was disappointed, "The first thing we need to do is to find where you are going to drill and the sooner the better."

Ken, George, Mohammed and Bill Brown came with me when we went to scout the land. We found nothing that first day. To be honest I had no idea what the engineer was looking for but he did. We would stop at what he said was a likely spot. We normally found it after he had consulted his map and his notes. Then he would dismount, take out a spade and dig a little.

It took three days and we were ten miles from Shardin when he found a likely place that satisfied the engineers. We had followed a sort of caravan trail and the site was just a hundred yards north of it. When we did, it looked different to a dozen others that we had explored.

"This is hopeful."

Ken nodded, "Aye, it is Mr Reynolds, this is as likely a spot as we have seen up to now."

"Bill, back to Shardin and fetch the others. Mohammed, go with him. I will act as a guard until you get back."

They mounted their camels and the corporal said, "Mind Sergeant Major Richardson's words, sir, no heroics."

He galloped off and I studied the ground. The two men were examining where they would drill. I had to avoid pitching tents there and I headed for a second flat piece of ground about three hundred paces from the drilling site. I did not know how much spread there would be and I wanted our camp to be safe. There was a rocky ridge that we could use for sentries. There were very few trees in this land and I had to tether Fatima to a rock. She had proved a well-trained animal. She would not wander. There were rocks that rose to a ridge to the north and I chose the flat ground just a few yards from that. We would have shelter and height. Mohammed had told me that whilst there was no regular rain, when it came it would be a deluge. We were slightly above the drilling site and any rainfall would disappear. There was, however, no water and that would be a problem. The other problem was the lack of firewood. I walked back to the trail and gathered the dried camel dung that lay there. I also found a few scattered sticks, blown there in one of the many sandstorms that they endured. I placed them where I deduced we would have a fire. I took Fatima's saddle from her and tethered her close to the rising ground but sheltered from the wind. She squatted down and began to eat the few scattered plants that sprouted in this harsh landscape. In England, we would have called them weeds but the camels seemed to like them and thrived.

That done and while Ken and George moved about the site, driving in little flags on sticks, I sat on a rock and lit my pipe. I found that it helped me to think in a logical and orderly fashion. Once the engineers were ready to work then my men and I would be their guards. However, we would also have to be the foragers. I looked up at the higher ground behind me. That would be the perfect place for a sentry. If we used three teams then one could guard the camp while the two others both scouted and foraged at the same time. Food would soon be a problem. The village of Shardin could sell us some and would, no doubt, be grateful for the income but the longer we were here then that would bring closer the necessity of returning to some larger place for food. That would either be Behbaben or the port. Both would mean riders had to be away for four or five days. By the time I heard the horses and camels as the others arrived, I had a plan.

The engineers began to unpack their equipment close to the little flags. "Sergeant Major, this is where I want the tents." I swept my hand in a line and he nodded.

"Right lads, nice and neat eh, this will be our home for a while."

Mohammed came over and I said, "Could you find the nearest water and any fuel for our fire? We shall need both."

He nodded and remounted his camel. He looked around and then headed off towards the east. I would not have had the first clue as to where to begin.

"Bill, rig two lines, one for the horses and one for the camels."

"Right, sir."

We had brought stakes with us for just such a purpose. He chose a place where the ground allowed the stakes to be driven in and, coincidentally, where there were some scrappy patches of grass and weeds. They would soon clear it and we would need to find better grazing for them. When we had been at Fort Desolation we had food sent from the coast. There it had not been a worry, here it was.

We had some kindling we had brought. When we had been in the port Jake had been to the quay and hauled up the driftwood. It had been soaking wet when we had left Bandar-e Deylam, now it had dried out in the Persian heat. Augmented by camel dung I estimated that we had a week of fuel and then we would struggle. We would not be able to afford a night fire. We would have a fire for cooking and that would be allowed to die and then relit for the morning meal.

Soon the camp took on organisation from the apparent chaos. The tents were in one neat row. I would share one with Syd and Jake. The others would share two tents while the engineers would live in the other four tents. I laid my gear in my tent. The two bags I had secured at Turnbull and Proctor had been a wise investment. They were cleverly made and I had my own storage bags. The kitbags of Syd and Jake were only useful for carrying and not for storing. We knew that dhobying was out of the question. There was not enough water for us. We would have to use the old soldier's trick of hanging underwear and shirts on clotheslines every three days to allow the wind to make them marginally fresher. We would all be growing beards. There would not be enough water to shave.

Mohammed returned before dark. He pointed back to the southeast, "There is a valley in that direction, perhaps two miles away. There is a farmer there with goats and a well. He will sell us water."

I was relieved. "Firewood?" He shook his head. "Then we will have to keep our eyes open while we search. When we go on patrol each day, Mohammed, I want you to look after the camels. They have served us well but we want them to be as fit as possible."

We all sat in a huge circle around the fire while we ate. I sat next to Ken and George Reynolds. Both were quite animated. "It will take all of tomorrow to set up the drill but this looks like a good place."

Syd asked, "How long to find oil, then sir?"

George gave him the sort of look a parent gives a child who has asked a simplistic question, "We may not find it here. What we will discover is what the rock structure is like beneath our feet. It could take weeks or months, perhaps and we might have to move many times but somewhere within four or five miles of where we are, there will be oil. How much I cannot say. With luck, it might be a huge field and that would please Mr D'Arcy."

Bill asked, "Why, sir? Won't the oil belong to the Persians too?"

"They will only get 16% of any profits. Mr D'Arcy knows how to negotiate."

That was not our problem, we were contracted for six months but such was our relationship with the engineers that I knew we would not abandon them at the end of the six months. I was not like that and neither were my men. Who knew, now, when I would get home?

I left Jake at the camp. He would make it more like a small fort. By moving rocks, he made firing positions above the tents where we could both watch and fight. Syd and I led our men in two different directions. I went north, over the ridge, and he went south. We were just trying to become familiar with the land whilst also looking for threats. I knew that Halil Rifat Bey would eventually hear of the Westerners in his land. He might even have heard of the gold we carried. I knew that such a warlord could come calling and we had to be ready. We had two advantages. We had the best weapon, the MLE, and I also had well-trained men. The pirate attack had shown me that the engineers were tough men who could handle themselves. We had enough men to make a stand.

At the end of the first week, we had established a routine. Each day men would ride to the goat farmer and buy water. The two patrols had discovered more grazing and as well as patrolling we would feed the animals. That was normally at noon. The heat in the desert was as hot if not hotter than it had been in Africa. It was good that we were all acclimatised. The

Desert War

engineers were not and George the Geordie had to deal with heat stroke.

As for the drilling, it all seemed a mystery to me but the engineers were all happy with their progress. George kept copious notes in his leatherbound notebook. He explained that he would need to write a report for Mr D'Arcy. One of our jobs, at the end of three months, would be to return to Bandar-e Deylam and send a telegram to the home office to report our progress.

It was the second week of our exploration when we met the men of the warlord. As luck would have it, I was leading the patrol. I had Bill with me as well as Fred and Dick. The eight men who approached us were not merchants. They rode scraggy camels and each had the long rifles favoured by the warriors of this land. At their waists hung swords. I had opened the flap on my pistol but kept my hand from it. I knew how to greet strangers and did so with a smile.

"You are in the land of Halil Rifat Bey. You did not ask his permission to be here."

I nodded, "We had permission from Shah Mozaffar ad-Din Shah Qajar and did not think we needed to seek your master's permission."

A thin smile played on the leader's lips, "The Shah has much to do in the north and it is my master who rules this land. You must pay for the privilege. Twenty gold pieces a week is the price you must pay."

He knew we had gold. I did not blame the headman. Faced with the choice of being loyal to western strangers or heeding the threats of a warlord it was clear that he would have caved. I shook my head, "We do not have that much gold with us."

"Then you must leave. I will give you one week to either leave or to find the gold."

I nodded but said nothing. My hand was close enough to draw my pistol if they became threatening. He nodded too, waved a farewell and turned to head back north. I waited. Bill said, "Sir, did you notice the one with them who was not an Arab?"

I shook my head. My attention had been on the leader, "No."

"He kept at the back but there was one with blond hair and skin that was yellower."

"Russian."

Desert War

He nodded, "What do we do, sir?"

"We wait until they are out of sight and then head back to the camp. We know that they will come and before a week is out. He has gone to get more warriors. We have three or four days at the most to prepare."

"For war, sir?"

"Aye, Bill, for war."

When we reached the camp I took Syd and Jake to speak to George and Ken. I told them what had happened and my assessment of the situation. George asked, "Could we not pay them off?"

Ken snorted, "I have met their type before, Mr Reynolds. The twenty pieces of gold would become thirty and whatever we paid we would find it increased week on week. Jack is right. They will come back and we will need to fight them."

George looked unhappy, "We can't afford to lose a day of drilling."

"You can keep on working. We will make the camp a fortress. I will just send out one patrol a day and that will be to get water. The rest of us will do the rest. However, when they return you will have to stop work. Ken, we will need you and your lads to help us fight. Have them keep their weapons to hand. One thing is for sure, the first time they come back will be in daylight. The second time will be at night."

Digging trenches was out of the question but we were able to haul rocks to make firing pits above the camp. We also moved the animal lines so that they were easier to defend. I sat with my officers and used a stick and the sand to illustrate my ideas. "We have eight pits. Each pit will hold three men. I want the engineers to be able to shelter there too. Two men will defend the animals. When they are finished, I want five men in the pits during the hours of daylight. They use their cloaks to keep themselves hidden. When the warriors return, I want them to think that the six of us and the engineers are all that we have. The men in the pits, when Bill sounds the bugle, will be able to pour bullets at them and that will give us the chance to take cover. Once the pits are ready I want every trooper to carry his rifle."

Jake said, "Then I will be in the pits, sir, you will need Bill to blow the bugle."

"Right, let's get started."

It took just two days to make the pits. Three men could easily shelter in each of them. Our cloaks made not only good camouflage but also shelter from the sun. Syd and I worked out that they would come in the afternoon. They would stay in Shardin and then leave. They would not travel in the noonday sun. Our daily water patrol would leave before dawn. We now knew the route. We had also bought a goat from the goat herder. It gave us milk and would be a source of food if we ran out of corned beef. The old man liked us and got on well with Mohammed.

The warlord's warriors returned on the fifth day. I had begun to wonder if I was wrong and they would just come when they said but the thirty men, mounted on a mixture of camels and horses arrived at about three in the afternoon. Hearing them approach Ken and his engineers had wandered back to the camp as though it was mealtime. I could not see Jake and his riflemen and that meant the warlord's men would have no chance of detecting them. All that they would see would be a rocky wall. I had the flap of my holster open and my sword hung from the tent post where I could get at it quickly. This time I sought out the Russian soldier and I spotted him just behind the leader. I spied his holster and his revolver. I had heard that the Russians now had a very effective six-shot double-action pistol called the Nagrant. When the firing began, and I knew it would, the Russian's weapon would be the best one. The warrior leading the warband had an old Navy Dragoon. A good weapon but with a long barrel it would be harder to draw and its action was not as good as my Webley. Syd also had a Webley.

They reined in and the leader smiled. It was the smile of a wolf about to devour a sheep. "You have a fine camp."

"Thank you. Would you care for some tea?"

He shook his head, "We have come for our gold. We will take eighty pieces and that will save us from returning too often."

Ken and his men had filtered up to the camp and although it looked as though they were simply sitting and eating, they were in fact preparing to draw their weapons, take cover and fire. The

Desert War

troopers that the warriors could see were all squatting with the butts of their rifles resting on the ground. I could not see Mohammed and knew that he would be finding a position from which he could fire at the warriors. Syd, Bill and I were almost surrounded by the leading warriors.

I shook my head, "I have told you, we are here at the request of the Shah and we do not have that much gold."

"You are Englishmen. The English are the richest men in the world. Do not lie to me."

I saw that he was becoming angry. I distracted him with my stump and that allowed me to rest my right hand on the butt of my pistol, "Do we look as though we are rich? We drink goat's milk and eat old beef from tins."

He raised his rifle. His men did the same. "Enough, pay me my gold or you will all die here and I will take it anyway."

Drawing my Webley I said, "Now, Brown."

The bugle blared. I fired two bullets at the Russian who flew back across the rump of his horse. Syd's Webley struck the leader. The volleys from Jack and his riflemen did the damage. The MLE was not a gun that was slow to reload. With a ten-bullet magazine and just a bolt to pull back, the men emptied their first magazines in under a minute. Fifty bullets tore into the warriors. I heard the distinctive boom of Mohammed's gun and the double boom from the shotgun. I fired at whoever was the closest. The rifles had a better range and were more accurate than my Webley at range. A few got shots off but more than half fell and just ten men survived to flee. The Colts and handguns of the engineers, not to mention the Purdey had been an unstoppable force. Next time there would be no surprise.

"Cease fire." Silence and smoke filled the air. The horses and camels that had not fled stood. Some had been restrained by their dying masters holding onto the reins, even in death.

"Any wounds?"

Dick Wilshaw said, "Just a nick, sir."

I saw that he had been wounded in the upper arm, "Geordie!"

"Righto, sir. Come into my surgery. No waiting today!" An easy victory like this made everyone feel relieved to be alive.

George Reynolds rested his shotgun against a rock, "Is this over or will it come back to haunt us, Lieutenant?"

"It will take some time to get back to the warlord and then they will come back. The difference is that the next time there will be no warning. If it is daylight, then they will come in charging and if it is night time then they will try to overwhelm us in the dark. We will have to use more sentries."

I walked over to the Russian. When I pulled off his keffiyeh I saw that he was blond and had a long duelling scar down one cheek. He was an officer. I took the pistol and holster and tossed it to Bill Brown, "Here, this is yours. Check his saddlebags for ammunition. It uses different ammo but it will be a handy weapon to have."

The Russian's horse was better than the rest and had stayed by the body. Brown searched the saddlebags and found documents but they were in Russian. He also found a purse. The Russian had a rifle in a scabbard. It was a Moison-Nagrant and like the pistol fired 7.62 ammo using a five-bullet magazine. Brown triumphantly held up a box of bullets. The other bodies yielded a variety of weapons but the best of them were those belonging to the Russian officer.

"What do we do with the bodies, sir?"

"We haven't got the kindling to burn them. Find some soft ground and we will bury them."

Syd nodded, "Right my lucky lads, grab a shovel and let us give these a send-off that they don't deserve. We should leave them for the foxes."

The action cost us the rest of the day. Little work was done. Mohammed took his camel and rode to follow them. We all doubted that they would hang around but it paid to be careful. We used the food in the saddlebags to augment our own and the Russian's saddlebags yielded some vodka. Geordie George could use it as an antiseptic.

Mohammed returned and said that the warriors had fled far to the north. They had passed through Shardin and would be heading for the warlord's lair. It was many days to the north. That night, as we sat, ate and reflected on the day none of us were certain what would happen next. Even Syd and Jake looked to me for answers.

I lit my pipe and as the smoke rose to deter the flies, even buried the corpses had attracted them, I said, "He could cut his losses and write this off as an unfortunate incident. He lost two-thirds of the warband he sent. He knows our firepower and I doubt that he has anything to compare. On the other hand, he may well decide he wants that firepower. Added to that he will have lost face. He can blame the defeat on the man who led this band but if men come again then he will have to lead them."

To the engineers, it was our problem but I could see that they were interested in our solution. They were used to solving problems of their own.

Syd had his pipe going too and he used the stem to point, "Jake and the lads fired from up there. You can bet that when they report back they will tell the warlord that. They will come over the ridge."

Jake said, "And that means they won't be using horses. It will be night."

Bill Brown was cleaning his new pistol, "But they could still come during daylight. If I was them I would charge in at dawn. They would be coming from the west."

I considered their words, "Then to counteract an attack over the ridge, put traps and tripwires there. You are right, Bill, and that means we need one night sentry with the animals, one at the western end and two on the ridge. It means four-hour shifts."

We had been speaking in English and Mohammed, although he had picked up a couple of words of English, had no chance of following the dialogue. He asked me what had been said. I translated and he said, "I will stand a night watch. I do not wish my throat to be slit by one of these desert snakes."

The engineers too all volunteered to provide one man for each shift and share the burden. I think that they knew how perilous our position was. Even though we felt safe for that night, at least, we initiated the new rota. We would all become more tired from now on.

Desert War

Jack

Chapter 12

The traps and tripwires were easy to fashion and we enjoyed solving the problems. We built another eyrie at the western end of our camp so that a sentry could watch and yet remain hidden. It meant we neither scouted nor collected water.

The next day we did visit with the goat farmer. He had heard the shooting and when we had not come for the water wondered if we had all died. He knew of the warlord, "There were many families who lived in this valley until he came. He made many of them leave but I am stubborn and hard to kill. I am pleased that you have bloodied his nose but he will seek revenge."

His words confirmed what I already knew. We rode, after the burning heat of noon, to visit with the headman in Shardin. Like the farmer, he was surprised that we had not only survived but defeated the plague that was the warlord and his men. "Perhaps you should leave before they return."

"My friend, we are here working for the Shah. Is there not an army that can deal with the likes of Halil Rifat Bey?"

"When we were part of the Ottoman Empire then there was law but there was also injustice. The warlord does not take everything. We are left with a little something. We have an army but the men who serve are still learning how to be soldiers."

As we rode back to the camp I reflected that it had been the same in Egypt. Until the army was given good officers and sergeants then no matter how brave were the soldiers they were doomed to failure.

The heat, the diet and the threat of an attack took its toll. The euphoria of the victory was now replaced by the constant fear of an attack, a knife in the night, the scream of a slaughtered sentry. There was less laughter and banter in the camp. Even Syd and George did not spend as much time talking about Newcastle. When we slept it was, generally, fully clothed. We kept loaded weapons by our bedrolls. In our case, there were now just two of us in our tent at night. The third was the captain of the guard. The first thing we each did when we went on duty was to check

Desert War

that the traps had not been triggered. They were not particularly sophisticated. They would just give a little warning. The noise of rocks tumbling or the cans jingling together would not hurt an enemy but we would know that they were coming.

While the days were so hot that you could have fried an egg on a rock, the nights were as cold as in an English winter and we wrapped in cloaks. I did not wear my sword hanging from my belt but hung it from my tent pole where I could grab it quickly. If it was hanging from my belt it would be a tripping hazard. Ten days had passed since the attack. I wondered if the warlord had decided that we were too dangerous a morsel. When Jake woke me I knew that it was just two hours before dawn. It seemed likely that this would be another night without an attack. Nerves would be stretched once more.

I went to make water first and just listened. Every man on watch with me would have been woken by a man coming off watch. That was how we did it. I knew that our guide had the ears of a hawk, Mohammed heard everything. He was making water at the same time as me. Suddenly he stopped and sniffed.

"What is it, Mohammed? Five-day-old dead goat again?"

He shook his head and pointed to our animals at the eastern end of the camp. "The night breeze is from the west and I can smell horses."

I now trusted my horse trader. Horse smells from the west meant an enemy. Ours were with our camels at the eastern end of the camp, "Wake the sergeants."

I went to Ken's tent and roused him, "There may be trouble. Wake the men and have them ready, Mohammed thinks there are horses to the west."

"Right lads, up and at 'em." He hissed the words and shook those closest to him.

I went to the sentry on the ridge. It was Dick. His wound was healing but I knew that it itched. He was scratching at it when I approached. It was as he turned that I heard the tiniest of noises. It was the sound of pebbles falling. Dick looked at me and I put my finger to my lips and drew my pistol. He loaded a bullet into the chamber of his Lee Enfield and dropped into the firing pit. I crouched and levelled my pistol. I sought the shadows that would be moving towards us. Until the rest of our men joined us

Desert War

it would be the two of us against an unknown number of men intent upon our deaths. The tripwires worked. The shadow fell, grunted and, in rising quickly, gave me a target. I fired and in the muzzle flash saw the eight men moving towards us. I fired at the nearest man whose face I had seen as Dick fired and chambered as fast as he was able. From the west, I heard the sound of hooves. Mohammed had saved us for a second time.

I heard Jake shout, "My watch with me to the pits."

Syd commanded, "Present and on my command, fire." He would be commanding half of our men as well as the engineers. Mohammed would fight his own war in his own way.

I fired again. The muzzle flashes from the warriors as well as that from Dick showed enough of the targets to aim at. Dick shouted, "Sir, get down!"

He was right and I jumped down into the pit next to him just as a bullet passed so close by that I felt the wind of its passage. I emptied my gun and shouted, "Reloading!"

Dick had more bullets than I did and he knew that even with my new metal arm I was still slow to reload. I could hear the sound of battle to my left as Syd ordered a volley and then gave the command for independent fire. If we had been lucky enough to have the Lee Enfield at Rorke's Drift then the battle would have been over sooner. I reloaded as Jake and the others joined us. With their firepower, we soon cleared the ridge.

I shouted, "Turn and support Syd. I am off to join him."

Jake said, "It is safer here, sir."

I ignored him and holstering my pistol hauled myself from my hole. It was clear now that the attack on the ridge had been to secure the firing pits and allow the main body to charge the camp and rely on their horses in the dark. The fact that we would be sleepy would have made them believe that they had an edge. I hurried towards the firing and levelled my pistol. Syd had his men and the engineers with their backs to the tents. It meant Jake and the men in the pits could support them. I emptied my Webley into the mass of horsemen, I was rewarded by screams and at least one man falling from his horse. I ran to my tent and drew my sword. I was just in time for a warrior slashed down at me with his sword. I managed to deflect the slice, aimed at my

Desert War

neck by using Geordie George's metal arm. I lunged up and felt my sword slide into the belly of the horseman.

The sun began to rise over the horizon behind us in the east. As its first rays penetrated the dark it showed that the warlord had brought more men this time. I moved towards the safety of our men. I saw that we had taken casualties. Bob Larriby lay on the ground and Geordie George was tending to him. I stuck my sword in the ground and picked up Bob's rifle. I rested the barrel on my metal-covered stump. It was not as easy as I had hoped to pull back the bolt but I managed and whilst the rate of fire was not as fast as the others it added to the withering wall of bullets that we sent at the enemy. This time they did not flee but when the sun burst from the east to clear the horizon a voice ordered the enemy to fall back.

"Anyone else hurt?"

Ken said, "Tommy Garstang has bought it. We have some scrapes but we can still fight."

I dropped the rifle, for I had emptied the magazine and I reloaded my Webley. I knelt. "How is it, Bob?"

He shook his head, "It is more than a scratch, sir."

I looked and saw that the bullet had hit his shoulder. Geordie George's fingers were covered in blood and he shook his head, "I am trying to get the bullet out, sir but…"

I went to the tent and brought out the vodka we had taken from the dead Russian. I poured some on the wound. Bob winced through gritted teeth but it showed, briefly, the tip of the bullet. George had some tweezers and he grabbed the end. I held out my hand, "Grab it, Bob, this will hurt."

He squeezed my good hand so hard that I wanted to shout out. When George shouted, triumphantly, "Gotcha, ya bugger!" Bob gave a wan smile and then laid back.

I stood and surveyed the scene. There were too many of us exposed. "Bill, take all but Syd, George, Eric and Bob. Put them in the firing pits. They are safer there and we can hold them better. Larriby, take the chest with you and get under cover." Bob used his good hand to drag the chest to the nearest tent. Geordie George had reloaded his Colt and was firing at the mass of horsemen who still remained.

Desert War

Syd had reloaded Bob's MLE. Just then we heard the distinctive sound of Mohammed's rifle. The enemy had retreated beyond the drilling but one had exposed himself and Mohammed had not missed. I looked back and saw that he was on the highest part of the ridge. The shot had to have been almost six hundred yards. It might have been an old weapon but at least it had the range. It was only one man that he had hit but that would both annoy and hurt the warlord.

"Syd, grab the bully beef cans and make a barrier here. Bob is exposed. George, you can join the others."

He shook his head, "Away with you, man, what kind of doctor would that make me? I will stay."

It seemed rude to point out that he was not a doctor.

Eric was a tower of strength and he positioned the boxes to afford protection to Bob. He was a solid and reliable trooper. I could trust him. I helped as best I could and we had a barrier of metal corned beef tins to protect Bob and George. Each tin held ten pounds of corned beef and was our staple. Syd asked as we rested the rifles on top of the tins, "What do you reckon they are planning?"

"I hope that they are not damaging the engineer's drilling equipment. If they are we shall have to shift them." Syd's look was one of disbelief, "We are here to help the drill. If their equipment is damaged then we have failed." I knew how important it was to keep the equipment safe.

"Aren't lives more important, Jack?"

"To you and me, yes, to Mr D'Arcy, no. Anyway, I think this warlord will still think he can take us and get his hands on the gold. Horses failed but Mohammed might have given him, inadvertently the answer."

"How so?"

"Their guns cannot fire fast but they have the range and, it seems, the accuracy."

As if to prove the point a bullet smacked into the corned beef tin just in front of Syd. He ducked and chuckled, "That settles it then. We will be eating beef filled with lead from now on."

I had the Webley hanging from its lanyard. Now that it was reloaded I felt better. I would not need my sword until they were at close quarters and with a loaded rifle and pistol then we could

Desert War

keep them at bay. Another bullet hit the tins. It was as I glanced at the smoke I thought I saw one of the Persian corpses moving. I put it down to a trick of the morning light but when I looked back I saw that the body was now three paces closer. One of them was feigning death. Even as I raised my Webley, like Lazarus, the warrior rose and ran at me. He was a fanatic. I had to empty the pistol to stop him. I sat with my back to the tins and reloaded. Syd and Eric were firing as though they were using a machine gun.

Mohammed was firing regularly although we could not gauge his success. I shouted, "Jake!"

"Yes, sir?"

"Can you hit them from where you are?"

"They have taken cover behind the spoil from the diggings, sir."

Syd said, "I bet you could hit them, sir."

"Jake, have a go. If you can make them move then the rest can open fire."

He began to fire. I could see that he was keeping their heads down but that was all. It was then I saw the spade. It had been left embedded in the sand but half of the blade was showing. I knelt and took aim at the spade. It was a gamble but I was gambling just one bullet. I fired and the bullet hit the spade at an angle. It ricocheted off and there was a cry.

I shouted, "Jake, use the rocks."

"Right, sir." Soon there was a regular rhythm to the bullets as men fired, not at the spoil but at the rocks behind and around the sheltering warriors. It had an effect. After half an hour the warriors mounted and raced off north. There were still more than twenty-five of them but we had hurt them. The men on the ridge managed to wound three more as they fled.

The engineers cheered. My men remained silent. We knew that they would be back and next time they would try something different.

The first thing we did, after we had collected all the weapons, was to bury our dead. Tommy Garstang had been hit by three bullets. He had died almost instantly. A big man, he had not been able to take cover quickly enough. We had managed to gain another pistol. It would be useful. After the funeral, we cooked food. I ensured that Mohammed and Dick were on watch, Mohammed led my trooper up to the vantage point he had used to snipe at the warriors.

"What do we do with the bodies of the enemy dead sir?"

"Make a wall of them to the west of the drill site. If nothing else it will slow them up the next time they come and, hopefully, the sight of the bodies might have an effect." I shrugged, "We have no fuel to burn them and no time to bury them. We will have to learn to live with the stink."

As we ate George Reynolds was despondent, "They will come back."

Ken said, "But the last time it took more days than we expected."

He was right, "Then our only chance is for someone to get to Bandar-e Deylam and send a telegram to London. Perhaps Mr D'Arcy can light a fire under the Shah. He is the only one who can stop this. If Mr D'Arcy threatens to stop paying the £20,000 then he may do something about the warlord."

Syd nodded, "Who are you going to send then, sir?"

"I will go and take Mohammed with me."

"Sir, why you?"

"It should be Mr Reynolds but he is needed here and the journey would be too much for him."

"I don't like it, sir."

"Neither do I but we haven't the number of men to keep fighting him. We lost one driller today and men were wounded. With this heat and with the enemy becoming cleverer if we don't get help then we are all doomed to die out here." I paused, "It is the only way. Make sure that Bob's wound does not get infected. Give him the pistol we took from the dead warrior. It is easier to use one handed and all he has to do is to guard the chest."

We left before dawn. Both of us were good riders and riding the two best camels Mohammed hoped to make the journey there and back in less than five days. It was a tall order but we had to try. I was surprised at how much faster we went with just the two of us and riding good camels. For the first few miles, Mohammed kept turning to ensure that I was keeping up. I was less than two camel lengths behind him and that gave him the confidence to keep pushing. We did not stop as long at noon as

Desert War

when we had the engineers with us. Instead, he used the shadows from the mountains to give us some shade. It meant that on the evening of the second day, we wearily plodded into his uncle's yard. We had to knock on the door to effect an entry.

His uncle looked not only pleased to see us but surprised, perhaps even shocked.

"My nephew, you are alive."

Mohammed looked puzzled, "And why would I not be?"

"We were told by Mohammed Ali Teymourtash that men came to tell him that you and the Westerners were slaughtered in the mountains by bandits."

Mohammed's face became angry, "That snake sent men to ambush us but thanks to the lieutenant here he failed." He looked at me, "Lieutenant, I think he will have told the company that we are all dead."

"Then in the morning, we will pay the agent a visit before we send a telegram to Mr D'Arcy."

His uncle said, "Where are my manners? Sit, Lieutenant," he clapped his hands, "water for washing, food and coffee." As I sat, he said to his nephew, "Where did you come from?"

"We left Shardin two days ago."

The businessman in him frowned, "The animals?"

"The animals did not suffer. The lieutenant knows how to ride. We have gained some animals; both horses and camels." While we ate and drank he told him of the two encounters.

When he had finished his uncle nodded, "I thought I had not seen Ahmed around. His death came not a day too soon. Mohammed Ali Teymourtash has men as bodyguards now, Mohammed."

"Then we will take some of our men when we pay him a visit. He is a bandit and we now have proof. The only way he could have known that we were attacked would be if he spoke to the bandits."

We rose early. I decided that we would visit the telegraph office first. I had the address and I sent a long and expensive telegram to the offices we had visited in Liverpool. Mr Milner and the Ice Maiden were our best hope of help. I had no idea where Mr D'Arcy might be found. I outlined the problem and told Mr Milner of the infidelity of his agent.

Mohammed had brought with us six men. They were tough-looking chaps. Mohammed sent four of them around the back of the office and we banged on the door. It was a servant who opened it and before he could shout a warning we had pushed past him. Leaving two of the men we had brought to secure the man, we raced through the house to the courtyard that Mohammed assured us the agent used. A young woman was stroking his hair. The agent did not look up but said, "Yussef, I hope this is important, Jasmine is preparing me for my day."

I said, in Arabic, "I think, Mohammed Ali Teymourtash, that your day has just become considerably worse."

He jumped up and I saw genuine shock, "You can't be here. The warlord slew you all."

He was even more treacherous than I had thought. Not only had he sent bandits to steal the gold he had colluded with our enemies.

I smiled, "No, he did not. I am guessing that you have told our employer that we are all dead and he has lost the money for the animals we hired. Have you asked him for more, already? Will the next engineers suffer the same fate?"

Mohammed Ali Teymourtash was a clever man but we had taken him by surprise and his mask slipped. I saw, from his face, that I was right. He recovered and spread his arms. "I do not know what you are talking about. I am just pleased that the news I received was false. I will send for the man and we can question him together."

Mohammed said, "When your deeds are known then there will be a swift trial and you will enjoy the punishment that you deserve."

He stood and without warning pushed the girl at me and Mohammed. He ran for the door. He shouted, "Ismail, guns!"

I guessed that there were men at the back of the building and they were armed. That was confirmed when I heard gunfire. Before we had even reached the door it opened and the agent held a gun in a two handed stance. Even as I drew my Webley I saw that it was the same type of gun used by the Russian we had killed. He opened fire. His bullet slammed into the girl and as she fell I had a clear shot. I took it. This was neither the time nor the place for charity. I could not afford for Mohammed to be

Desert War

killed or wounded. I had to get back to the camp and Mohammed was my best chance of doing so. My bullet hit his chest and, at that close range, threw him back across the room.

Mohammed's men came in and one said, "There were three men. They are dead."

The girl was also dead. That she had been something of a concubine did not mitigate the circumstances of her death. The shooting meant we could not leave straightaway. We had to give statements. Mohammed Ali Teymourtash had not been a popular man and none mourned his death but the officials were thorough.

That night Mohammed's uncle said, "When you return tomorrow, take four of our men. They can return here with the animals you have taken and, perhaps, give your engineers a little help. Perhaps there may be help from Tehran but our king likes to play the westerner and may not even be in his own kingdom. I am sorry, Lieutenant Roberts, it may well be that your exploration is doomed."

Part of me thought that he was right but I still had a contract to fulfil and it was not in my nature to quit.

Desert War

Jack

Chapter 13

The four men were some of the ones who had come with us to take the agent. They were relatives of Mohammed and I realised that this was more of a clan thing than anything. The officials had been concerned about the Russian connection. The Russian pistol that Mohammed now wore around his waist was clear evidence of collusion. The British brought money but the Russian bear just brought control. We rode hard and we rode fast back to Shardin. When we reached the camp, however, it was deserted. What had happened to my men and the engineers? We had been away for just five days. We rode to the goat farmer and he pointed to the east. "Your men, Lieutenant, came yesterday. They said that the engineers wanted to find somewhere else to drill. They are in a valley two miles to the east. Shall I take you there?"

I shook my head, "No, my friend, you watch your flock. You have been more than helpful. Did the warlord return?"

"Not yet." He looked troubled, "If he returns, Lieutenant, I will have to tell him where you have gone."

"Of course, and do so without being prompted. We will be ready."

We soon found the camp. They had not yet begun to drill. The tents were up and the toilets dug but that was all. This time the ground ran northwest to southeast. The ground rose on both sides but was not as high as on the first camp. One thing we had brought back with us was kindling and Mohammed set his men to unload the camels. We would have fires to help us to cook. George Reynolds, Ken and Syd joined us.

"Well?"

"The agent told London that we were dead. They now know that we are not but who knows what damage that has caused?"

Ken was angry, "When I get my hands around his scrawny neck I…"

"He is dead but something else you should know is that he was colluding with the warlord. He had a Russian gun and he knew of the attack on the camp. They will return." The three nodded. "Is that why you moved?"

George shook his head, "We discovered that the last camp was not one where we could find oil. This one seems likelier."

Ken saw my disappointed face and said, "Drilling for oil is a hit-and-miss activity, Jack. We may still be here long after your contract has expired."

"We can't leave you here without protection."

George shrugged, "And I would not expect you to stay here without pay. We will manage."

"Then the least we can do is to make this more defensible. While you set up your drilling rigs we will make this into Fort Hopeful."

I went with Syd and we walked to the highest point we could find. "This is not as good a defensive position, sir. If they had come to the other place we might have held them up but here...I tried to dissuade Mr Reynolds from moving but he was adamant."

"Syd, the purpose of this expedition is to find oil, not to be safe from attack." I took out my pipe and filled it. Riding was not conducive to smoking a pipe. I sat on a rock and lit it, "Did I ever tell you about Rorke's Drift, Syd?"

"Bits and bobs, aye,"

"We had walls and buildings but they did not stop the Zulus. We had to make a defensive position and to make one we used mealie bags. We can do that here." I took my dagger from my belt and dug around at my feet. "This is soil and not rock. It is not as high as the other camp but we can dig six firing pits here. We keep them occupied and disguise them as we did with the other site by using cloaks. We have four more men and we can use them. We know that they are good shots." I pointed to the nearest other high spot. It lay beyond where the drilling rig was being set up. "We hide Mohammed and his men up there. We now have another four allies." I pointed to the camp. "The men on the two flanks can give supporting fire. Down there we will have the rest of the men and the engineers. We build two walls of bully beef and rocks."

"They will see it and know that is where were are defending."

"Exactly and when they come, this time on foot, they will be more confident. They will use the rocks on the approach for cover."

"How does that help us, Jack?"

"We don't need to use those rocks and so we make them deadly traps. When we camped on the way back Mohammed told me about the snakes and scorpions they have around here. If we can find some and put them in the rocks then when they are used for cover they will give them a shock. We move rocks so that while they appear to give cover, they will be precariously positioned. You know yourself, Syd, when you are running for cover you don't stop to think. Falling stones will either expose or hurt them. When Bill sounds his bugle then we open fire from the flanks." The pipe had gone out and I tapped it on my metal-encased stump. "What do you think?"

"It might work if they come this way."

"And they will. When we came today and found the deserted old camp and the graves we headed for the goat herder. They will do the same. I told him to collaborate with them. We need to work hard today but, if we do then even if they come in the next couple of days we can give them a shock."

It was a plan.

"By the way, how is Bob?"

"The wound itches but that is a good sign, it means it is healing."

My one arm meant I was of little use in the actual digging of the pits but I could help to move rocks. We had learned from our first camp and we were able to disguise the appearance of the pits so that they looked natural. This time the riflemen would not be able to fire down on the enemy, it would be a flatter trajectory but they would still be able to fire over the tents from the marginally higher ground. Mohammed and his men were happy about both the tasks I assigned them. They liked the idea of gathering deadly creatures and hiding them. The thought of surprising the warlord and his warriors with their rifles was equally appealing. More than anything they were the ace trick we were keeping up our sleeve. The warlord could not know we had four more men.

Desert War

That night we were exhausted but as we had brought fresh food as well as water and kindling, when we ate it was almost like a feast. While they devoured the food, I explained my plan. "Tomorrow morning Jake and his men and Mohammed and his men will leave the camp as soon as we have eaten and they will wait all day in their positions. It will be the rest of us who move around the camp. Those men with Syd and me have to look like a dozen. Jake and Mohammed's men will only open fire when the bugle sounds. I want the warlord's men committed to an attack. I will shout the order for the engineers." They nodded that they understood. My plan had worked the first time and they had confidence in me. I hoped it was not misplaced. Much could go wrong.

This time the camp was closer to the drill site. We had learned our lesson. We also tethered the animals in a dell to the east of the camp where there was a pool. There must have been some rain and the rock had held it. The animals would soon drink it, but it meant we did not have to go as often to the goat herd. I wanted as few visits to him as possible. I did not want our presence to put him in any more jeopardy than he already was.

George was concerned about the death of the agent, "I am not sure how Mr D'Arcy will view the incident, Jack."

I shrugged, "I could have done little about it, George. The poor girl he shot was evidence of that. The locals assured me that had he and his men not been killed they would have been tried and executed. They seemed pleased that we had saved them a trial and rid them of a parasite." George Reynolds had different priorities from the rest of us.

Syd and I took a turn around the sentries before we retired, "How is the ammo holding out?"

The sergeant major shrugged, "It depends on how many we expend on their next attack. The last one used a fifth of our ammo. With what we had already used we have less than two-thirds of what we started with. It is not enough, sir."

"And there is little likelihood of getting any more. Who would have thought that .303 ammunition would be so hard to come by?"

Despite everyone begging me not to I took a duty. They were concerned about my arm. The metal sleeve had worked and it had protected me in the two attacks. We had few enough men without the officer skiving off.

My new plan meant that we all rose before dawn and ate while it was still dark and cool. The engineers were able to begin drilling earlier and we had our surprises hidden. For the men who were hiding it was a day spent covered with a cloak. While it afforded shade and rest, it was boring beyond words. They would have to sneak from under their cover to make water but that became part of their game, to see who could do so quietly. Mohammed and his men had decided to collect their nasty surprises at the end of the day. I was relieved when the sun began to set and the warband had not returned.

When Mohammed and his men returned from having seeded the rocks they were in high spirits. Geordie George shivered when I explained what they had done, "I cannot abide creepy crawlies and as for snakes, why man, we have none in England and a damned good thing too."

Ken chuckled, "Mind you, George, they are not as big here. Do you remember those bloody big ones in the Dutch East Indies? And the spiders?"

Geordie George turned to Syd, "They were as big as me hand and used to hunt birds if you can believe it."

Syd nodded, "I believe you. There were some nasty ones in Sudan. And the scorpions…"

George said, "We had none of those in the East Indies. Are they big?"

Syd shook his head, "The rule with scorpions is the smaller they are the deadlier they are. A bite off a big one was like a nasty bee sting. A little one would, more often than not, be deadly."

With those cheery thoughts, we retired. When I woke, for my early duty, I made water in the latrine and then walked up to the sentry, Eric, at the firing pits. It was still pitch black and I sniffed the air. The wind was from the west and that was the direction we had taken when we had arrived. There was no trail. This was the land of goats and they needed no trail. However, any enemy coming would take the line of least resistance and that would be from the northwest. Since Mohammed's words, I had been more

Desert War

aware of my senses. I could smell horses, camels and men and yet our horses and camels were downwind of me.

"Eric, keep your eye to the northwest. Look for signs of men and animals."

Taking off the safety, he slid the bolt to chamber a round, "Right, sir. Trouble?"

"Could be."

I went down to the camp and roused Mohammed, Syd and Jake, "I can smell something to the northwest. Let us get men in position now. If it is nothing then they can return and we will eat."

Mohammed said, "I will put my men in their holes and then see if I can detect that which you suspect."

Syd roused George who moaned, "Away man, it's the middle of the night."

"The lieutenant can smell something. Start cooking the food but have your lads armed and ready."

He became all business, "Right. Come on, bonny lads, time to be up and at 'em."

I donned my sword. Jake quite liked the captured Russian rifle and I used his Lee Enfield. The corned beef boxes allowed me to use the weapon as I could rest the barrel along their tops. I was not as accurate as I would have been with two hands, but I could add to the fusillade. I rested it on the flat part of the boxes. Our men were in position and the rest of us moved around as much as we could to give the impression that there were more of us than there actually were.

The fried corned beef was not the same as bacon but the smell was just as enticing and one luxury we had in abundance was English mustard. The flatbreads we had brought from Bandar-e Deylam were a little stale but by frying them in the oil they were more than palatable. Even though we were in danger the hot food encouraged laughter and smiles among engineers and soldiers alike. If we were being watched then they would think that we were unsuspecting and unaware of danger. Nothing could have been further from the truth. We were as prepared as it was possible to be. Our keffiyeh covered our helmets and while they could not stop a bullet they could, as we had discovered, deflect one. More importantly, they would stop a sword from slicing into an unprotected skull.

I had the flap of my holster open and my sword hung from my tent post. I was standing close enough to my tent so that I could grab the weapon quickly enough if I needed to. I took the flatbread with mustard and corned beef from Bill and bit into it. Fred put my mug of tea on the top of the corned beef tin. It was still dark. The glow of the fire was the only illumination and would pinpoint our position to an enemy. We would still be shadows moving around the fire but as I had found, you could aim at shadows. If they were coming then they would want to be much closer before they opened fire to ensure that they killed us. I finished the bread and beef and sipped the strong sweet tea.

Ken came over to me, his eyes flicking to the northwest, "Do we go and start drilling as normal, Jack?"

"That is the plan but the hairs prickling on my neck and what I smelled this morning make me think that, perhaps they are out there and getting as close as they can in the dark. We..."

I got no further. There was a shout. One of Mohammed's creepies had been disturbed and a warrior had been surprised. Syd shouted, "Stand to!"

We all dropped behind the tins. A thin crack of light in the eastern sky told us that the day would soon be upon us. There was a scream as this time a creepy found a warrior and either bit or stung him. Muzzle flashes in the dark identified where the enemy warriors were. Syd shouted, "Hold your fire until you can see a target."

That was easier said than done although we knew their position from where we had seeded the rocks. We knew where they were hiding. They were within one hundred and fifty yards of us. That was very close and if they rushed us, especially in the dark, then we were doomed. We were all safe for the moment. More of their rifles fired and I heard the bullets slam into the tins. It was a waiting game and their single-shot rifles took time to reload. They did not fire volleys.

I heard the shouted command from someone leading the warriors, "Charge them!" I had been too clever. My men on the flanks could not fire down in the dark. Until the sun rose, we would have to fight for our lives.

Desert War

I shouted, "Open fire!"

I fired the MLE at the muzzle flashes and the shadows. The rest of my men fired faster and the handguns of the engineers rattled like a machine gun. George's Purdey sounded like a cannon and in its flash I saw the huge numbers of swarming men. It was when they were just twenty yards from us and we could smell them that the sun flared from the east.

"Now, Brown, now!"

The bugle's strident notes sounded and almost instantly the two flanking groups opened fire, Jake and the men above us rattled bullets while Mohammed and his men were slow and regular. I still had half a magazine but they were so close now that I dropped the MLE and drew my pistol. The warrior who appeared from nowhere and swung the butt of his long rifle at my head almost succeeded. I fired and he was so close that his face disappeared. He dropped like a stone. I had no time for self-congratulation, and I fired another four shots in quick succession. We were winning but only just. The warlord must have scoured his lands for men. It would not now be simply about the gold. His pride had been hurt, not to mention his reputation. He had to destroy us. I saw him, even as he raised his rifle to end my life. He was less than ten yards from me and the end of his barrel looked close enough to touch. I fired. It was just in time. My bullet did not hit him but the firing mechanism of his rifle. The end of the rifle rose in the air. I dropped my pistol and grabbed my sword.

It was at that moment that the two men flanking the warlord were shot, probably by Jake and his men. Instead of falling backwards they fell forward and crashed into the corned beef tins. The falling bodies destroyed the defences in front of me. They also distracted me. There was a triumphant look on the warlord's face as he saw his chance. It was made to look all the more sinister in the shadows created by the sun in the east. He raised the rifle and pulled the trigger. The gun did not fire. My bullet had damaged it. He hurled the weapon at me and I ducked. I was not quite quick enough and the butt caught my keffiyeh and hidden helmet. The helmet saved me. He drew his sword and used the bodies of his two dead men to leap in the air and swing his sword at me. He was a powerful man and if I had not had the metal covering for my arm I am not sure what the outcome would have been. As it was his blade slid down the metal sleeve and I found my arm being forced back. I used my left arm to support my right and his blade was held between my sword and stump. He spat at me and as I jerked my head instinctively back I found myself falling. I hoped that there was nothing behind me and I relaxed into the fall. Sensing victory he strode after me and that was his undoing. As my back hit the ground my right foot came up and connected with his groin. Although I had not intended it the kick proved decisive. It stopped him and allowed me to roll to the side. As he swung his sword, belatedly at where my body had been, I slashed sideways and connected with his knee. Not a mortal blow, it was a painful one and it drew blood. It also bought me the time to stand.

He was angry and cursed me, "You and all your men shall die. Your bodies will rot and no one will remember the Englishmen who died here in the desert." He swung his sword at me and I blocked it. He swung it the other way but I had anticipated it and my blade parried his.

All around us men were fighting. The handguns of the engineers now proved their worth. The warlord was weakening slightly. The wound from his knee was taking effect. In desperation or perhaps he had always planned it, he drew his dagger and slashed it at me. I was forced to block it with my sword and he took advantage, swinging his sword in a scything slash at my neck. My left arm came up and not only blocked the blow but as the sword slid down the polished metal of my stump, the metal end of the protection Geordie George had made for me connected with his cheek. As a punch, it would have done little harm but the screw fitting on the end, although finished off still had an edge and it ripped across his cheek. He reeled and I punched at his head with my sword hilt. The two blows made him step back and it was at that moment that the rifle bullet from the direction of Mohammed and his men slammed into his head and he fell, dead.

Now was the time to end it and I shouted, "Brown, sound the charge!"

Neither the engineers nor Mohammed and his men understood the call but when we ran at the disheartened warriors

Desert War

they joined us. The enemy broke. We chased them. Those with pistols were able to shoot their enemies in the back. I slashed and stabbed at anyone within range. By the time we reached their horses and camels, less than twenty were there to mount and to flee. Many of the other camels and horses joined them.

I pointed out, "Mohammed, there is your bonus." He grinned at the twenty horses and camels that had been hobbled and could not flee. After ensuring that there were none feigning death we took the animals back to the camp. We passed the two men who had been bitten by snakes. It was as we walked back that I realised a man was missing. I saw him at the camp. Eric Wise, quiet Eric as we had named him, had died. An unassuming trooper, he was reliable and had obeyed every order ever given to him. His head had been split open by a sabre. His killer lay dead.

The death took the edge off the victory. John Jones and Bert Willis had been wounded but neither was life-threatening. The search for the oil had cost the drillers one man and now a soldier had died. We collected the bodies of the enemy and made a pyre beyond the horses and camels. We would be upwind of any stink. Using half a can of cooking oil we doused their bodies and burned them. In the early evening, while Brown played 'Last Post,' we buried Eric Wise in a deep grave. We covered his body with stones and found a huge slab to cover it. His remains would not be disturbed by animals.

Desert War

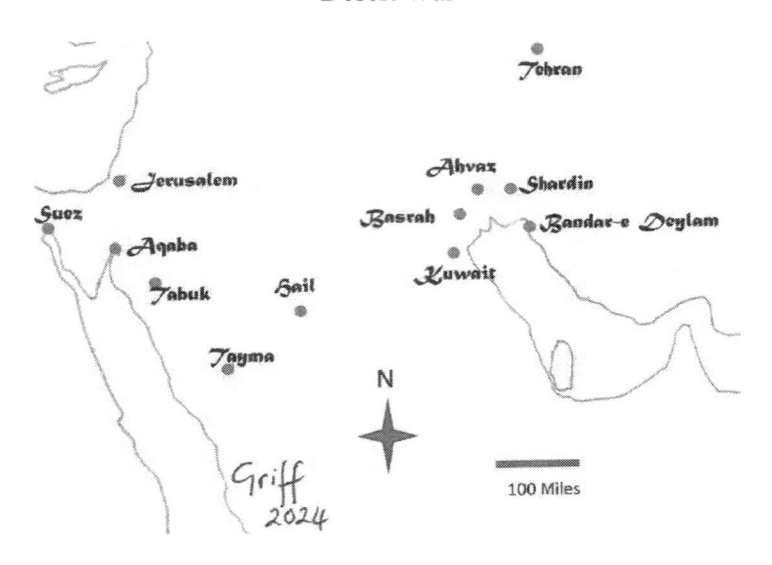

Desert War

Jack

Chapter 14

The bodies burned for the whole night and in the morning were still smoking. George and Ken were anxious to get on with the drilling. Geordie George, aided by Syd, made a makeshift hospital in one of the tents for those who had been injured or wounded in the attack. Mohammed and his men did our job. They rode for ten miles in a northern direction to look for signs of danger. There was none. The headman at Shardin told us that the survivors had fled through the village so fast it was like a sudden sandstorm.

A week after the attack Mohammed and his men left us. They had stayed longer than they had needed to and that was due to the bonds of war. This was not an official war but as Mohammed told me, there is always war in the desert and men have to fight to hold on to what they have. George had paid for the camels and animals before we had left Badar-e Deylam. Mohamed said that when we were done he would happily buy them back from us. He saw that we had cared for them. He was happy for he now had a string of horses and camels that he could sell. I was sad to see the Arab leave. He felt like Saeed had done and was a friend. A man did not make many good friends in the short time he spent on earth.

Our life fell into a routine once more. We resumed our patrols but kept them more limited. It was high summer and the temperature at noon was so high that none of us could bear to be in the sun. We rigged our cloaks to make shady areas and just endured the painful heat for a couple of hours. George and his drillers used the cool of the evening and the morning to work and they were the productive hours. Syd and I could see little progress but the engineers seemed happy that they had found a potential oil field.

Eric had been the quiet one and his loss should have caused us the least problems yet he was the sole topic of conversation for the first week after the skirmish. He had a mother. As Jake had said, we all had a mother but, in Eric's case, they were close.

He had taken the contract so that he could make her more comfortable in her old age. His father had died in South Africa and Eric was her only support.

"I will make sure that she gets all his back pay."

George Reynolds was a kind man and he felt bad about the death of such a pleasant young man. Tommy Garstang had been a loner with no family. Everyone got on with him but when he had been killed there was not the mourning that followed Eric's demise. "When you go home, Jack, I will give ten gold pieces to the widow. God knows you have all earned a bonus and I am happy to use Mr D'Arcy's gold."

I shook my head, "I will take the gold for Eric, George, but we cannot leave you here unprotected. We will stay on beyond the end of the contract."

George smiled, "You are a good man, Jack, an honourable one but we may be here for years. We are used to danger and you have done your duty and more. With the warlord gone, we are safer. Your contract is up in the middle of September. You should leave then."

"And how do we get home? There is no SS Carnic waiting to give us a voyage back to England. No, like it or not, until Mr D'Arcy contacts us we are stuck here."

Mohammed had already promised that he would bring any telegram that arrived in Bandar-e Deylam for us. The clerk was his cousin. At the end of each week, I had looked to the northwest for a sight of a rider from Bandar-e Deylam. None had come by the start of September.

Despite the uncertainty, we got on well with the drillers. We appreciated their skill and hard work and I know that they were impressed by our diligence and vigilance. Ken knew that they had all been saved at least three times by our skills.

"When we were in the Dutch East Indies some natives raided our camp. We had no soldiers with us then. We fought them off but we lost half of our men." He patted his pistol, "We became far more proficient with these things then. Don't you worry about leaving, we have learned from you. I wish we had more rifles though."

Desert War

"That is easily solved, you can have the Nagrant we took from the Russian and Eric's MLE. You will have to husband the ammo but..."

"So, you will be leaving at the end of September?"

I laughed, "Don't put words in my mouth. I am giving you the two rifles as a gift. We will not abandon you."

It was Jake's patrol that brought us, in the last week of September, the news that riders were approaching. "They are wearing uniforms, sir, and I don't think that they are the warlord's men."

Even so, I sent men up to the firing pits in case this was a trap. There were twenty horsemen and they had a wagon with them. The captain who dismounted had flecks of grey in his beard. I saluted him and said, "Sir."

He spoke in Arabic. George wandered over. He had picked up some Arabic when Mohammed had been with us. "I am Captain Nadar Afshar of the 1st Tabriz Cavalry and I am here to relieve you."

"Relieve?"

He snapped his fingers and a sergeant dismounted and brought over a piece of paper. It was a telegram. "It is in English and I cannot read it."

It was addressed jointly to George and to me. It was from Mr Milner who explained that the defence of the drilling crew would now be the responsibility of the Persian army. Our contract was up and we were ordered to leave the camp and make our way back to Suez. There was an agent in Suez who would arrange for our passage. George was asked to find oil as soon as possible and I was informed that we would be paid until we returned to Liverpool. It was all a little perfunctory, not to say cold.

I handed it to George so that he could study the details and spoke to the Persian soldier, "Thank you, Captain. We will leave tomorrow. Do you need me to take you for a tour of the camp and our defences?"

He gave me a haughty look. I had seen the same look on some British officers when they were speaking to what they thought to be an inferior. "This is my country and we know how to defend it."

Desert War

I was angry and, with nothing to lose retorted, "It is a pity that you did not control the warlord. If you had then we would not have lost men. However, you needn't worry about Halil Rifat Bey, we defeated him and his body is now part of the desert."

I think he would have liked to smack me with the switch he held but my men had heard the interchange and four of them were behind me. "The sooner you leave the better." He hissed the words at us. Not all the reptiles in this land hid in the rocks.

I joined George and Ken along with Syd. I pointed to the tents. "We don't need all of those. We can make do with just two."

Ken nodded, "And we don't need the camels either."

Syd nodded, "We will take the bully beef with the bullet holes. That should last us. How far is it, sir?"

I shrugged, "George, can we have a look at your map?" We went to his tent and he unfolded the map of Persia. "I will make a copy of this." I traced the route we would take. "It looks to be a thousand miles. Some of it will be in the land ruled by the Ottomans. They won't take kindly to our presence."

Syd shook his head, "Looking at this map, sir, there will be no bugger there to question us. We will struggle to get water."

I jabbed a finger at Basrah. It was the largest place I could see, "There will be water there. We buy extra skins."

George said, "As well as the gold for Eric, I will give you some as well, Jack. You deserve to be treated better than this. Mr Milner could have arranged for a ship to pick you up from Bandar-e Deylam."

"We have served our purpose. Don't worry, George, we are used to being discarded when we are no longer needed. We all knew that when we took this contract. We have been paid well. When we reach Suez, we shall sell the camels and that money will be shared out too."

The rest of the day was taken up in preparing to leave. The two tents were taken down. We would sleep with the drillers. We took them down efficiently and quickly in contrast to the Persians who were trying to establish their own camp. They chose the far side of the drilling site. Not only was it not flat, they chose not to use straight lines. Bill Brown chuckled, "Wait until they have to use the toilet at night!"

Desert War

The meal that night was a feast. Geordie George used some of the vodka to enliven the stew. When Mohammed and I had returned from Bandar we had brought some spices and dried fruit. They were also used up. The Persian soldiers had brought fresh supplies and the sergeant, who was less offensive than the officer, also told us that there would be a monthly wagon bringing water and food. George and the drillers would not starve.

While the food was being prepared and cooked George and I made a copy of his map. I saw that we faced a journey of one hundred and seventy miles to reach Basrah but there was water on the way. It was once we left that ancient city where we would struggle.

"The good news is that there is an English presence in the city not least of which is the East India Company. You should be able to ask them for help and guidance for your journey across the desert. Perhaps you could take a ship from there to Suez?"

"The journey across the desert will be hard but it will be a shorter one than a sea voyage and besides you said yourself that ships sailing west were more likely to be preyed on by pirates. We are desert soldiers and we will use that as our means to get home."

There was a great deal of laughter that night. Addresses were exchanged but, in most cases, they were optimistic rather than realistic ones. The exceptions were Syd and George. George had every intention of returning to Newcastle and if Syd bought a pub, which was his plan, then it would be a perfect match.

I sat with George Reynolds, "I am still not happy about abandoning you like this. Do you think you will find oil?"

"Oh, I can guarantee that. What is less certain is the time scale. Still, it will be the high point of my career if I find oil where it has never been found before, eh?"

We all had different dreams and George would endure the desert to make his come true.

We left, before dawn, after a hearty breakfast and a dixie of tea to take with us. Before we mounted our camels we went, as a group, to Eric's grave. While Brown played the Last Post once more, we saluted. I could not but feel guilty somehow. I had lost a man. We mounted our camels and left the camp. It felt like

Desert War

leaving home and we rode in silence. We had the draught camels we had bought in Bandar-e Deylam, and they carried water, tents and food. The troopers rode with rifles hanging from the pommels of their saddles. We might have ended the threat of one warlord but there could well be others and there would be bandits. I just hoped that the open display of weapons would discourage them. The first leg of our journey, to Ahvaz, was sixty miles and we did it in one day. Since my return from Bandar-e Deylam, we had not worked the animals. Ahvaz was a sizeable town with about a thousand people living there and, most importantly, it lay on a river. Our camels could fill up with water. We were also able to buy food. Speaking Arabic made all the difference. Had we spoken English then we would have been the object of suspicion. We had water all the way to the great city of Basrah. We reached it after one night sleeping in the open. We had not bothered with tents but we had lit a fire to keep away the many flies that infested the land. Leaving the rest of the troop to buy food and the necessary waterskins, Syd and I sought out the representative of the East India Company.

Archibald Lewis had the mahogany skin of a man who had lived most of his adult life in the tropics. He was delighted to see us not only because we were English but also because we were soldiers. He happily provided us with maps and advice. I was pleased with the meeting but, as we turned to leave, he said, "Lieutenant, how would you like to earn a little extra money?"

"We are on our way home, Mr Lewis. We want a peaceful journey."

"I understand but your best route to Suez is not in a straight line. You need water and this," he plotted the route with his finger, "is the one with water and places to find food: Kuwait, Ha'il, Tabuk, Aqaba and then Suez."

"Thank you, we are indebted to you."

"I have a caravan which is heading to Kuwait. I would pay you to ride with them as an escort. It would be mutually beneficial. While there are many bandits on the road you shall take the one which is afflicted the most and the largest number of them lie between here and Kuwait." He took out ten gold pieces. He did not know how many men I had but it would mean a gold piece each.

Desert War

Syd saw my hesitation, "Sir, we are going that way anyway. It makes sense to have company."

I was defeated, "Very well then, when do we leave?"

"First thing in the morning. You can meet the caravan master, Ali Ben Faisal, at the south gate." He pushed over the money.

I said, "One more thing, have you any .303 ammunition?"

He beamed, "Of course." He shouted, "Carter, fetch two boxes of .303 ammunition, please. It is a gift from the East India Company." He smiled, "You say there is a British company exploring for oil around Shardin?"

"Yes." I did not divulge any more information.

"Interesting. Our own geologists seem to think that there might be some here. Perhaps I will send to your surveyors and offer them the chance to come here."

I gave a noncommittal nod. I doubted that Mr D'Arcy would wish to share the bounty. The two boxes of ammunition were a godsend. I should have been a little worried that Mr Lewis was being so generous but I could not see that there would be a problem.

The men had the extra waterskins ready and we filled them all. We ate well that night. Mr Lewis had recommended a place that cooked and sold food. It was not a restaurant, we ate beneath the awning of a building, but the food was filling and cheap. More importantly, we did not have to use our supplies. I distributed both the gold and the ammunition. With the gold from Mr Reynolds and the back pay due to us when we reached England then they would all be richer men. For soldiers of the queen that was unusual. Even though she was dead I still felt as though I served the queen, the queen had been not only Queen of England and Great Britain but Empress of the Empire. Most old soldiers were either too crippled to work or unable to cope in a world without the barking of orders and the inevitable structure that came from a life in the army. It was why Ged had been so keen to serve as my batman. He could not face a life away from the army.

We slept in the stable where we had paid to house our camels. They were fed grain and it was warm. We rose early and were at the gate as it opened. Ali Ben Faisal and his caravan were there waiting for us. There were forty camels and I could see why we

Desert War

were needed. With just twenty camel riders and the leader, they would have been hard-pressed to defend themselves if they were attacked.

He was pleased that we spoke Arabic. He spoke English but not well. When he saw the rifles my men carried he was delighted that we were to be his guards.

I took charge, "I will ride at the fore with you, my sergeant and two men. The rest of my men will be the rearguard."

He touched his forehead and bowed, "I am in your hands, my friend."

I had already studied a map and knew that the ninety-odd miles could not be covered in one journey. We would need to camp. Ali Ben Faisal told me that there was an oasis and we would use that to camp.

"Is it popular with merchants?"

"It is."

"Then the bandits will know that you will camp there."

He shook his head, "They will not attack us while you are protecting the caravan."

"Do not be too sure. They might well think that this is a larger-than-usual caravan and an even more tempting target. Syd, make sure the lads all have one up the spout."

He wheeled his camel around. We were now all familiar with our animals and Syd rode him as though he had been born to his back. Ali Ben Faisal said, "You could make a small fortune, Lieutenant, hiring yourself out as caravan guards."

"We are going home, Ali, this is the last time we go to war."

He laughed, "This is not war."

"The moment you believe that is the moment that you will die. If we have to fight then it is better to view those who attack us as enemies. If we just see them as unfortunates who have chosen a career poorly then they will win and we will die."

"And how did you lose the arm?" I told him the story of Omdurman. He nodded, "I have heard of that fight. The Dervishes were a fanatical people. You were lucky just to lose your arm and not your life." He was right, I was lucky.

As with all such merchants we stopped before noon to rest from the heat of the sun. Ali found us an oasis which, whilst crowded, allowed us to be shaded from the sun and for the

Desert War

camels to enjoy a little water although I would not have touched the oily-looking liquid. We left when the sun was becoming hot but not unbearable. Our goggles had proved a godsend. They were tinted so we did not risk sun blindness. The fact that they kept out the sand was also important.

The bandits, when they came, were just a mile from the oasis we were seeking. Perhaps they counted on us being complacent and eager for food, shade and rest. They did not reckon on my men. Fred Emerson was with Syd and me. His eyesight was second to none and it was he who spotted the unnatural lump in the sand.

"Sir, am I going daft or is that small dune in totally the wrong place and the wrong shape?"

Holding my hand up to stop the caravan, I took out my binoculars and peered through them. While the man-made dune might have fooled at a distance I could see, through the binoculars, the distinctive shape of a camel covered by a cloak.

"Syd, fire a bullet at that mound of sand in the distance."

"Sir, that is a thousand yards away."

"It is alright. I just want you to get close. If Fred and I are right, then there is a bandit and his camel hiding in the sand there."

He leaned his forearm on the hump of his camel and squeezed off a shot. It was close but he had aimed too high and it whizzed over the top of the sand. It worked, however, and suddenly other sandy lumps rose like so many wraiths. There were thirty bandits.

I shouted, "Skirmish line!" This was a manoeuvre we had not used yet but I knew that Syd had trained the men well. The ones leading camels dropped their reins and joined the rest of us as we formed a line in front of the caravan. I drew my Webley. The rest all did as Syd had done and rested their forearms on their camels' humps. The screaming bandits galloped at us.

Ali Ben Faisal said, "Should we not run?"

I shook my head and shouted, "There are just thirty of them." It was not arrogance or overconfidence. There were ten of us armed with the best rifles in the world. The twenty camel drivers all had weapons of one sort or another. Even had they outnumbered us I would not have run. Colour Sergeant Bourne had instilled in me to face your front. It was not foolish heroics. As long as you faced an enemy then you had the chance to beat him. If you turned your back, you were inviting death.

I shouted, "Hold your fire until I give the order." The bandits were spread out in a long line. They would be used to fighting single-shot weapons. The MLE could fire ten bullets in the time it took one of their ancient guns to fire two. Their long line would avail them nothing. I could sense the nervousness of the Arabs. It manifested itself when Ali Ben Faisal raised his gun and fired. He missed. I heard the cluck of annoyance from Syd but I said nothing. Even when some of the other men in the caravan opened fire I said nothing. I knew it could only help us. The bandits, who were unharmed by the random shots would be thinking that while the rifles were reloaded they had a chance. The Lee Enfield would give them a rude shock.

Ali Ben Faisal was panicking, "They are on us. For the love of God open fire."

I waited. When they were just three hundred yards I shouted, "ESEG, open fire!"

The nine rifles all cracked not just once but again and again. Those at the rear, commanded by Jake, fired at the extreme left of their line. Syd and those at the fore aimed at the right of the line and then both sets of rifles worked their way to the middle. The bandits sent a desultory volley in our direction. One bullet came close but hit neither me nor Fatima. I rested my Webley on Fatima's hump. Saddles had been emptied and some of the bandits had realised the futility of their charge. In the centre, however, four riders seemed hellbent on getting to grips with us. I squeezed the trigger four times in quick succession. The leader, in the centre, was thrown from his camel. When the two men flanking him fell then the survivors, all eight of them, turned and fled. I saw that in all, twelve men had survived the attack but they also had some who were wounded. Most importantly, their leaders and bravest warriors, lay dead. We had not destroyed the bandits but we had ensured that they would leave large caravans alone.

"Cease fire. Sergeant Major, collect the weapons and the camels."

Desert War

Four camels had failed to flee. They would make handy remounts and when we reached Suez, whatever money they fetched would be a bonus.

We camped at the oasis. I set the sentries. The merchant was delighted with the outcome of the failed attack. His terror was now replaced by euphoria. We ate well that night and we did not have to cook.

When we reached Kuwait the next day I saw that it was a better port than Basrah had been. There were larger ships tied up there. I recognised the distinctive flag of the East India Company. There were not as many as there once had been but they still plied the seas. We camped by the sea and were feted again by the merchant while his men unloaded the camels and the dock workers loaded them onto the ships. The next day they would take landed cargo and head back to Basrah. He was grateful because he would have lost everything but for us and he wanted us to know that. I used his friendly attitude to ask him about our journey. I showed him the map and he marked on it the oases we would find. He also marked where we might expect to find bandits.

We headed southwest when we left the merchant. We had full waterskins and fresh supplies from the city. By my estimate, we had another two weeks in the desert and then we would reach Suez. It was when we camped that night that I realised what we should have done in either Basrah or Kuwait. It was out of character for me when I cursed and my men were startled.

"What is up, sir?"

"It is me, Jake, I must be getting old or something. We should have sent a telegram from one of those two places to tell our families that we are alive."

"Surely, they will know, sir. I meant Mr Milner knows."

"And Mr Milner is running a business. It might not even cross his mind. When we reach Suez the first order of the day is to send a telegram to Colonel Dickenson. He got us into this, and he can tell our families."

Desert War

Jack

Chapter 15

That journey through the desert had a profound effect on me. Firstly, it was longer than any we had undertaken in Sudan and it taxed us all. It also brought us so close together that it felt like the time I had first joined the army. That was the time when I found friends. I might not have seen Hooky and the other survivors of Rorke's Drift for years but they still felt like my friends and I knew that the nine who rode with me, even though we might never see each other again once we reached England, would always be close to me. It was also a strange crossing of the desert. When we had ridden in Sudan and Egypt we had been on the lookout for danger. Here it soon became apparent that the Arab travellers that we met, and we met many, were just crossing the desert to get home or to seek supplies. We found all the oases that Ali Ben Faisal had told us about and none of them were ever empty. We shared the water and the shade with other travellers. In most cases, they were travelling east while we were travelling west. We always shared our food with them and found that they were generous in what they shared. Sometimes it was food but more often it was information and that was just as valuable. I was able to add to the map I had copied from Mr Reynolds.

The other valuable commodity we shared was the stories we told each other. In my case, it was our tales of the warlord and Omdurman. In the case of the Arabs, it was about the uneasy relationship they had with their Ottoman overlords. As we were English we were seen as relatively safe and they confided in us that there were many who wished to revolt against their masters. We listened, sympathetically, to their stories. I wondered if those ruled by the new king, those in Africa and India would take to a revolt as the American colonies had done. I thought of the soldiers with whom I had served who had transferred to the Egyptian, Sudanese and Indian armies. What would happen to them?

The crossing of the desert changed me. I was able to look at the desert in the morning, blue and chilled and then again at sunset when it was pink, red and almost purple and I marvelled at its majesty. I could not believe that it could be so beautiful and yet so deadly at the same time. I had never been a religious person. I believed in God, of course I did. I had yet to meet a real soldier who was an atheist. You had to believe that when you died there was something beyond. A soldier was always a bullet away from death. The desert showed me that there was a God and he had made this. We were now close to the centre of three religions: Christianity, Judaism and Islam. God could be seen all around us. Speaking to the Arabs I discovered that they had the same God and the same wonder about the deity. They were all pious. We respected their frequent prayers and did nothing to offend them. I prayed too but that was always just before I retired. I found it comforting.

The last part of the journey from Aqaba to Suez was across the Sinai Peninsula. We knew that our journey was almost at an end. We were all bearded and as brown as mahogany. We looked, our goggles apart, like Arabs. That we stank was obvious and that we were leaner was visibly clear. We were not the same men who had left Suez back in March. We had lost track of time but I estimated that it was either the end of October or the beginning of November. The journey had taken longer than I had expected. I knew that we had left Shardin at the start of October. George Reynolds kept a diary and he told us the date every day. Often it would be to announce some historical event that had occurred on that day. Now it was as though we had passed through another world where time was of no importance.

We reined in and looked down at the port which had changed beyond recognition since the first time we had seen it all those years ago. It lay across the canal from where we reined in. "Well boys, when we reach the agent and secure our berths you will cease to be soldiers."

I saw grins. Jake shook his head, "Sorry sir, but you are wrong. We will never stop being soldiers. One thing riding through the desert dressed like an Arab has taught me is that it is not the uniform that makes a soldier, it is something in here." He patted his heart. "We will take off the uniform and wear civvies but you will still be, sir. You have earned that respect."

Desert War

"I don't mind being called Jack, you know. Syd calls me that."

"Yes sir, but you and Syd were non-coms together, you have a history."

Fred asked, "What about the Lee Enfields, sir? Won't the army want them back?"

I shrugged, "I don't know. Let us play that by ear." I banged some of the dust from my cloak and said, "Right, let us show these chaps that we are still soldiers, even if it is for just a short time." I took off the keffiyeh and shook the dust from it. I fastened it about my neck. The others did the same. I draped my cloak over the back of Fatima. The helmets marked us as soldiers and the uniforms of the troopers, faded as they were, confirmed it.

We moved into a column of twos and with straight back and our left arms hanging from our sides we rode the last few hundred yards to the simple raft-like ferry that carried those travelling from the east across the canal to Suez. It was a lucrative business but also a precarious one. It had to be timed so that it did not interfere with the passage of ships. It took two trips.

The ferry meant that we landed outside the port and had to pass the barrier into the town. It would not have stopped a determined force and was more to deter those who might wish to cause mischief. There was a guard hut. Two men were by the simple barrier. It was the Egyptian army that guarded the port. I heard an Egyptian shout, "Sergeant Major, soldiers approaching."

The sergeant major came from the guard house. He saw my pips and saluted, "Sir. Can I ask your business?"

I ordered Fatima to lower herself to the ground and I dismounted. "We are here to meet the agent of the Anglo-Persian Oil Company and take a ship back to England."

He looked relieved, "I was worried when we saw British soldiers coming from the south that there was more trouble. Life has been peaceful these last years."

"And that is due in no small part to you, Effendi."

I looked around and saw Saeed. Saeed had been a sergeant who had served with us at Fort Desolation and been promoted to

Desert War

become an officer in the Egyptian army. His uniform showed that he was now a major. I grinned and held out my hand, "Saeed, sorry, Major, it is good to see you. Congratulations on your promotion."

His smile turned to a frown when he saw my metal arm, "You were wounded?"

I shook my head, "It is in the past."

"This is my command now and I would be honoured if you would stay with us while you are in Suez. We are not yet at full compliment and I can offer you all a comfortable bed."

Syd had dismounted and he grinned, "Saeed, old friend, make it a bed and a bath and we are in your debt forever."

"Syd, Sergeant Major, good to see you. I can offer both."

We passed through the gate and he led us to a track to the right that led to some wooden huts. I recognised the design. "Saeed, I must find the agent of the company that hired us."

"Of course, there is your bed for the night, sir." He pointed to the hut and I continued walking down the main road into the bustling port of Suez.

I had been given a name in the telegram from Mr Milner, John Sharp. I headed for the offices that lined the road leading to the port and canal. It did not take me long to find out which office was Mr Sharp's. A French clerk directed me. I knocked on the door and an Egyptian voice said, "Enter."

It was not a large office. The Egyptian clerk was in a cubby hole of an outer office and I saw a door leading to an inner one. The clerk saw my uniform and switched to English, "Yes, sir, how can I help you?"

"I am Lieutenant Jack Roberts and I am looking for a Mr John Sharp."

The door opened and a young man stood there. He had the reddened skin of one who had not been in the tropics for long. He also had a thin pencil moustache. I could not but help be reminded of Billy, my dead brother. Was he another one seduced by money and promotion? Who was I to talk? I had taken gold to fight as a mercenary.

He beamed, "I wondered when you would get here. You crossed the desert?"

I smiled at his infectious enthusiasm, "I did."

Desert War

"Mehmet, tea."

"Yes, effendi."

I entered the office which was filled with box files and papers. All were neatly organised. "How did you manage to navigate through a sea of sand, Lieutenant, if you don't mind me asking? Did you have a guide?"

I shook my head, "My men and I served in Sudan and Egypt during the war. We know the desert."

He shook his head, "I admire you immensely, Lieutenant Roberts. I would have loved to be a soldier but...Mr Milner said that he hoped you would be here by December but if you were not here by January then I had to assume you were dead." He pointed to a calendar on the wall. "I have been checking the days and imagined you crossing the desert. You look just as I imagined."

Mehmet brought in the tea. It was not Sergeant Major tea but welcome for all that. There was proper milk for one thing. It was not cow's milk but it was better than tinned.

"Sorry, there are no biscuits."

I smiled, "The least of your problems I should imagine."

He nodded and sipped his tea, "Yes, there is just Mehmet and me and we run this office."

"I am surprised that Mr D'Arcy keeps an office here. "

He smiled, "It is a new venture. He has begun to use the canal to send goods from his home in Australia to England and vice versa. Having lived in both countries he is in the unique position of knowing what the other needs. We have a ship a week passing through." He reached up for a clipboard, "And the next ship to England is the SS Waltham Abbey. She is due in Suez three days from now. I will reserve berths for you and your men." He put it down triumphantly, "Everything will be organised. You will be accommodated in cabins for two and everything is found. She docks in Liverpool."

I was relieved. Three days was not long to have to wait. Of course, I was not naïve enough to think that the ship would arrive exactly when the confident young man thought it would. I stood and held out my hand, "Thank you."

"And where can I find you? Where will you be staying?"

"At the barracks by the gate from the desert."

Desert War

"With Egyptian soldiers?" I could hear the shock in his voice.

I smiled, "We fought alongside them, Mr Sharp, and they are fine fellows and brave too." I paused, "Tell me, have you learned any Arabic yet?"

He shook his head, "I find that English and my limited French get me by."

"Your life out here will improve considerably if you learn to speak to the people in their own language. Get Mehmet to teach you. I guarantee you will be more successful if you do so."

"I will take your advice, Lieutenant, for I can see that you have experience but I fail to see how life will become better."

I was about to leave when a thought struck me, "Is there a telegraph office here?"

"Of course."

I took a piece of paper and wrote down Colonel Dickenson's details as well as a simple message. "Could you send that for me, please? Our families think we are dead."

He looked appalled, "Of course. I didn't know."

"But your Mr Milner did."

I headed back to the barracks. When I entered barely half the men were there, "Where are the others, Jake?"

"Bath time, sir. We are on the next shift."

He produced a bottle of rum, courtesy of Saeed. "He says he doesn't drink but he knows that we do."

I beamed, "And when I have bathed and shaved, I shall enjoy a pipe and a glass of rum."

The Turks had occupied Egypt for many years and one of the benefits was the bathing facilities. By the time I had washed the dirt and detritus of the desert from my body and shaved the unruly beard and moustache, I felt more like a civilised man again. One of Saeed's men had cut my hair. I looked in the mirror and smiled at the paler skin where my beard and moustache had been. By the time we reached England, the pale patches would be as tanned as the rest of my face.

Being an Egyptian regiment they had dhobi wallers and we gave them our dirtiest clothes to wash. It cost just sixpence and they would be well laundered. The hot sun ensured that they would be dried and ironed ready for dinner. Our friend was the commanding officer of this small camel unit and we dined that evening in the mess that they all shared. We were treated as guests of honour and Syd and I flanked Saeed. Our friend must have regaled his mess with tales of Fort Desolation and they were eager to hear the stories, first, of Omdurman and then Persia. I could see that the young men envied us the action.

When it came to coffee and our pipes, Saeed and I sat apart from the others on the veranda and just talked about our lives. He was interested in Griff. I had to explain the notion of a military college to him. He, like me, had risen through the ranks. "Young men from military families can win a place there and in the year that they spend at the college, they are trained to be officers. They will learn to shoot, fence and ride horses as well as have the necessary lessons in science and mathematics."

"And does that make them better officers?"

I laughed, "Probably not but it will gain Griff a commission and that is better than rising through the ranks. For a start, there will be no ceiling and the pay will be better."

"It is what you wanted?"

I shook my head, "Not really but his heart was set upon it. I hope that he makes good friends like I have. We are friends, are we not?"

He beamed, "We are more than that, Jack, we are brothers in arms and there is no closer bond between men than that."

That night we slept between crisply laundered white sheets for the first time since we had left the Carnic. With a glass of rum to warm me, I slept like a baby. We had no reason to rise early but the reveille woke us and we joined the Egyptians at breakfast. While we were eating Saeed said, "My adjutant and I looked at your camels. They are fine animals. What are your plans for them?"

I shrugged, "Sell them I suppose."

He nodded, "That is what I hoped, we will buy them from you. They are seasoned and, from what you have told us, can withstand gunfire."

"Then it is agreed."

"I fear that the price is the one set by our government."

"And that means less than the market price. It matters not to us and my men will be pleased to know that their animals will be looked after."

Desert War

"Good and that allows me to broach another subject, perhaps thornier. The rifles your men use, what are your plans for them?"

"Technically they belong to the British army but…ask the men, they may well agree to sell them to you, or even give them."

"Such a fine weapon deserves payment."

My old scout negotiated with the men and they all agreed to sell their rifles. They would have little use for one at home. With cash in their pockets, they spent two days in the souk in Suez. My men knew how to barter and unlike the passengers from the passing ships who paid the first price that was suggested, they haggled and paid far less. We also found a Chinese Tailor who made us all civilian clothes. With fine Egyptian cotton shirts, bought at a fraction of the price of those we might have bought in England, we were well set to impress our families when we landed.

Mehmet came for us the day after the troopers had finished their shopping. "Mr Sharp says that your ship has arrived. She is taking on supplies and then she leaves."

It was typical that we would have to leave quickly like thieves in the night. While the others went to pack I went to say farewell to Saeed. He was devastated, "We planned a feast for you, my friend. This is so sudden."

"It is the way of soldiers and we have many memories do we not?"

I held out my arm for him to clasp, "I am happy that you came into my life again, Jack Roberts. We can share the knowledge that we have good lives and we are still alive."

"The song is sung by every soldier who survives combat. Farewell, Saeed."

"I would come and say farewell at the port but duty calls. I must lead a patrol into the Sinai."

By the time I reached the barracks everything was packed, including my bags. Mehmet waited to direct us safely to the ship. The sentries saluted us as we left the camp and we marched proudly to the ship. Mr Sharp was there already with his clipboard and papers in his hand. He was speaking to the purser on the quayside.

When he spied us he turned and said, "Mr Jones, these are the passengers. They have done great service for Mr D'Arcy and he wants them treated well."

The purser was a portly man and middle-aged. He beamed, "For soldiers who have served Britain in foreign climes nothing is too good. You gentlemen are fortunate, some passengers who should have joined us at Bombay were delayed by the monsoon, I have five first-class cabins available."

You would have thought that it was Mr Sharp who was going to be the recipient of such a stroke of luck. He said, "Splendid. That will suit, won't it, Lieutenant Roberts?"

"It will indeed, and we are grateful to both of you."

The purser waved over a steward, "Show these gentlemen to cabins 16, 17, 18, 19 and 20."

Syd and Jake took my bags, "We will take your stuff, sir."

"Mr Sharp, did you have a reply to my telegram?" I was anxious to know if it had been received. The last thing I wanted was for it to be sat in an in-tray in Whitehall.

"Yes, Lieutenant Roberts. Colonel Dickenson was most delighted with the information and promised that he would tell your family the news. The telegram said something about speaking to Griff personally?"

I nodded, "Griff is my son and he is at military college." I held out my hand, "Well thank you for your help, Mr Sharp, and good luck with your position."

"And thank you, sir, for your advice. I have begun to learn Arabic and the difference with the locals when you try is nothing short of astounding."

"Simple things, Mr Sharp, often bring the greatest rewards."

I strode up the gangplank. Was this the last time I would set foot in Africa? I had thought so the last time. I did not go to my cabin but stood watching the last of the supplies being loaded and taking in the sight of Suez. I lit my pipe and leaned on the rail. Syd and the lads joined me. They also smoked: some a pipe but most cigarettes.

Syd said, "Well, lads, take a last look at Africa. We have left some good friends here."

They all nodded. Each of them would remember a face. For me it was not only Ged and Eric that I thought about but also my brother Billy. If we had had more time, I had planned on visiting his grave. The best-laid plans and all that...

The captain was anxious to make his passage through the canal and he wasted no time setting off. We all waited until we could no longer see the port before we went to the cabin. Mine was the only single one. That would have been Syd's doing. My clothes were all neatly hung up in the wardrobe. I changed into my civilian clothes. I had found that if you wore your uniform when there were civilians, especially ones with money, they all seemed to think that they could offer military comments. We could do without that.

The one hundred and twenty miles up the canal would be taken at a steady, sedate pace. Travelling at between six and eight knots would take us about sixteen hours. We would reach the Mediterranean Sea in the early afternoon and have a fine sunset to look forward to. A steward knocked on the door, "Do you have all that you wish, sir?"

"It is all good. What is your name?"

"Patterson, sir. I am serving all of these cabins."

I handed him half a crown, "If there is anything we need to know, I trust that you will tell us. We are just simple soldiers."

He shook his head, "I can't take your money, sir, my dad was a soldier. He served in the Zulu Wars."

I pressed the coin into his hand, "As did I and that is all the more reason to reward you. I can afford it, son."

"Very well, sir. What sort of thing do you need to know?"

"Simple things like the time we dine; any ritual that is observed. Will we be seated at the same table?"

"The times of dinner are simple, sir." He flourished a printed sheet with the times. "As for rituals, sir, we have none and the purser has already arranged for you gentlemen to be seated at one table. He has put two together."

"Then the money is well spent for I have knowledge." He was about to leave when I added, "And I would like to be woken when we leave the canal, sort of say goodbye to it?"

"Right you are, sir."

After he left, I organised my money. I had English money. I had kept it in my bags but now I would need it. I transferred it to my wallet. I had tipped Mehmet with the last of my Egyptian money. I was going home clean. My gold coins were safely in my bag. I would not need them. When Saeed had paid us for the horses and the guns it had been with pounds, shillings and pence. I had bought more tobacco in Suez. It was not as good as that which I usually smoked but it would do. I mixed some with the last of my English tobacco and closed my pouch.

Syd and Jake knocked on my door. I opened it. "Ready for a bevvy, sir?"

"I am indeed." As I closed the door I said, "This is not like the Carnic. I am guessing that we pay for our own drinks."

Jake shook his head, "No we are not, sir. When I went to the bar to scout it out, like, I had a swift half and was chatting to the barman. He said that the purser has said that the drinks for the soldiers were all free."

Before I said anything, Syd said, "Don't worry, sir. I have spoken to the lads and they will not abuse it. The desert matured them. They saw what happened to Eric and know that could have been any one of them. They just want to get home and start a new life."

That was the thing about sudden death. It gave you a better perspective on life.

It was still hot despite the breeze generated by the ship and the fans above our heads. Iced beer was the order of the day. We drank two or three before the gong summoned us to dine. As we drank we discussed Eric. Jake knew where his mother lived and he promised that he would take Eric's share of the money we had been paid as well as the gold. I was relieved. I felt I owed the quiet man something. There had been just a handful of people in the bar. The dining room was also small. It seemed to me that there were just twenty cabins for 1st Class as there were fewer than forty people in the dining room. We were the only all-male party. There were a couple of families but no young children. We nodded politely as we entered and waited until the ladies were all seated before we took our seats.

The food was 1st Class. I preferred the food on the Carnic but there they had catered for drillers and soldiers. This was what I would have termed posh food. Very nice to look at but not robust enough for our palates. However, beggars can't be choosers and it was free. We had endured bully beef for weeks and we cleared

Desert War

our plates. The desserts and the cheese board were a delight. Dessert in the desert had been fruit when we could get it. I waved over the steward, it was Patterson, "That was very nice, Patterson, now what we need to finish it off is a port, have you got one?"

He beamed, "We have a lovely ruby port sir and plenty of it. I shall get you a bottle." He leaned in, "Oh, by the way, sir, one of the rituals is that you don't smoke in the dining room. I shall bring the port and the glasses into the bar."

"Good man."

I was happy to leave the dining room as there were a few of the men who had looked down their noses at us. They had dressed for dinner with dinner jackets and black ties. We had newly bought bow ties but just lounge suits. They clearly disapproved.

The bar was empty and the port was just as good as Patterson had said. We finished the bottle. For the last hour before bed, we played cards. It was not the game of bridge I had enjoyed in the desert but whist was somehow easier when you had played bridge.

I confess that I preferred the motion of the sea rather than the canal. I found that sleep came easier when the ship rocked from side to side.

I was woken by a gentle knock on my door, "Sir?"

"Yes, Patterson?"

"Just thought you should know that we are about to leave the canal."

"Thank you, Patterson."

I dressed and hurried up to the deck. I knew that Africa would be to our left, the larboard side, all the way to Gibraltar but the Africa I knew was Egypt and the canal. I wanted to say goodbye. I went to the bow and stood watching the land. This was the delta, a very productive part of Egypt and where many people lived. Their houses were small and mean but the people eked out a living and ate. There would always be hope that one child out of the many that they raised might drag themselves from their poverty-stricken life and achieve something. As the land gave way to the sea I saw the ships queuing to use the canal. I saw a couple of British warships. Britain could never release her hold on Egypt, not while we had India. There would continue to be a British presence in this part of the world.

I stayed on deck, smoking my first pipe of the day until Syd joined me, "The lads are heading for breakfast sir. Bacon!"

Bacon was the one food we had all missed and that single word was enough for me to knock the ash from my pipe and follow Syd to the dining room.

Life followed a pattern. After breakfast, we would all go on deck. The awnings gave protection from the sun and the air passing over the moving ship kept us cooler. Patterson and the other stewards seemed to enjoy serving us. After a few days, I saw why. Some of the other 1st Class passengers were obnoxious. They carped and complained about everything. Perhaps our expectations were lower for we found no reason to complain about anything. The service and the food were of the highest quality. They moaned that there was too much shade, not enough shade, the wrong kind of shade. They whinged about the smoke from the funnel. When we had passed houses they had objected to the smell from the land. It was no wonder that the stewards took to serving us quicker than they did some of the others.

We played cards and I took to writing in the notebook I had bought in Suez. I had no idea if my book had been published but I found that I missed the process of writing each day. Every morning I would write a few pages. They were mainly notes recording what had happened while we had been in Persia. Men like Mohammed and the drillers would make good characters in a novel. I would, of course, have to change the names. I found that quite a challenge but one that kept my mind active. Even if no one read my books I would still write them. One day Griff would have a family and if I was not there then my stories would be a reminder of what I did when I was a British soldier.

When we reached Gibraltar we picked up British newspapers that were more recent than the ones we had read in Suez. The papers were full of the failure of the British Army to subdue the irregular army of the Boers in South Africa. The name of Herbert Kitchener leapt out at me. I read, with interest, how he had now taken charge of trying to defeat the guerrillas. We were sympathetic to the problems faced when fighting an enemy who knew the land better. It would be a thankless task for the soldiers.

That evening in the bar we heard different views expressed by some of the other 1st Class passengers. We had come to know the names of some of our fellow travellers. There was a missionary and his family, John Ponsonby, returning to England after a life bringing God to New Guinea. He always looked weary to me. There were others who had been visiting their estates in India. They were all arrogant but the worst was Richard St John-Wilson. Patterson had told us when we had asked, that he was incredibly rich and powerful. His brother was in the House of Lords and his estates in India amounted to a small kingdom. It was he who was holding court when we entered the bar.

"The trouble is we are too damn soft with these rebels. Hang 'em all. That would stop them."

John Ponsonby shook his head, "That will only make them struggle even harder."

"Pah! Turning the other cheek never works, Reverend. What we need are better soldiers. The rank and file we send out to fight our wars are little better than the sweepings of the gutter. If we had better soldiers then this war would have been over for months."

That was too much for Syd. He had just taken a sip of his beer and before he sat down he said, "Sir, you have no idea what you are talking about. I find your words offensive."

The rest of my men murmured their agreement. He turned and gave them what he hoped was a withering stare. It had, of course, no effect. He sneered, "I would have expected nothing less from someone like you." He waved his glass of whisky, spilling some. "You are the very sweepings of the gutter. Why on earth you are allowed to inhabit 1st Class is beyond me and I shall write a strongly worded letter to the chairman when we land."

Syd strode over to the pompous man and squared up to him, "Who are you calling the sweepings of a gutter? I have served the Queen for half of my life."

"Are you threatening me? I shall have you put in a cell. I was an officer in the army and I do not take threats lightly."

I stood and smiled, "There have been no threats so far as I can tell. There was an insult for which you should apologise. If you are a gentleman, then you will do so and realise that perhaps the drink has got the better of you."

He stared at me, "And I will not be lectured to by a damn cripple."

John Ponsonby said, "Mr St John-Wilson, your words were inflammatory. Perhaps Lieutenant Roberts is right and an apology would calm things down."

The others who had been standing in support of the unpleasant man had drifted away and he was alone. He looked around and saw that he was isolated. He downed his whisky and slammed the glass down. "I have had enough of this. I am going to speak to the captain." He stormed out. The effect was ruined when he could not get the door open and a steward had to help him.

Syd was angry, "I just wanted to give him a good smack, sir."

The missionary shook his head, "It would have done no good, my friend. I have met his type before. They were raised to believe that Britain was theirs to rule. He has lands so vast in India that he can travel for days without leaving them. Who is there to tell him he is wrong?"

"We want no trouble, Mr Ponsonby."

"I can see that. We are on the last leg now. Hopefully, this squall will pass and peace will descend."

It was after dinner that night, a chilly affair, when the captain sought me out, "Lieutenant, I have had a complaint from one of the other passengers. He said he was threatened by one of your men."

I shook my head, "Mr St John-Wilson. He was not threatened. He called my men the sweepings of the gutter and when my sergeant major asked him what he meant he said he was threatened. He was not."

"That is what my steward said but I am in a difficult position. He has friends in high places."

I sighed, "And what is it you want us to do?"

"If you would apologise it would make my life easier."

I shook my head, "And that is not going to happen for we did nothing wrong."

Syd had been listening and when the captain left us he said, "It is all wrong. I thought we were all equal. What gives the likes of that man the right to lie and get his own way simply because he has money?"

"It is the way of the world. One day it might change but not, I think, in our lifetime. Can you imagine serving under him when he was an officer? Men like Kitchener and Colonel Dickenson are rare. It is men like my son who are the hope for the army."

"Aye, you may be right." He chuckled, "I bet Mr St John bloody Wilson will be less than happy when he sees that we have not been punished."

A combination of events conspired to keep us apart. His party took to dining in their suite. Allied to that we had a storm just off Portugal that ensured many passengers could not keep food down. By the time we neared Southampton, we had not seen St John-Wilson for almost a week. He and most of the other 1st Class passengers disembarked there. The cargo and the 2nd and 3rd class passengers were bound for Liverpool. We stood watching as they descended. When he reached the land Mr St John-Wilson stood and pointedly stared at us. Syd and the lads gave him a cheery wave. It was a victory, of sorts.

The last part of the voyage fairly flew by and we landed at Liverpool on October the 30th. We were home.

Desert War

Griff

Chapter 16

Meeting Lieutenant Dunn gave me hope. When Geoffrey had run I thought that the blue bloods had won. I saw only despair. We four musketeers were, in my view, in a minority and I anticipated that we would be ground down and defeated. I looked for little victories. It annoyed the life out of St John-Wilson and his cronies when the lieutenant and I spoke in Arabic. They had no idea what we were saying. I, of course, told my friends, in the safety of our own dorm, what had been said. Lieutenant Dunn was a kind officer. I knew that he would be a good leader and he became my role model. When he taught his classes, he did not have to raise his voice, even when others in the class were disruptive. He had the ability to establish order quickly. He did punish gross misbehaviour and the eight soon realised that they could not win. They hated the lessons and saw no reason to study map reading. They saw war being fought over a land with roads and signs. Lieutenant Dunn pointed out that in many parts of the empire, there were no roads and certainly no signs. It confused them.

It was a Sunday in March that I was summoned to the commandant's office. It was our free time and we were all in the lounge, playing cards, reading the paper and the like. A senior cadet took me from the lounge. When we reached the office I saw that as well as Captain Collins there was a colonel with the red tabs of the General Staff. Captain Collins said, "This is Colonel Dickenson, from Whitehall. I shall leave you alone." He paused at the door, "Oh, by the by, Roberts, the cadet who ran, Fairbrother, he was found drowned."

"Drowned, sir?"

"Not sure if it was an accident or…anyway, I thought you and the others should know."

I felt my stomach lurch. I had hoped that Geoffrey would have simply gone home. That he was dead had never occurred to me. It made me feel physically sick. The colonel, with the red tabs on his collar, said, "Everything all right, Roberts, Griff?"

170

Desert War

I shook my head, "One of the other cadets was bullied and he ran. I hoped…"

The colonel nodded, "You are just like your father. I was his commanding officer in Sudan, you know."

"Yes sir, I recognise the name and I want to thank you for helping me to get a place here."

"From what I hear from Captain Collins you more than deserve a place here. All the instructors speak highly of you."

That came as news to me, "Thank you, sir. I always do my best."

He nodded and looked ill at ease, "There is no easy way to tell you this, Griff, but your father is on active service once more."

"Lieutenant Dunn told me, sir but I thought after he lost his arm that the army had finished with him."

"I am afraid that it was me who recalled him. He has volunteered to take a six-month contract protecting some engineers drilling for oil. He is sailing, even as we speak. I am telling you this because it may well be that there will be no letters. I, of course, will keep you informed if anything changes. I do not live far away."

I was in shock. How could a one-armed man protect anyone? I feared for my father. He was being used. Suddenly all the good feelings I had for the colonel disappeared. I stood, "Is that all, sir?"

"Yes. I heard that Lieutenant Dunn is one of your instructors?"

"Yes sir."

"He is a good chap. While you are here talk to him."

I went directly back to the other cadets. The business about my father I would keep to myself for the moment but they had to know about Geoffrey. This was the first time that I had to break the news of a death to someone and I found it hard. We had all barely known Geoffrey and yet we had been part of his life and he part of ours. Our fates were interwoven. The blue bloods were laughing about something or other. It somehow seemed wrong and yet I knew that they could not have known the news. The others were as shocked as I was.

"I hope it was an accident. I should hate to think it was ... you know?"

James voiced what we all thought. To be so full of despair as to take your own life seemed more horrible than a simple accident. The result was the same but an accident could be shrugged away easier than a suicide.

"It was those that drove him to it. They got away with it."

"Yes Bob, and their type always gets away with it. If you worry and stress about such inequalities, well, there lies the road to madness."

James was wise. I wondered if his broken heart had somehow made him wiser. I had yet to fall for a young woman. Would it affect me the same way?

Peter nodded, "You are right, Griff has shown us the best way to deal with them. Excel at everything. They might have begun as the best fencers and horsemen but we have shown them that we are getting better. They have not improved. They will get the commissions in the fancy regiments but if we get high marks then who knows where we might end up."

Peter's positive note made it easier for all of us but, that night, at Evensong in the chapel, we four attended and I prayed for the soul of Geoffrey.

April was the time when the next set of cadets graduated and another tranche of recruits would arrive. It also coincided with a week of leave for Lieutenant Dunn and I found that I missed my talks with him more than I would have believed. Senior Cadet Watson graduated as the top student and won the Sword of Honour. Our congratulations were sincere ones.

"Where are you bound then?"

"The Durham Light Infantry. It is a fine regiment with a long tradition. I shall enjoy the life." He smiled, "You four have done well. You must know that the sergeant instructors are impressed with you and you are highly thought of."

In truth I did but that was only because Colonel Dickenson had told me.

"Stick in and who knows you may get the regiment of your choice."

That evening there was a feast and afterwards, as we sat in the lounge, we speculated about that future. James was still determined to join an Indian regiment. He had said as much to Captain Collins who was disappointed. Once he realised how determined James was he had told my friend that if he graduated then he could choose any Indian regiment. James was happy about that.

Peter wanted the cavalry. He had become a proficient rider and had excelled at fencing. Both were seen as attributes needed for a cavalry officer. Bob wanted action and that meant an infantry regiment. James said, "You never say what you want, Griff. Why is that?"

"I don't know. My father was in three regiments. The Loyal Lancashires did no fighting, the 24th did but the one he enjoyed the most was the ESEG. The trouble is that was disbanded. I would like to use my Arabic but I don't see how."

"Speak to Lieutenant Dunn. He seems like a nice chap and he knows your father."

When he did return we all had a surprise. He had been promoted. As usual, he told me the story behind it in Arabic. It maintained my skills and my companions all knew I would tell them all. That night, as we played cards I gave them the story.

"His commission in the Egyptian Army was captain. Back here he was just a lieutenant. However, Colonel Dickenson, you know the chap who told me about my father and got me the place here," they nodded, "he has secured him a promotion. When he finishes here, in June, he is to go to Egypt. They want a new unit on the lines of the ESEG to be created."

"Sudan?"

I shook my head, "No, Peter." I took a piece of paper and a pencil to illustrate. I drew a rough map of North Africa, "Egypt is, officially, part of the Turkish Empire, the Ottoman Empire but the ruler of Egypt is the Khedive, Ismail the Magnificent."

Bob laughed, "And who gave him that title?"

"Why he did, of course. He bankrupted the Khedivate and had to sell the shares he had in the Suez Canal back to Britain and France. It means that Britain and France rule Egypt in all but name. The Ottoman ruler of Tripolitania and Cyrenaica is rattling his sabre. Whitehall, and by that I mean Colonel Dickenson, have decided to create an Anglo-Egyptian force of camel-mounted cavalry to operate on the border. That means Captain Dunn will be in command."

"Sounds exciting. Perhaps I should ask for a posting there."

I smiled, "Peter, from what my father and Captain Dunn have told me it is a most inhospitable part of the planet. There is little water and the noon day temperatures can kill a man. It is filled with scorpions, snakes and spiders and every one of them can kill you."

They took that in and James said, quietly, "And that is where your father is now, eh, Griff, back in the desert? You must be worried."

"Of course I am, but Captain Dunn told me that my father had no peer in the desert. He will survive. Of that I am certain. I just don't know why he went back."

"Adventure I suppose. From what you have told me your father has spent the last thirty years fighting for Queen Victoria. It must be hard to give that up."

With the older cadets graduated there was another raft of cadets promoted to Senior Cadet. We learned that because of the Fairbrother incident, as it was known, none of our intake would be considered. It was Captain Collins who told us that. While the four of us accepted the decision the blue bloods did not. They blamed us. They had expected to be given the position. At public school, they had all been head boys or prefects. They felt that we had taken that away from them.

I received letters from home. I could tell from the tone of Aunt Sarah's that she was less than pleased with my father's decision. It was understandable. He had been almost as much her son as my nan's. I knew that James was right and that my father was having a last adventure. I just wished that he wasn't. I wrote letters back and told them of my progress. I did not mention the blue bloods. There was little point. It was my problem and I would have to deal with it. My prowess with my fists allied with the fact that the four of us kept together ensured that there was no violence. Instead, we just suffered snide and nasty comments and allusions to our lack of any sort of breeding. It became clear that they thought we had no place at such a prestigious military college. In the lounge we had heard them talk of their breeding and how it was the likes of them that had fought for England

Desert War

against Napoleon. They seemed to take credit for the victory. As James pointed out it was those same officers who had lost us the war against the Americans and almost cost us the war in Crimea.

We all scored highly in the frequent tests we were given. Captain Dunn told me that the sergeant instructors thought that one of us should win the Sword of Honour. I doubted that it would be given to any of us. The Fairbrother incident had tarnished us all in the eyes of the commandant. It was as though they wished it forgotten, erased from the annals of the college.

It was at the end of June that Captain Dunn sought me out. We were in a mathematics class and I was taken out. He had with him Sergeant Instructor Windridge. I knew that Windridge liked me and I wondered why the two of them had sought me out. "Griff, could we take a little walk together?"

"Of course, sir. Have I done something wrong?"

Sergeant Windridge's voice was remarkably gentle as he shook his head and said, "No, son, you have done nowt wrong."

We left the college and headed to the village. Everyone else would be in classes or on the range or riding. The village was almost empty. They headed to the pub. I sat with Sergeant Instructor Windridge while the captain brought over three pints. The sergeant took out his pipe and filled it. I could not help but be reminded of my father. When the tobacco was lit and the smell drifted over to me I realised it was almost the same smell as my father's. It was somehow comforting.

They raised their glasses and said, "Cheers."

I responded but I wondered what was coming.

"There is no easy way to tell you this, Griff, but your dad, my friend Jack, has been killed in Persia. He and the men with him were ambushed by Persian bandits. So far as we can tell they are all dead."

I felt numb. I raised the glass to my lips but I could not feel it.

Sergeant Instructor Windridge said, "I am sorry, son, from all that I have been told your father was a brave man and a great soldier. I would have been proud to have served with him."

I nodded and turned to Captain Dunn, "Did they find his body then?"

"We don't know. A Mr Milner, who is based in Liverpool, sent the message to Colonel Dickenson. He told us. Your family will be receiving a telegram even as we speak. I wanted to tell you face to face."

"And I appreciate that. The thing is, sir, if they haven't found his body then how do they know he is dead?"

"It is a wild and empty country out there, Griff. It might take months to find the bodies or for the survivors to reach civilisation."

I drank more of the beer. This time I could taste it, "I am sorry sir, but until it is confirmed then I refuse to believe that he is dead."

Sergeant Instructor Windridge shook his head, "Just accept it, son, it is for the best."

I sighed, "My father spent more of his life away from me than with me. I grew used to that. In here," I tapped my heart, "I knew he would come back safe. Even when we heard of disasters or that many men had been killed in battles then I knew he was alive. I think he is alive. He is a tough man, Captain Dunn, you know that. I can't believe that he and his men would all have been killed by bandits. They were too good for that."

"That is called blind faith, son."

Captain Dunn suddenly smiled, "You know, Griff, you may be right. Syd and the men with him were, are, good soldiers. The only time we lost more than one man was when our officer let us down and your father managed to save the rest." He raised his glass, "Here's to Jack. Come back alive."

Sergeant Instructor Windridge looked from me to the captain and back, "Well, I don't know." He shook his head in disbelief at our attitude. "You can have a leave if you like Cadet Roberts. Compassionate leave."

I shook my head, "I don't need it. There is nothing I could do in Liverpool except dwell on this. If he is alive then he will want me to score as highly as I could. I want to graduate. We are halfway through the course. Now is not the time. I will focus on my work and pray that God looks after him."

As we walked back from the pub Captain Dunn said, "How is the bullying?"

I shrugged, "Annoying and I want to lash out but…"

"It will pass. Your father would have said, 'Choose your battles'. Sometimes it is wiser to run or simply hide. I know we

Desert War

did that in the desert and men's lives were saved. When we fought we fought and died hard but there is no point in dying for no reason."

I was not sure if he was talking about my father or Geoffrey Fairbrother but I had heard my father say the same. He had told me that at Rorke's Drift, they had no choice but to fight. They were surrounded and alone. His words gave me some comfort for I realised that St John-Wilson and his ilk were irrelevant in the scheme of things. They made my time at college unpleasant but we had less time to go than we had already served. When we graduated I would never see them again.

In her letters, Aunt Sarah begged me to come home so that we could all be together at this sad time. I tried to say the same thing in the letter that I had told to Captain Dunn. It was not as easy. My friends did what friends do, they rallied around and life became a sort of normal once more. When Captain Dunn, having finished his course with us left to take up his new post, it was like losing a friend. I would miss the conversations in Arabic. His face at the weekly lesson had been something I looked forward to seeing. Now it was gone. Sergeant Instructor Windridge seemed to realise that and he went out of his way to be there whenever he could. He had heard our conversation on the way back from the pub and was doing what he was able to. His presence helped make my life easier as whenever he was around the blue bloods could not make our lives unpleasant. He was quite happy to bark out orders and give them punishments. The pan bash and the cleaning of the latrines were two duties that they did not want to endure a second time.

The summer passed and still, there was no news from Persia. It was at the start of October that Colonel Dickenson reappeared. We were with Sergeant Instructor Hargreaves. It was drill time. I quite enjoyed the precision of it and also the fact that the blue bloods hated it. Part of their annoyance came from the fact that a non-commissioned officer was ordering them around. It happened in other classes too but drill was one bounded by shouts and orders. Captain Collins came with the colonel. They waited until we were all at attention and then Captain Collins said, "Cadet Roberts, could we have a word?"

Desert War

Sergeant Instructor Hargreaves smiled, "Off you go then, Roberts, do as the captain has asked."

The captain waited until the platoon was marched off across the parade ground. "The colonel has news, Roberts."

"My father, sir..."

"Is alive. He sent a telegram from Suez and he is on his way home. He has no further wounds."

I could not help the smile filling my face and I said, "Thank God."

He nodded, "I think you are right, Griff, we do need to thank him. Captain Collins, if I might have a word with Cadet Roberts."

"Of course, sir." He smiled at me, "We are all pleased, Cadet Roberts. The team have all been impressed with the way you handled yourself through this. It bodes well for your career as an officer. You behaved impeccably." He saluted the colonel and marched off.

"He is right, Griff. Archie Dunn was also impressed by you. When I saw him off at Southampton he said he would like you as an officer in his new command. How do you feel about that?"

"Sir, I have a month of the course yet to go."

"You are at the top of your class, Griff. You will become an officer. I can't see you losing sight of the prize this close to the end. You will graduate but you could have your choice of regiment."

"It is an easy choice, sir, I would like to become an officer and work under Captain Dunn."

"Good, then I will begin the paperwork. Of course, you realise it will mean just a short leave with your family before you have to take a ship for Egypt?"

"That will be hard, sir, but if I am going to be like my father and be the best soldier that I can be then it has to be done."

I wrote a letter to my father so that it would be waiting for him when he reached home. His ship was due into Liverpool at the end of the month. When I told the others they were envious but for different reasons. Peter because I would be in the cavalry, Bob because I would be seeing action and James because Suez was on the way to India. I told no one else but the word must have spread through the sergeant instructors. Each one

Desert War

congratulated me in private. I was touched by their affection. They were all big gruff men but they seemed to have a soft spot for both me and my three comrades.

We graduated at the start of December. The Sword of Honour was won by a cadet from a different platoon. I did not mind. I had my prize. The last night before we all parted, probably for the last time, we exchanged addresses and made unrealistic plans to meet up. I knew it would not happen. James had his wish. He had gained a commission in a regiment with a battalion in India. He would be closer to his Dorothea although as India was a vast continent it was not the end of his journey, but rather the start. Bob had landed a position in the 3rd East Kent, the Buffs and he was delighted. Peter was the most excited of all. He managed to become an officer in the 21st Lancers, the regiment that had charged the Dervishes at Omdurman. We did not begrudge the blue bloods their commissions in the Guards. They rarely went to war and had so many ceremonial duties that it was all spit and polish. As James wryly pointed out, as they would have a servant each the spit and polish would not be their own. I was just glad that I would never have to see any of them again.

The four of us all travelled to London together and then took our separate trains home. I wondered if we would ever meet again.

Desert War

Griff

Chapter 17

My father had sent me a letter when he had returned home and I knew that he was whole and he was safe. The details of the actions in which he had fought would not be committed to a letter. He would save those for when we went to the pub. The train journey north was a dreary one. The weather was wet and the days short. I sat alone in the carriage wearing my new lieutenant's uniform for the first time. Colonel Dickenson himself had brought it to the college. As it was a new unit there were no regimental markings. He had been there for the graduation. He had told me that the rest of my uniform and the tropical service gear I would need would be waiting for me on the ship that I would take from Southampton. I would have a bare two weeks in Liverpool. The steamer with the others who were being sent to join Captain Dunn would be leaving on the 1st of January. My father and I would be passing each other like ships in the night.

He was at the station with a taxi, waiting as the train pulled in. I had anticipated a wait in line and the inevitable delay. This was not like the day I arrived at Sandhurst. I saw pride in his eyes as he held out his hand, "What a smart soldier you look, Griff. The uniform suits you."

"Just the one chest, sir?"

I nodded, "Here I will give you a hand."

The driver shook his head, "I can manage, you two get in the cab and under that rug. It is too cold to stand around here."

He was right but I was just pleased to see that dad was whole although he had a metal covering for his arm. As we sat and I pulled up the rug I said, "What is that on your arm?"

He smiled, "One of the engineers, George, made it for me. There is a screw attachment at the end and I have some tools that I can use. It makes life much easier, you know."

As we set off, I said, "They said you were dead but I knew you were not. How is that?"

He shook his head, "I don't know, Griff, but there are many things that happen in our lives that are inexplicable. I am glad that the lie did not hurt you."

"The lie?"

He told me of the treacherous agent who had tried to steal their gold and how that had set off the line of dominoes that had ended with a telegram.

"And you, your letter home mentioned Captain Dunn, Middy?"

"Yes. As I said I have been given a commission in his new unit. It sounds like a newer version of the ESEG."

"Archie is a good soldier and I am pleased he has done well. It will not please your Aunt Sarah though. She knows that if you are in the desert then news will be in short supply."

"And I will be away, well, it might well be for six months or a year."

"Griff, when you said you wanted this, a life in the army, you knew that was inevitable."

"What I didn't know then was that you were going to put yourself in harm's way once more."

"I did it because it was Syd and the other lads. I had been their officer and this was the end of their military career. I felt a loyalty to them. It is over now. They are all back in England and, thanks to the contract, richer men. They will have a better life now than many who served their country. I promise my days of soldiering are over for definite this time."

"Whoa, here we are gentlemen, safe and sound."

The door to the house opened and Aunt Sarah stood framed in its golden glow. I thought she looked older and frailer but that could have been my imagination. Once the chest was inside, the driver paid and the door closed, she embraced me and wept. "You are home but the uniform is a harbinger of ill. I wish you were not a soldier."

"But I am, Aunt Sarah and I want to make the most of every minute I am home so no more tears, eh? This is Christmas. Let us make it a joyous one."

She took out her handkerchief and dabbed her eyes, "You are right and I am a silly old woman." She shook her head, "You are your father's son."

Aunt Bet, Jack and Victoria appeared at the door to the dining room. Victoria hurled herself at me, "Our Griff, my but you are smart."

Jack, sporting a moustache, held out his hand, "Good to see you, cuz."

Aunt Bet enveloped me in her arms, "You and your father...you do suit a uniform."

The welcoming smell of the stew enticed us into the dining room. The three ladies all went to fetch the food from the kitchen while Jack opened us each a bottle of beer. "So, Jack, how is life working for the White Star line?"

"Grand. We have new ships planned and liners that are so big that the Carnic, the ship Uncle Jack here sailed in, would be dwarfed. I work in the department that finds the supplies for the ships. Fascinating work. Uncle Jack says that you are to serve in the desert, like him."

I nodded but as the food was being brought in my father said, "We will leave that for another time, eh, Griff. I am so hungry that I could eat a horse..."

Jack and I finished off the sentence for him, "With its skin on."

We all laughed and that was the sign that I was home. We were a family. We were not a normal family with a father, wife and children, but I knew that it worked. When the four of us, the musketeers, had played cards and spoken of our homes I knew I was lucky. Poor James felt estranged from his parents and the rift caused by the forceable break up of his chance of happiness meant he would never go home. Bob's father and mother bickered and fought the whole time and Bob was glad to be away. Peter was not the favoured one in his home, that was his brother and Peter had felt more warmth from the three of us than he enjoyed at home. In theory, they all had normal homes but none of them was happy. I was.

"Have you told him your news, our Jack?"

My father shook his head, "Not yet, Aunt Sarah."

"News?"

"Yes, Mr Kipling's agent has been in touch. My book is to be published. It will be out next year."

I beamed, "Splendid news! My father, a published writer!"

Desert War

"I am not sure that it will sell many. Mr Kipling told me that he has to go on lecture tours to make real money."

Bet smiled, "But Jack, you told me it is not about the money. You enjoy writing. Since you came back you have spent most of your time scribbling away."

I knew that it was just modesty and low self-esteem. In my long talks with his old comrade at the college, I had learned much about my father. Captain Dunn had not told tales out of school but I had pieced together a picture of my father the soldier, from his words. Supremely confident about being a soldier he was less sure about other matters. I knew that I was different from him in that respect. I had seen those who were supposedly my betters and knew that they were not. I had seen those who were seen as inferiors behaving far better than the ones born with every advantage.

The next day my father took me into town. "Turnbull and Proctor kitted me out. The Anglo-Persian Oil Company paid but they have excellent equipment. My goggles and the like you shall have but they do light tropical underwear and socks. They are more durable than the kit issued by the army. I still have some of George Reynold's gold. I would like to buy them for you."

The assistant in the shop remembered my father. I suppose it was the one arm that made him memorable. He saw me in civilian clothes but when my father told him I was an officer he became more than helpful. Within an hour we had all our purchases made and wrapped up. We went to the nearest pub to celebrate and it was while we were there that he began to tell me of the events in the desert.

"I lost a man in Persia and his death haunts me still. Poor Eric was a quiet man and his death happened without anyone noticing. You will find, Griff, that you will have a bond with the men you lead. It is a double-edged sword. You will feel their hurts as well as your own."

I nodded and told him about Geoffrey Fairbrother and the Blue Bloods. "All he wanted was to be one of them and they destroyed him."

"Perhaps the drill sergeant had something to do with that. I would never have ordered such a punishment."

I had not thought of that. Had I misjudged them? On the way back home I was silent as I tried to rationalise what my father had said. I came to the conclusion that Geoffrey would not have made those mistakes that led to his punishment if he had not been trying to impress others. However, we four had not been completely innocent. We could have made him want to be like us. I would remember Geoffrey when I led my own men. There was not one way to treat a man. Every man is different and, from what my father had said, a good leader treats each man according to his nature.

I saw a different side to life in the build-up to Christmas. Both Victoria and Jack worked and both had what was termed *'a work's do'*. Jack and I escorted Victoria there and brought her home. She had enjoyed a couple of sherries and was tipsy but she was full of the gaiety of the night. There had been dancing and she had been popular. Father and I did the same for Jack. As we made our way home and passed a streetlight I saw the lipstick on his cheek.

"You had better wipe that away before Aunt Sarah sees it."

He did so and smiled, "I kissed a girl tonight, Griff, under the mistletoe."

I looked at my father who shrugged. Such things were not in our world. Jack and Victoria would have normal and predictable lives. They would meet someone, court, marry and have children. They would live in houses much like Aunt Bet's and bring up children like they were. My father and I were soldiers. Our lives were, perforce, different.

That Christmas was a fine one. There were presents but we were never a family that set great store with material things. The gifts we gave were personal. Christmas was joyous because we were all together. The food was delicious and the day warm and cosy. There was no snow but it was cold and that made the fire seem a little brighter and more welcoming. We enjoyed wine and, after dinner, port. My father had bought cigars and we enjoyed the Christmas ritual once more.

The leave went all too quickly and I had to prepare to join the army. My father helped me to pack my chest. He gave me his keffiyeh, goggles, cloak and Webley as well as the swagger stick he had used when he had been a sergeant major. "I know you will be issued a pistol but a second one won't hurt. I know that Middy will employ the keffiyeh but if you wear mine, well, it will be as though I am there, with you, I shan't need any of these again." He produced the two bags he had brought back from Persia. "The chest you took to college is a bit bulky. You can put these on the back of a camel. A gift from the Anglo-Persian oil company.

They were touching gifts. I packed them all along with my new tropical gear. The new leather valises were only half full. The rest of my equipment was waiting for me on the ship. The uniform I wore was the uniform for England. Once I reached the tropics the heavier uniform would remain in my bags and I would don the lighter one more suitable for the desert.

The morning I left, my father went with me to the station. The money he had been paid in his Persian adventure meant he could afford taxis. It was the same driver who had picked me up. He waited while we found my carriage and the leather valises were placed in the luggage van.

"I know better than anyone, Griff, that communication will be hard. All I ask is that when you can, write home. It is for Aunt Sarah. She will miss you."

"But she will have you and that will bring her comfort."

"All aboard."

I shook his hand, "We seem to be saying goodbye all the time."

He nodded and touched his head, "But in here we never part. I think of you each night before I go to sleep." He paused, "And your mother. I find it comforting. You might do the same."

"I shall."

I climbed aboard and lowered the window. The whistle of the guard initiated the hiss of steam and the grinding and clanking of the wheels as they sought purchase on the rails. I raised my hand and my father did the same. The smoke and steam from the engine wreathed him, making him look like a ghost. He would not be alone on the journey back to Bet's. The taxi driver would chatter like a magpie and that would help. In contrast, I would have a long journey to London and then Southampton alone. I would have to make do with my own company.

In the event, I was not completely alone. A family joined the train in the Midlands. The boy was fascinated by my uniform and I faced a veritable bombardment of questions. His mother chastised him but I shook my head and said I was quite happy to answer the questions. It stopped me from becoming melancholy. The parting from my father had been hard.

I said farewell at the station and took a taxi to my next station. My father had ensured that I had plenty of change to tip the porters and taxi drivers. "You are an officer now and with it comes responsibility. I know I was one for the briefest of times but I served enough good officers to know what makes a good one. You are now a gentleman and there are obligations."

As I boarded the Southampton train, I saw the khaki of other soldiers in Third Class. I wondered if they were bound, as I was, for Africa. There were more soldiers in South Africa these days but the British still had a strong presence in both Egypt and Sudan. Omdurman had ended the Dervish threat but the British would not allow it to rise again. The railways that were being built were the way to make that vast country more accessible.

I knew what to expect at Southampton from what my father had told me. I had the taxi driver drop me next to the hut at the foot of the gangplank. I paid him off and entered. A sergeant and his corporal stood to attention, "Sir!"

"At ease, Sergeant, Corporal. Second Lieutenant Roberts reporting."

He sat and ran his finger down a list. "Ah, here you are, cabin B124. Jenkins, have the lieutenant's bags taken aboard."

"Right, Sarge."

I saw the sergeant roll his eyes at the informality. "Sorry about that, sir, some of these lads...Anyway, you are prompt, sir. The rest of those travelling with you have yet to arrive. I believe they are getting the morning train." He held up a letter, "A Colonel Dickenson was very precise about the arrivals. He said that you would have the furthest to come and be the first here."

"How many are there?"

"Just a dozen although there are other units aboard." He handed me a list of names. "You will only be on this ship, the Doric, until Gibraltar, sir. She is bound for Cape Town with reinforcements for General Buller. You will take," he looked down his list, "the SS Carnic."

I smiled, "The Carnic?"

"You know the ship, sir?"

I nodded, "In a way, yes."

"Your tropical gear and weapons are in the cabin, sir. I will send Corporal Jenkins with the inventory for you to check. No rush sir, you don't sail until tomorrow."

I knew all about lists and inventories. "Thank you, Sergeant. B124?"

"That's right, sir. There will be an orderly at the top of the gangplank. He can direct you. Good luck, sir."

As I stepped onto the gangplank I felt excited. This was the beginning of my new life. The college had just been a preparation. No matter what I had learned there my real lessons would come when I joined Captain Dunn. Nothing that the college had taught me could fully prepare me for a life in the desert. This would be my test. Had I made the right decision?

I found the cabin easily enough. It was a good one. My father had described life aboard a troopship and I knew from the position of the cabin, that I had a porthole, and its size, that I had been treated well. The corporal had placed my two bags at the foot of the bed and I saw that my new tropical gear was hanging in the wardrobe. I unpacked the rest of my belongings and arranged my toiletries over the sink. I had the luxury of running water in my cabin. That done I explored the ship. The sentry at the gangplank gave me a rough idea of where things were to be found. I sought the officer's mess first. As I had expected it was the 1st Class lounge and dining room. There were two officers there already enjoying gins. They did not see me and I left. I found the mess for other ranks. It was, perforce, much larger. It was also noisier. I heard the hubbub of chatter and the laughter of men who had just enjoyed a leave and were regaling their comrades with their stories.

I headed back to my cabin and as I neared it heard a discreet cough and, "Ah, sir. The inventory?"

It was the corporal. I nodded, "Let's do it now. What time is dinner?"

"I believe it is seven thirty, sir."

Desert War

As I had expected, the list and the contents of my wardrobe matched. I signed it and he left. I sat at the desk and began my first letter home. I addressed it to my father. I remembered what he had written in his letters and I did the same. I had put my watch on the desk and it showed me that it was almost time for dinner. I doubted that it would be formal. My father had told me that but I made sure that I looked as smart as I could. I arrived at the dining room just ten minutes before it was due to start. I saw two second lieutenants waiting to enter. They were the Argyll and Sutherland Highlands. I approached them.

"Do you mind if I join you?"

"Of course not. You are English are you not?"

"Yes, why?"

"The rest of the ship is made up of the Highland Brigade."

"Ah, my men and I will be leaving the ship at Gibraltar. We are bound for Egypt and the desert. I am Second Lieutenant Griff Roberts of the 1st Desert Group."

"I am Robert Kilbride, and this is Donal MacIntyre. Never heard of your unit."

"It is newly formed." I gave them an outline of what we would be doing and they both nodded, enviously.

Robert Kilbride sounded a little down when he said, "Sounds more exciting than what we are going to be doing. The war in South Africa is against civilians and that does not sit well. The newspapers are being very critical of the army."

Donal shook his head, "Don't worry about newspapers. As Sergeant Campbell said, *'Newspapers are good for one thing. Wrapping up your fish supper.'*"

We three dined together and it was pleasant talking to officers who had joined a regiment because of familial connections. Their fathers had both served in the regiment, although in different battalions. I knew from my father that the Highland Brigade had a fierce reputation. They were reliable and tough.

I was anxious to see the men who would be sailing with me. Captain Dunn had not known who he would have under his command when he had offered me the position. He just knew the idea. He had said, *'We will operate from an old Egyptian fort close to the Qattara Depression. You and I will be the only officers and, along with whoever is the sergeant major, will lead*

Desert War

patrols to discourage the Ottomans from Tripolitania and Cyrenaica from causing mischief.'

The list I had was just that, a list of names. It told me nothing about the makeup of the men or their history. I knew the role of one of them. Trooper Cartwright had a star next to his name and the title, Officer's Servant. I knew from the letter sent by my father's old batman the relationship between an officer and his servant. I doubted that the blue bloods would have such a relationship. The other names meant little. There was a sergeant and a corporal and the rest were troopers. I had been told that the train would reach Southampton by noon and, allowing for transport from the station they could be expected by one. The ship was due to sail at five and I doubted that the captain would brook delays. After breakfast, I used the time to add more to my letter home. I would be able to post it at Gibraltar by which time I would be able to give my father a picture of the men I would be leading. He would be interested.

I had the list in my hand as I waited at the gangplank. A dozen men marched down the road. They had not waited for public transport and that boded well. Their marching was smart enough although as troopers we would be riding more than marching. I saw that they were all wearing their greatcoats, a necessary precaution in England in January. They halted at the hut on the quay and I saw the sergeant, new white stripes on his uniform, enter. He was not in the hut for long and when he emerged, with a sheet of paper in his hand, he slung his bag over his shoulder and marched up the gangplank followed by the men of what would be my first command. I was excited. I moved away from the gangplank so that they could all stand close together.

I was wearing my hat and when they all came to attention I saluted, "Stand easy, Sergeant. I am Lieutenant Roberts."

The sergeant and the corporal grinned. "I am Sergeant Shaw, sir, and if your father is Jack Roberts then I served under him at Omdurman."

I was taken aback, "He is my father, how..."

"Sorry sir, but you look just like him. I was a corporal back then and Corporal Atkinson here was a trooper. The other lads are all new."

Desert War

I nodded, "Welcome all. We will only be on this ship until Gibraltar. The rest of the troops are bound for South Africa." I looked at the sheet of paper in the sergeant's hand. "You know your cabins?"

"Yes sir."

"There will be food in the mess until one. I suggest you find your cabins, get some food and then meet me on the foredeck at two. That will give you the opportunity to find your feet, so to speak." They saluted. "Dismiss."

I did not know Shaw and Atkinson but the fact that they were old comrades of my father made life better somehow.

I had chosen the foredeck as there were deck chairs there. It was not the weather for sunbathing but as there was an awning above they would be able to sit while I spoke and be protected from the weather. I could have used one of the lounges but there would have been other soldiers there and I needed to speak to them all privately. I wanted to get to know them.

I had my greatcoat on but I did not bother with gloves. I had my list of names and a pencil. They all arrived together. Clearly, Shaw and Atkinson had organised them. I smiled, "Sit, you can smoke if you wish."

Unlike my father, I did not smoke. I saw some of the men took out a pipe but most opted for cigarettes. I waited until they had lit them before I spoke. "I am guessing that most of you know the purpose of this unit. You have all volunteered. Sergeant Shaw and Corporal Atkinson know what to expect. They have served in the desert. While I am new to command I do know what to expect." I took the keffiyeh from my greatcoat pocket, "This is a keffiyeh and, along with your puggaree will prove to be useful in the desert. We will all have much to learn and I know that Captain Dunn, Sergeant Shaw and Corporal Atkinson will help us all make the transition from what we are today into desert warriors. I will read out your names and if you would just tell me a little about your background."

It proved an illuminating talk. Most had been in cavalry regiments. What I did not discover, as it was a public meeting, were the reasons for their move. In the case of my sergeant and corporal, it was obvious. When their unit had been disbanded they had wanted to get back to what they enjoyed. I dismissed them at four. I had decided that I would try to teach them some Arabic. I knew that Shaw and Atkinson would have a few words but Captain Dunn had impressed on me the need for the new men to speak Arabic. It would pass the time on the way south and would not be a wasted effort. Cartwright, Shaw and Atkinson waited when the others had been dismissed.

"They seem keen, Shaw."

"They are that, sir. Tommy and I had them for a week at the holding camp in Aldershot. We tried to give them a picture of what life would be like." He shook his head, "Until you have been out there, you can't know."

"You know my father went back to the desert, last year?"

Both non-coms looked shocked, "But he lost his arm, sir."

"I know, Atkinson. He and Syd Richardson, along with Jake Johnson served in Persia for six months. They are all back in England now. I mention this to let you know that my father has prepared me as much as possible for the life ahead." I smiled, "Let us hope I have inherited more than his looks, eh? I am happy that two of his old comrades are serving with me and I hope that it bodes well for the future."

"It will, sir. Come on Tommy, let us find the mess. I could do with a pint."

Left alone with Cartwright I studied the trooper. He looked to be a little older than the other troopers and more of an age with Shaw and Atkinson. "So, Cartwright, why did they make you an officer's servant?"

He smiled, "Because I asked to be, sir." He hesitated.

"Cartwright, you and I are going to be closer than any in this section. There can be no secrets. Whatever your reason you can tell me."

He sighed, "I was brought up on a large estate, sir, in Yorkshire. My father was a butler and my mother a housekeeper. I was destined to be a servant and I trained to be a gentleman's gentleman. The young man I served, well, sir, he was a bit of a wild youth and, well, sir, he managed to fall off a horse whilst drunk and killed himself."

"I see, but I don't see the connection."

"They had to blame someone and his lordship said it was my fault and I should have helped him." He shrugged, "It was easier to blame me than his son."

"That is ridiculous."

"Yes, sir but I was still dismissed and without references. I was trained for one thing and one thing only. It was my father who suggested the army. I had learned to ride with my young gentleman and it seemed the only choice."

"Cartwright, you have chosen a difficult life. This troop will not be operating in England. We will be in the desert."

"I know, sir. I promise that I will not complain and serve you well."

"The thing is, Cartwright, I don't need a servant. The troop needs soldiers."

He brightened, "That is not a problem, sir. During training, I was the best shot amongst the recruits."

I sighed, "Very well."

"If you would show me your cabin, sir, I can get to work. I shall have to get to know your little ways."

I was not thrilled by the prospect but the fact that my father had got on so well with Ged, his batman, made it slightly more palatable.

We set sail and the next day I began the lessons in Arabic. Had I not enjoyed so many conversations with Captain Dunn then my Arabic would not have been as fluent as it was. I learned that I could speak it better than either Shaw or Atkinson. The progress with the troopers was varied. Cartwright took to it easily. He had a little French already and that helped. So long as they all understood some basic words then life would be easier in the desert. The lessons themselves told me much about the men. Geoffrey Bates always crewed his face up as he struggled with the sounds but he persevered. Peters had a tendency to give up too easily and had to be coaxed. Dixon found it hard to emulate the sounds. He was from the north country and every vowel was flattened. I was patient, more so than either Shaw or Atkinson. After three days I took them to one side, "Don't hector them so much. This is a hard skill to learn. Technically, they should not need it at all but Captain Dunn wished them to speak some."

"Sir."

Desert War

I knew why it was, of course, it was the spectre of my father. They wanted me to be as successful as he was. I was under no illusions. I was not my father and my skills were not his. I was not trying to measure up to him but they were using him as a yardstick.

As we neared Spain the weather improved. It was still overcast but slightly warmer. We were able to move around the deck without our greatcoats. It meant our time on the ship was coming to an end. Soon we would disembark. I had not socialised as much with the other officers for I wanted to spend as much time getting to know my men as I could. However, I did have a drink each night with the two second lieutenants from the Argylls. I doubted that I would ever see them again but it was good to know that I could get on with other officers. My experience at the college had made me wonder about my fellow officers.

Griff

Chapter 18

The Carnic was waiting for us in Gibraltar. She looked like a smart ship although smaller than the troopship we were on. We had just one hundred yards to carry our gear. Cartwright and my non-commissioned officers insisted that my bags would be carried by the men. I did not like it but I allowed them to carry my leather bags.

Captain Hall greeted us at the gangplank, "Lieutenant Roberts?"

"Yes, Captain."

"Welcome aboard. Your face and name are familiar to me."

"I believe you carried my father to Persia."

"I did, indeed. How is he?"

"Back in England."

"Good. We are empty at the moment. We dropped off wounded soldiers here in Gibraltar and we are heading to Alexandria to pick up some reinforcements for South Africa. You will have the whole ship to yourself although it will be a relatively short trip."

When we found the cabins it was as though the men had been given the keys to the kingdom. They each had a cabin of their own and we had the freedom of the ship. We sailed almost as soon as we boarded and headed into a Mediterranean that was far warmer than the Atlantic had been, even in mid-January.

As we passed Tripolitania and Cyrenaica I stood with my officers and pointed, "That will be where we will be operating."

Charlie Atkinson nodded, "Be a bit different from where we used to patrol, sir. No river. The Nile was always handy as both a marker and a source of water. I think where we are going will be a little drier."

I had the report which had been waiting for me at Southampton. In it, Captain Dunn had outlined where we would be. "I think it is another version of Fort Desolation. There is an oasis and the fort guards a caravan route but it is close to the border."

"Is there a garrison, sir?"

I looked at the report and nodded, "A sergeant and fifteen men are its garrison. Captain Dunn has already scouted it out with the first of his new troop. I think we can assume that he will have identified weaknesses and problems." I tapped the report, "He is meeting us in Alexandria, and we will be travelling by train to Faiyum. There we will be picking up our camels and then heading to Farafra. As far as I can see from the map it is the last oasis before Tripolitania and Cyrenaica."

"The edge of the world then, sir,"

"Yes, Shaw, the edge of our world. We have no telegraph and no way of communicating with the army. We will be on our own."

Charlie Atkinson chuckled, "Sounds like it is right up our street then, sir."

Alexandria came as a shock to me. I had lived in Liverpool for a long time but it was empty compared with the crowded Egyptian city.

We had learned that there was equipment for the troop that would need to be unloaded once we landed. The troops to be embarked were waiting patiently as we nudged our way next to the quay. I saw a familiar figure moving through them. There was a ripple in the soldiers as Captain Dunn and a trooper passed through them. By the time we had tied up and the gangplank was in place he was waiting patiently at the bottom of the gangplank.

The first mate approached, "Yes, Mr Seymour?"

"The captain's compliments, Lieutenant. He says to tell you that your supplies will be at the forward hold. They are unloading them first."

"Thank you and thank the captain and the crew. We have been made to feel more than welcome."

"We shall miss you, sir. You and your men have behaved well."

A seaman saluted, "Ship secured, Mr Seymour."

"Very well. You may leave the ship, Lieutenant."

As at Gibraltar, the men insisted upon carrying my equipment. When we reached the bottom, I stepped to the side to allow the men to leave the gangplank. A sergeant major barked to the waiting troops, "Hold fast there. Let these chaps off first." He saluted me, "Sorry sir. They are a bit keen."

"Not a problem Sergeant Major." We made our way past the troops and found the captain.

Captain Dunn held out his hand, "Good to see you, Lieutenant."

I shook his hand and said, "Our supplies are at the forward hold."

"Good." He turned to the trooper, "Burton, fetch the wagon."

"Sir."

We made our way down the quay. The barking sergeant major had organised the waiting men and even as we walked down they began to board, section by section.

"Good trip?"

"It was and that was the ship my father used to sail to Persia."

"Well, I never."

"A small world, eh, sir?"

"You and these men along with the equipment you have brought, are the last piece of the puzzle. The other half of the troop is waiting for us at Faiyum with the camels. We have visited the oasis and they are expecting us. We will have to hit the ground running though as there have been a number of incursions from the east. Thus far they have been exploratory. Our intelligence is that there is a new local commander of the Ottoman troops there and he is a little belligerent and keen to impress his masters in Constantinople."

We reached the forward hold and the crane was already lowering the crates to the quayside. Two seamen stood ready to unhook the ropes.

"Sergeant Shaw, stack our gear over there and then be ready to unpack the cases."

"Sir."

"I assume we will be unpacking the crates, sir?"

I saw that the horse-drawn wagon that was approaching would not take the crate whole.

"Yes, Lieutenant. This equipment consists of rifles, ammunition and tins of bully beef and tea. The rest awaits us at Faiyum."

Desert War

As soon as the first crate was down Shaw ordered the men to open it. The second crate was lowered next to it. Trooper Burton joined our men as they took the cases of rifles and ammunition from the crate. Captain Dunn and I stood to one side to watch them load the wagon.

"What are they like? I know their service record. A couple served with your father but I don't know them."

"They seem a good lot, sir. We have made progress with Arabic but like the curate's egg, it is good in parts. They are all keen. Shaw and Atkinson are good NCOs."

"And your chap? Cartwright, isn't it?"

"Yes, he is an enigma. Destined to be a gentleman's gentleman he seemed, at first, a most unlikely soldier but he has impressed me."

"Burton is my chap and he is as solid as they come. Sergeant Major Leonard transferred from the Camel Corps. He was in the Egyptian Army at Omdurman. He is at Faiyum and he is a good organiser. As for the rest…You can never know a man until he has been under fire. I am confident that the two of us will manage."

I said, quietly, "I am honoured that you asked for me, sir, but I don't want to let you down…or my father."

"That you are your father's son is a bonus, Griff. I wanted you here because you impressed me at Sandhurst. Even if you were not Jack Roberts' son, I would still want you. Your scores were high and everyone at the college was impressed with your leadership skills. You led your little band well and handled the bullies perfectly. I think you are destined for greatness."

It did not take long for the wagon to be loaded. Captain Dunn said, "Sergeant Shaw, load your gear on the top of the wagon and then you and the men climb aboard. Lieutenant Roberts and I will ride with the driver."

"Sir. You heard the officer, shift yourselves and look like soldiers you slovenly shower."

It was pride in the troop that made the sergeant bark.

The Egyptian handled the four horses pulling the wagon well and he negotiated the crowds skilfully as we headed for the station. It was not a long journey but I was overwhelmed by the crowds. "A lot of people here, sir."

"And that is in direct contrast to the desert where we will be lucky to see another person from one week to the next but, if we do, then it probably means danger. You are going to a lonely sea of sand, Griff. The skills I began to teach you at Sandhurst will be honed well in the furnace of the Libyan Desert."

When we reached the station the carter took us to a side line. There was no platform and no train but there was a wooden roof that clearly afforded shade from the sun rather than protection from the rain. Captain Dunn said, "Stack the gear under the roof and then relax. We have to wait until the train arrives."

The driver had gone by the time that everything was organised. Captain Dunn said, "There is little point in unpacking the rifles until we get to Faiyum. The cases will be useful as kindling. There is little wood where we are going and we need fuel to cook and water is vital." He pointed to the waterskins I had not noticed before. They had been in the wagon when my men had loaded it. In England, we would not have given water a second thought. My father had told me that out here it was as valuable as gold. There were so many things I wished I had asked my father about. He had tried to give me as clear a picture as he could before we had left but there were many gaps. Further down the platform, I saw a handful of Egyptians. They would also be boarding the train.

"I take it this isn't a military train, sir."

"No, there are just two trains a day to Faiyum. The main line follows the Nile but this is a branch line. We have one hundred and eighty miles to travel."

The train which pulled the carriages into the station was a familiar one. It was British-designed although crewed by Egyptians. The guard who greeted us directed us to a goods van close to the guard's van at the end of the train. He spoke English. "You can load your supplies in the van and we have kept the last carriage for you and your men."

"Sergeant, load the guard's van. I want two men on duty there for the whole journey."

"Sir."

The compartment we had been given was a basic one. The wooden seats would be uncomfortable. I saw Charlie Atkinson advise the men to use their greatcoats as cushions. Captain Dunn

Desert War

said, when we were all aboard, "This will be a hot journey. Feel free to loosen collars and take off your jackets. Smoking is allowed."

When it was loaded the train chugged its way from the station and headed south, to its first stop, Cairo. I sat with Captain Dunn and looked out of the window as the train passed through the suburbs, then the poorer quarters of Alexandria until we reached the farms and the green swathe that was the Nile.

"It is one hundred and twenty miles to Cairo. That will take us three hours. We have water aboard and Burton has some fruit, bread and cheese. We will not starve." As we headed south he explained to me the way we would be operating. "The garrison of the fort are not the best warriors in the world. They are mainly old men who like the order of the army and are close to the end of their enlistment. They guard the walls and will cook the food but that is all. If we are attacked then it is our men who will defend it. When Lord Kitchener set up the first unit, under Colonel Dickenson, he made the rules by which we operate. There are four Egyptian servants in the fort. They do not fight but will do the dhobying and keep the barracks tidy. You and I will be charged with the patrols. I will take you out for the first one. After that, Griff, you will be on your own." He saw the look on my face and smiled. "Don't worry. Shaw and Atkinson have done this before. The two of them will always be with you. We will juggle the troopers around so that we all get to know them but the core of each patrol will be the same."

"And if we see an enemy?"

"Ah, there's the rub. Until you are fired upon then they are not the enemy. They may be innocent travellers. That is why your language skills are so important. We talk first and fight later. If you are fired upon then, of course, you can return fire."

"And do you expect that we will have to fight?"

"This is the desert. There is always a war. Most of the time it is against the desert but any strangers you meet may well be an enemy."

The fruit we had was dates and the cheese was not English cheese but it was a good way to become acclimatised to the land of Egypt. The cuisine on the ship would be our last taste of England for a while. Variations on bully beef would be the order of the day. The water was clean and tasted of chemicals. Captain Dunn had told me that the water had purifying tablets in it. We would only be using the tablets when we were using water for drinking. Any time we boiled the water for tea it would be safe to drink.

"I take it, sir, that the rifles we will be using will be the Lee Enfield, the ones the sergeant instructors called 'Emily'."

"Yes, they are not perfect for us as we will be riding camels and firing from the back of a camel is not easy anyway, but they have a prodigious rate of fire."

"I confess, sir, I am a little worried about riding a camel."

"It is not as easy as riding a horse I agree but you soon find out the right way. Shaw and Atkinson know the ropes and you can trust them to give good advice. It helps if you don't try to ride them like a horse. It will come to you."

I glanced at the men, "But I don't want to fail in front of the men." I was thinking of Fairbrother when he fell from his horse.

He smiled, "If there was one thing I learned from your father it was to be honest with the men you lead. They don't need you to be perfect. God knows that is impossible in any case. They need you to do the best you can. In the same vein, don't expect them to be perfect. Just pray that any mistakes we make are not fatal."

I know why he said what he did but it filled me with even more trepidation.

Cairo station was busy. It was not just soldiers and Egyptians who thronged the station. As Captain Hall had told me there were now tourists, rich Europeans who wanted to see the wonders of ancient Greece and wonders like the Pyramids and the Sphinx. The railway was a lifeline to Egypt's past.

Captain Dunn sent Cartwright and Burton to purchase a jug of tea for us. The pair had got on well during the journey from Alexandria and when they returned it was with tea as well as some sweet pastries. We had finished the tea and pastries by the time the train left the mainline to take the branch line towards the oasis of Faiyum. We passed, not through the desert but through green and fertile fields. Captain Dunn explained that engineers had managed to irrigate the desert as far as Faiyum and that was why the branch line had been built. It was for the carrying of

Desert War

goods and not people. The track was a single track. We passed two passing places but with just two trains a day, at the moment, there was no need for a second line.

It was late afternoon when we chugged into the station. The advice about the greatcoats had helped on the journey but we were all glad to be off the train. We had all taken the opportunity, during the journey, to walk to the guards' van. Despite the swirling smoke the colder air rushing over the train was a relief. The sergeant major and most of the troop were waiting for us at the station. I saw the herd of camels and my heart sank. They were far bigger than the horses we had ridden at college.

It took half an hour to unload the equipment. Captain Dunn ordered the rifles to be unpacked and then the packing boxes were carefully broken up. They would provide kindling.

Corporal Higgins was acting quartermaster and he had a checklist. He assigned each rifle to a trooper and then a camel. Sergeant Shaw sorted out the new men. The ammunition and food were distributed amongst the pack camels.

"Sergeant Major Leonard."

"Sir."

"This is Lieutenant Roberts. He is my second in command and will be the adjutant for the troop. We now have a sergeant and another corporal."

The sergeant major saluted, "Welcome, sir. The captain has told me of your father although I had already heard of him. He must be proud that his son went to Sandhurst."

"He is Sergeant Major."

"Corporal Higgins, show the lieutenant to his camel."

"Sir."

Cartwright dutifully followed me with my gear as we headed for the camel. The corporal spoke as we approached the beast which was squatting on its forelegs. "Scheherazade is a sound camel, sir. I understand you speak Arabic?"

"I do."

"That will help. This one can be an awkward bugger if you just try English. Sorry, sir, pardon my French. Your man can load your bags on the side. There is a scabbard for your MLE." Cartwright had picked up my gun.

"Should I mount now, Higgins?"

He smiled, "You might as well, sir. Get it over with so to speak. We haven't got far to ride tonight. Our camp is just a mile away."

Cartwright had managed to secure my bags to the straps and slip my rifle into the scabbard. I took off my sword and hung that from the pommel. The last thing I needed was to get it tangled in my legs.

Higgins noticed my swagger stick, "That will come in handy, sir. Use it to help guide her. She is a good beastie and won't need too much of a smack."

I sighed. I could not delay any longer. I went to the camel and stroking its head said, in Arabic, "Scheherazade, I am your new rider. When I am able, I shall get treats for you. For now, all that I ask is that you do not throw me."

Cartwright did not have much Arabic and it was clear that Higgins did not understand my words. The camel, however, turned a baleful eye to look at me as she chewed.

"Right, sir, climb aboard, so to speak. We call them ships of the desert for good reason."

I saw that Captain Dunn was mounted already and the sergeant major and the others were helping my men to mount. I put my foot in the stirrup and used the pommel to haul myself up. It didn't feel so bad.

Higgins said, "Well done, sir. Now just say, Scheherazade, up and pull on the reins. If you encourage her with the stick it will help and if you can use Arabic then so much the better."

I used Arabic again and waited. It took a few moments but eventually, the hind legs rose and I was in danger of being pitched forward but I had a good sense of balance and rectified the move.

"Well done, sir."

I was upright and I seemed to be so high that if I fell I would surely break my neck.

"Now, if you just wait there, I will get your man sorted and then, when I mount, we can try to move."

Glancing over at the others I saw that the sergeant major had used one of the troopers to demonstrate how to make the camels move. Having watched me Cartwright had an easier time of it.

Desert War

Higgins told him that his camel was an older animal and the most placid of the troop's camels. It showed that Captain Dunn had prepared well. Cartwright might be the perfect servant but it was clear, from his conversation with me, that he might have shortcomings as a soldier. Higgins had ensured that Cartwright was next to me and he said, "They will stay still until they are ordered to move. Camels are lazy beasts. I will go and get Elsie."

"Elsie?"

"Yes, sir, I couldn't pronounce the name she had. It was a bit like Elsie. Anyway, she seems to understand the new one. It was my wife's name." He grinned, "Similar nature too!"

He mounted easily and he used a switch to start the camel. I noticed that he used what sounded like made-up words, "Hai, Hai, Elsie." The camel started to move and Higgins used the reins to steer her in a circle. When he neared us, he said, "Whoa."

"There you are, sir. Now give it a go."

I took a deep breath and said, "Hai, hai, Scheherazade." I used my heels and the swagger stick and she took off like a train. I did what my instructor at Sandhurst had told me not to do. I gripped the pommel with my left hand. Unless I could turn her, I would end up deep in the desert. I pulled the reins to the left and used my body weight, knees and heels to make her move in the direction I had chosen. I pulled back on the reins and said, "Whoa, Scheherazade."

She stopped. I was forty yards from the others. I used the time to calm myself. I dropped my left hand and breathed slowly. Instead of 'Hai,' I said, in Arabic, "Walk on, Scheherazade."

When she obeyed I almost cheered. I reached Corporal Higgins who applauded me, "Well done sir. Now, Cartwright, you have seen what your officer can do. Let's see if you can emulate him."

I think the wild charge had frightened Cartwright and he held back on the reins. That, allied to the camel's nature meant he moved at a more sedate pace and returned safely.

Sergeant Major Leonard shouted, "Well done. Now that we are all mounted. Let us head to our camp. You new chaps will each ride next to one of us."

Trooper Burton ghosted up next to Cartwright, "I shall be your partner. You did well." Cartwright nodded. "Lieutenant, if you would join the captain at the head of the column."

"Walk on, Scheherazade." She obeyed and I was soon next to Captain Dunn.

He grinned, "Good first lesson and it will get easier. Let us try to get to the camp before dark. The last thing we need is for one of the camels to be spooked by a snake in the dark."

With those reassuring words ringing in my ear we headed along the road from the station towards the distant camp. I was in Africa and I was riding a camel. What had I volunteered for?

Desert War

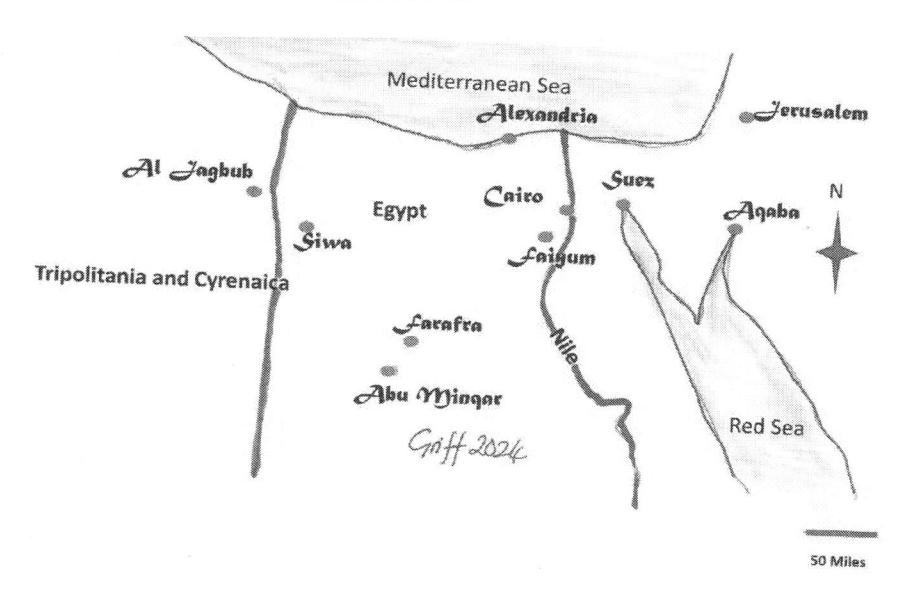

Egypt 1900

Desert War

Griff

Chapter 19

I was surprised that there was only one tent at the camp. As we neared the camp, its position identified by the fire and the smell drifting towards us of a stew, Captain Dunn said, "We will not be using tents. It is a waste of time to put them up and take them down. We have two hundred and sixty miles to travel through the desert. We will probably have more sleep at the noon day rest than in the night. There is enough camel dung to be had for fuel and we can keep a fire going all night. This close to civilisation there are flies aplenty. The fire will work. You and the new lads can enjoy a good night of sleep tonight but from tomorrow, they will stand a watch like the rest. As will you."

"Not a problem, sir."

When we stopped, I realised that I had not yet been taught to dismount. I listened to the captain, "Down, Jinni, down." He used his switch to emphasise the command.

I saw which way the camel lurched. "Down, Scheherazade, down." She obeyed and I dismounted.

Cartwright struggled a little but Burton was on hand to help. He immediately came over to take my bags. "No tents, sir?"

"No, Cartwright. Ask Burton where we sleep. Lay out my blanket and my greatcoat. There is a cloak in my bags. I will use that to cover me."

That first night I felt like a passenger. Captain Dunn and the sergeant major were patient but I knew that I had to pull my weight the next day. I went to Sergeant Shaw, after we had eaten, grateful that he was a veteran. He knew the desert and he knew camels. "How did the men cope?"

"Generally, quite well. Flynn is the one struggling the most. I thought it would have been your servant but he coped well. Flynn is finding the motion of the camel difficult. Tomorrow will be the test." He smiled, "Don't worry sir. This is your first command, and you are doing well. Keep your keffiyeh wrapped around your face. You have caught the sun already. Sunburn is a nasty thing."

Desert War

    I spoke to all the men who had sailed with me. I knew that the whole troop were my responsibility but having travelled with them from England I was closer to them. Mindful of Captain Dunn's words and the possibility of the presence of snakes, I lifted my bedding and shook it before retiring for the night. Thanks to the fire we had burning not to mention the pipe smoke and cigarettes, we were not plagued by flies, despite the proximity of water.

    I was woken when the sentries were changed. It was not dawn but being awake I went to make water. The men on watch were heating water for tea and I went over to them. It was Corporal Higgins who was captain of the watch, "Morning, sir. I would say it was going to be a hot one but as every day is hot... Tea will be ready in fifteen minutes, sir. Just have to boil the water. There is some bread and cold bacon. Make the most of it. It is the last treat. From now on it is bully beef and beans."

    While I waited I loaded my pistol and my father's. I had not travelled with them loaded but now that we were in the desert it seemed right. I had two holsters. When he had seen them Captain Dunn had commented that I looked like someone from the Buffalo Bill show. He did not say it mockingly. I also loaded the MLE. Cartwright had spent some time the previous night cleaning the grease from it. We would travel across the desert loaded and ready for action.

    Trooper Wilson was the bugler and when reveille was sounded the whole camp came to life. Like me, I suspected that the freshly arrived men had felt every rock and bump on the ground and were ready to rise while the veterans knew that we had to move while it was cool and dark. Once the sun rose we would be riding through a furnace.

    Sergeant Major Leonard bellowed, "Water your camels at the oasis before we leave."

    I think his comment was for the benefit of we new men as the others were already leading their camels to the open patch of water. It did not look appealing but we did not have to drink it.

    The camels all drank as the tent was dismantled. We mounted and headed south and west along, not a road, but an ancient caravan route. With my keffiyeh wrapped around my face and my puggaree over my neck it was just the backs of my hands that were exposed to the sun. Despite the fact that the sand was not being blown I wore the goggles my father had given to me. They were better quality than those issued to the troopers.

The captain began to teach me from the moment we left the camp. It was a continuation of the lessons in the classroom at college. The difference was that these were practical lessons. He pointed to stars and the sky. Once daylight came he took out his compass and used that. He pointed to his map. What looked featureless in two dimensions suddenly became clearer when he pointed out the wadis, humps and bumps.

"Once we reach Farafra and start our real work then those wadis, humps and bumps will represent danger. We will have to hone the skills of the troopers who are going to be our scouts. I do not yet know the men you brought although Corporal Atkinson, from his service record, appears to possess scouting ability." He pointed to the odd bird flying in the sky. "If you see buzzards gathering then you know there is a kill there. It may be animals but every gathering of scavengers is worth an investigation. When you do then do so cautiously. Expect the worst and if it none manifests itself then that is a good thing." We rode in silence for a while.

"When do we stop to rest from the sun, sir?"

"This is not yet hot." He tapped the pocket watch in his top pocket. Mine was in a side pocket. "By the time it is eleven or approaching eleven we look for somewhere to rest. It may be a dune or a rock which might give a little shade but if not we make shade through the use of the camels and the cloaks we have brought. We need sentries while we rest and believe me that is the hardest duty of the day. Peering through a heat haze for danger is not easy."

"Sir, I have good goggles, I would like to volunteer for the watch today. I have been a passenger up to now. It is time I showed that I am an officer."

"Are you sure? No one will think badly of you if you wait."

I shrugged, "I have to do it sometime. Better now than when I am tired."

Desert War

Over the next five days I became an officer. I was not afraid to seek advice and I learned. I resisted the desire to drink all the time. I watched Sergeant Shaw and, as he did, drank a mouthful regularly. I watched how he rolled it around his mouth before swallowing. I learned to make water every time we stopped. Corporal Higgins told me that you peed when the chance came rather than having to. By the time the mud-walled fort came into view, my hands had changed from bright red to brown, my buttocks had become used to the motion of the camel and I had learned to eat dates whenever I could. I had stood a couple of noon watches and knew how to discriminate from haze and recognise movement.

We passed the oasis, which was tiny. There were trees but the water was like a village pond. The Egyptian soldiers stood to attention as we passed through the gates. There were three small towers and a larger one with a flagpole. The gatehouse had a man there as did the tallest tower. It looked too small to house our troop and animals. Sergeant Major Leonard roared, "Troop dismount."

The same manoeuvre performed from the backs of horses looked smart. The camels sank to their knees in a less ordered fashion. Sergeant Instructor Hargreaves would not have approved. When they were all dismounted the sergeant major held the reins of Captain Dunn's camel. The captain removed his keffiyeh and swept his arm around the parade ground. "This, gentlemen, is your new home. It is cosy. You passed the oasis on the way in. This is not like Faiyum. We husband our water. Sergeant Major Leonard will give you standing orders regarding the watering and grazing for the camels. Sergeant Abn Hamed commands the cooks and the garrison. They will share the barracks with you. The barracks are also your mess." He smiled,

"We are a small troop and the officers will share that mess with you." He pointed behind him at the long low building that stretched from the tall tower to the smaller corner tower. He pointed to his left, "There are the stables and beyond them at the southeast corner are the stores. The kitchens are at the southwest corner and on the west side of the walls are the offices and the officers' quarters. Finally, the armoury is located at the base of the northwest tower. This is an ancient fort but it is our home, As well as the standing orders Sergeant Major Leonard will issue your duties." He paused and walked along the double line of camels and men. "We are the first line of defence in these parts. I do not think that we shall be fighting battles but we will be fighting a war. That war is to keep Egypt's western border safe. We are here to protect those who live and work in this part of Egypt. We did not come here for glory. We came because we are all soldiers. We were soldiers of the queen and now we are soldiers of the new king. If you need to speak to either Lieutenant Roberts or myself know that we will listen." He turned, "Sergeant Major Leonard."

"Right then, let us get you sorted, eh?"

I followed the captain into the office. It was small and could hold barely four people. He took off his helmet, "Sit, Griff. Here is where you and I can talk." We sat and I saw behind him a map of Egypt. There were some red dots which looked few and far between. We were one of them. There was also a red line which marked the border. It looked close.

"Well Griff, what do you think?"

"You are right, sir, it is cosy. The men will be living on top of one another."

He nodded, "I chose the men from the many volunteers we had. Like you, I wanted men who could cope. I think I have chosen well." He stood and pointed to a red dot. "This is us. To the north is Siwa Oasis. There is a fort there and a garrison like this one. The difference is that their oasis is much bigger and the place is busier than we are. There are archaeologists looking for evidence of Alexander the Great. There are many people who believe his tomb lies at Siwa. They guard the caravan route from the coast. They are Egyptian soldiers under the command of Major Lowery."

Desert War

"Then why are we not there, sir?"

"Good question." He ran a finger from the coast down the border, "It is because we can cover the ground between Siwa and Mut. The desert is vast and empty. The wind covers tracks quickly but our job is to investigate any threat to this land. We have six months and then we will be relieved. We get a month's leave and then we return. We are allowed a month to travel back to England. The two months we will not be here is high summer. Our relief will be a troop from the Camel Corps and they will be here to guard the oasis, no more. That will be our life; six months on and two months off."

"That is more leave than my father enjoyed."

"Lessons were learned, Griff. If we are to do our job, then the weapon that is this troop needs to be sharp. We cannot afford to be either complacent or dull."

There was a knock on the door. It was Burton, "Sir, we have stowed the officers' equipment in your quarters. The cook would like to serve the food within the next hour."

He smiled, "And the men can't eat until Mr Dunn has stopped nattering, is that right, Burton?"

The batman kept a straight face, "Of course not, sir. Take all the time you like. I am sure the troopers will relish cold food and lukewarm tea."

"Be off with you. We are done."

"Sir." He left with a smile on his face.

"He is a good fellow and as you will find with Cartwright, something of a nagging wife. Still, he is right. We have lots of time to chat."

We rose and with our helmets under our arms left the office and walked the few paces to the door that Burton held ajar. "These are our quarters, Lieutenant. I will go to speak with Sergeant Abn Hamed. The bugle will let you know when it is time to eat."

I saw Cartwright holding the door to our quarters open. "These are our rooms, sir." He shook his head, "Back at the big house the scullery maid had more room."

I entered the rooms and saw what he meant. There was a cot and a rail for clothes and then another door. I opened the door and saw that my room was little bigger than Cartwright's cell.

There was a bed, a bedside table, a chair and a wardrobe. It was like the sleeping compartment on a train.

He pointed to a pot in the corner, "And that, sir, is where you make water. Apparently, the dhobi wallers use it to clean clothes."

I nodded, "I read that was how the Romans did it." He looked dubious, "We shall just have to make the best of it."

He pointed to the wardrobe, "Your clothes are hung, sir. Trooper Burton has explained to me the washing arrangements. They call it dhobying out here." He shook his head.

"Cartwright, I know that your assigned role is as my batman but you have to know that I do not need a servant. What I need is someone who is a good soldier and, when we ride on patrol, someone who can look after Scheherazade. This is not the big house. This is an outpost of the British Army."

He gave me a wan smile, "I know, sir, and I confess that the dirt and cramped quarters apart, I quite like being part of the troop. They are all good chaps. They are not what I am used to but I feel part of something I did not feel back in England even with my father as a butler. It will just take some getting used to."

"And that is just as true for me."

The bugle summoned us and we headed for the mess hall. It was the barracks. The beds were along two sides of the long low building and the table was in the centre. Cartwright said as we entered, "Sir, I believe that you sit at the opposite end of the table to Captain Dunn." Burton had clearly briefed him.

He held the chair out but I did not sit. I waited until Captain Dunn had done so and then I sat. The rest all followed. The troop had clearly been told of the arrangements for, along with Burton and Cartwright, four of the troop went to the waiting cooks to collect the food. Cartwright served me the stew. It was bully beef, bouillon, reconstituted beans spiced and with some strange vegetables. A dixie of tea was placed in the middle. The food was tasty but I suspected Aunt Sarah would have complained that it was too spicy.

"Cartwright, when do the Egyptians eat?"

"When we are done, sir. Sometimes, I believe, they eat outside." He said it as though it was hard to believe that one would eat in such a manner.

Desert War

There was no duty for us that night but we would have to rise early for the first patrol. There would be ten of us on the patrol. Four would be new men and that included me and Cartwright. Hunter and Foulkes would be the other new men. Shaw and Atkinson would be the non-commissioned officers. They were not new to the desert but they were new to this part of it. Captain Dunn and Sergeant Major Leonard knew how to organise.

I woke early for I was nervous. I tried to be quiet but the lighting of the lamp and the sound of me making water in the pot must have woken Cartwright who came in with a fresh jug of water. "Shall I heat it for you to shave, sir?"

I shook my head, "Shaving is a luxury out here, Cartwright. If you shave it must be a dry shave. I shall grow a beard."

Reveille was at five am. We were dressed and ready. We made our way to the mess hall. It was more casual at breakfast. There was a bread oven and we had bread to go with the porridge and fried bully beef. Along with tea it would set us up for the day. I was keen to set an example and Cartwright and I were ready with our camels in the parade ground before anyone else. We stood in the shade of the stables and two corner towers although the sun had barely risen. There was no heat as yet. I had my father's cloak and I was grateful for it. The troopers had to make do with their greatcoats, puggarees and keffiyeh.

Sergeant Shaw checked that the saddles were secured and we mounted. We had to duck beneath the gatehouse as we left and Captain Dunn led us north along what was barely a trail. "We will ride towards Siwa. It is two hundred miles away. Today I expect us to cover just twenty-five miles. At the end of the month you, Lieutenant Roberts, will be ready to lead a long patrol to Siwa. Today is just to give you a feel for the land."

Captain Dunn was a good teacher. He pointed out features for me to recognise. The trail, which had appeared as just a slightly harder piece of ground became clearer. I learned to identify what to look for. There were no large oases on our route but there were remnants of trees that afforded shade. There might be some greenery for the camels and even puddles of water at such places. When we found one we stopped. The camel dung we discovered showed that others had used the shade too.

Desert War

"Sir, how do we know that this dung was not deposited by enemies?"

"We don't. That is our problem, Lieutenant. We have to investigate every traveller we meet."

We met just one group of travellers that first day. We were on our way back to Farafra and they were heading for Siwa. It was not merchants and a caravan but a party of archaeologists. We had just turned around when we met them. They had horses as well as camels.

I saw that there were thirteen in the party. Three Europeans and ten Egyptians. We stopped. "I am Captain Dunn of the Egyptian Border patrol and this is Lieutenant Roberts." It was not a question but the statement invited an answer. I realised that there was a young woman with them. She looked to be even younger than I was.

"I am Richard Cowley and this is John Bannerman-Carlisle. This is my daughter, Lucinda. We are heading towards Siwa. We left your fort yesterday." He gave a smile, "We are still getting used to travelling in the desert and we move slowly. That is the thing about being an archaeologist. What you seek is old before you start. We rarely have to rush." The young woman looked to be in her late teens. Although she was well protected from the sun and looking at ease amongst the all-male company I wondered at the wisdom of bringing a young English woman to this most inhospitable of places.

Captain Dunn nodded towards the picks and shovels, "A new dig or an existing one?"

"We were here two years ago at Siwa. We found some evidence of a possible tomb between Siwa and your fort. We are going to do some exploratory work there. My daughter has just finished school and it seemed a good time to come. There will be more archaeologists joining us in a couple of weeks. We are to do the groundwork. If we find the evidence we are seeking then it will become a major dig."

"And if not?"

"Then we will either return to England or join the main dig at Siwa."

"Good luck."

Desert War

"We may see you again as your water is as close as that of Siwa. We have enough for a month."

Captain Dunn frowned, "If there was a tomb surely it would be close to some water."

"There was water at the dig site when we found the evidence but you know the desert, Captain," Captain Dunn nodded. "That is what we hope but things change and we have plans in place. The tomb we seek is more than two thousand years old. This land had more water back then."

"Have you any protection? This is a wild part of the world."

He nodded towards their bags. I saw that they had a couple of shotguns and the two men had pistols. "We are armed and prepared."

"I wish you luck." As we parted Captain Dunn turned to me, "We will need to keep an eye on those fellows. I had planned on heading south tomorrow but this means I must return and see where they are digging." He rubbed his chin. "You will lead tomorrow's patrol. Take these men. I will take the rest of the troop. We might have to camp overnight. You will be in command of the fort until I return."

He said it as though it was the most routine of orders. I felt nothing but fear. The patrol did not daunt me but the thought of being the commander of the fort did.

Desert War

Griff

Chapter 20

By 6 am the whole troop was ready to leave. Captain Dunn and the bulk of the men had two spare camels with extra water, food and blankets. They would spend one night away from the fort. My orders were clear. I was to ride twenty-five miles to the south and west and then return. The eight men I led did not seem sufficient enough and I felt a little vulnerable. Sergeant Shaw must have sensed my feelings for four miles from the fort and with the flag still visibly fluttering he nudged his camel next to me.

"I spoke to the Egyptian sergeant, he is a good bloke. He said that there is little traffic to the south of us. Most of the caravans head to Siwa and Marsa Matruh. The last caravan that headed south passed the fort a week ago. Caravans go north from Mut. The one that passed through does the trip three times a year."

"Good to know, Sergeant. I think that Mr Dunn just wanted me to get a feel for the land."

"It is a funny old place. This is different to Sudan. There we had mountains and hills and then the river valley. Everything came back to the Nile. Here it all looks the same. I know it is not. This is proper desert."

I did as Captain Dunn had done the previous day. I stopped whenever we saw what passed for shade. If we saw movement we headed towards it. Once we found a patch of brackish water and some weedy plants. The camels were grateful for the morsels of food they represented. Distance was hard to estimate without signs and I stopped at eleven. We would spend three hours under our cloaks and then return. I set sentries but I was too nervous to take advantage of the rest. Even though the sun burned down I climbed the rocky outcrop that gave us a little shade and taking my regulation binoculars from their case I scanned the horizon. The heat haze made it hard to see clearly but to the southwest I saw movement. I focused on the movements and relaxed when I realised it was birds. I was about to descend when I looked again. They were birds but they were not roosting. They were

Desert War

vultures and moving along the ground. I remembered Captain Dunn's words. They were feasting on something.

I went back to the others and as I approached Sergeant Shaw opened his eyes, "Sir?"

"Instead of heading directly back to the fort, I want to investigate something to the southwest. I saw vultures." I was not sure if my suggestion would be dismissed by the sergeant and when he nodded, I felt relief.

I lay down in the shade afforded by my camel and rested my eyes. It was not sleep but I was not making heat and conserving my energy. Captain Dunn had stressed the importance of doing so in the desert. When it was a little cooler we mounted and moved. The terms cooler and hotter did not mean the same here as in England. Cooler could still mean that a man without water or shade cou'd die quickly.

Sergeant Shaw said, "One up the spout, lads and be wary. Lieutenant Roberts has spotted vultures."

As we neared the huge and ungainly birds they took to the air but did not move far. They gathered like hooded sentries and watched us. There were bodies on the ground and from the skulls they had once been human. The bones had been largely stripped of flesh but the clothing and skulls were unmistakeable. These were men.

"Atkinson, sentries."

"Sir."

He assigned four men who rode their camels twenty yards away at the four points of the compass. I dismounted as did Cartwright and Shaw. I handed my reins to my batman, "It looks like the remains of three men. I can see no animals."

Shaw said, "There is camel dung over there, sir. It is dry but soft in the centre so it is a few days old."

"And these bodies do not look fresh." I stood. "Whoever they are they deserve to be buried."

"Sir. Corporal, get two men to dig a grave for the remains."

"Hunter and Cartwright, get some spades, find a patch of soft sand and dig one deep grave."

As the two men began to dig I used my mind to work out the sequence of events. We were on the camel trail from the fort. The sergeant had said that the last caravan to pass south had been

Desert War

a few days earlier. This had to be that caravan. They had been attacked and their goods and animals were taken. Was it a bandit attack or raiders from across the border? In either case, they would have taken everything. I left the men to the digging and moved west. I passed the sentry there, it was one of the new men, Foulkes, and kept going. I found the evidence of camels just forty paces from the sentry, two hundred from the attack. The dung was dried but when I picked it and squeezed it there was dampness in the centre. It was less than a week old. These men had been attacked by raiders who had headed back to the border. I knew I was speculating but Captain Dunn had told me on the train south, that soldiers in the desert had to think more than those based in regular garrisons.

The delay helped us in one way. We neared the fort just before dark and the last part was cooler. We dismounted at the oasis and I left my camel with Cartwright to water for me while I went to the fort. The sergeant was clearly worried by our late arrival, "Was there trouble, Lieutenant Roberts?"

I nodded, "Tell me, Sergeant, how many men were with the caravan that passed through here going south?"

"It was a small one. There were just three of them. They had six camels with them."

"They were attacked about twenty-eight miles southwest of here."

He shook his head, "Poor men. They had three ancient rifles with which to defend themselves."

The fact that I was in command that night weighed heavily on my shoulders. Although we did not have to stand a duty Stan and I both took a walk around the walls before we retired. The sentries were vigilant but they were used to looking out over the same scene each night. Stan and I were not. We might see something they would overlook. There was nothing.

As we stood over the gatehouse looking towards the oasis, Stan said, "You are doing well, sir. You did the right thing at our noon break. If you hadn't spotted the birds then we would never have known about the attack."

"You may be right, Sergeant, but I can't help but think that this task is too great for the paltry number of men we have."

Desert War

"And that is always the way, sir. A few dead merchants won't worry the powers that be. Captain Dunn is a clever chap. He will know what to do when he gets back."

His words gave some comfort to me but I still woke early and I was on the wall before the bugle was sounded for reveille. Until Captain Dunn returned I would have to organise the day. I did not want to risk leaving the fort empty but I did not want the men idle either. I saw that the ditch around the fort was not as deep as it ought to have been. I summoned my handful of men. "I want this ditch empty of sand."

Trooper Foulkes looked down at the ditch, "But sir, it will just fill up again."

I waved over the waiting Egyptian sergeant, "Sergeant, when was the last time the ditch was cleaned of sand?"

He shrugged, "I have been here for two years, Lieutenant Roberts and I have never seen it cleaned. Should it be?"

I pointed to the walls, "Those walls are not high. If I were to stand beneath them on the back of my camel I could reach the top. The ditch is there as a protection for the wall. That is why the gatehouse is higher. There is no ditch there. The ditch is not meant to be filled with sand. We will start with the gatehouse wall and see how far we can get." I turned to Cartwright, "Fetch me a spade, too,"

The fact that I was going to dig meant that all the men not standing a duty, or preparing food joined me in the work. As the sand was shifted to the top I had men move it further from the fort. By noon we had made such progress that we had reached the rock at the bottom of the ditch. It was more than four feet deep and now that it had been cleaned was, once more, an obstacle.

The Egyptian sergeant shook his head, "I thought it would be a shallow thing, Lieutenant. This is a barrier."

"Not yet but it will be." I pointed to some dead spikey branches close by the oasis. Not big enough for kindling they would do as a primitive alarm. Animals had grazed the foliage leaving bare sticks. "If we embed those in fissures at the bottom then, at night when the fort is at its most vulnerable, there will be something to deter men from descending into the ditch."

Desert War

We ate and rested from the heat of the sun. We were able to use the shade afforded by the north wall to begin work earlier than we might have expected and by the time the sentry in the tower reported the return of the patrol, we had cleared the north ditch too.

I had the spades stored and I had cleaned myself up by the time the patrol returned. They looked weary. For the new men who had come from England, it must have been a baptism of fire to spend a night in the desert and two days in the saddle.

Captain Dunn dismounted, "Burton, take my camel. Sergeant Major Leonard, the men did well. Give them a double ration of spirits tonight."

I smiled. Captain Dunn had not been a midshipman for long but the traditions of the sea were still embedded. We were allowed a ration of grog while stationed in the desert. Captain Dunn had ensured that it was rum rather than the local arrack.

I saluted, "A good patrol, sir?"

He saluted, "Yes. Let us go to the office and we can fill each other in. I see you have been busy today."

Once in the office and with mugs of tea before us, I made my report. He frowned. "Of course, there is no way of knowing if the attack was by bandits or Ottomans."

I had thought about the problem as we toiled in the ditch, "Sir, why not give the next caravan an escort? Even just four or five men would help."

"Good idea. The dig is fifty miles from here. There is a small oasis and someone found the remains of stone buildings beneath the sand. As they have not yet found the tomb of Alexander at Siwa they are excited about the discovery. There may be more men coming at the end of the month with supplies. I promised that we would escort them to the dig."

I drained my mug, "It seems strange to me, sir, that the remains of such a man as Alexander the Great would be buried in the desert."

He nodded, "Me too. I had a chat with the chap in charge of the dig. It seems that when Alexander died he was supposed to be buried in Macedon but Ptolemy took the remains and had them entombed at Memphis. They were then taken to a tomb in Alexandria where they remained for some time. It was after the

Desert War

time of Cleopatra that they disappeared. The tomb in Alexandria might have been pillaged. The archaeologist said that Emperor Caligula took some of the items from the tomb. The body was moved almost two thousand years ago."

"I also wonder at the wisdom of bringing a young girl out here."

"I spoke to Richard Cowley. He is a widower and with him here his daughter would be alone in England. She has finished school and is as keen as her father is on archaeology. Rather like you, Griff, she is following in her father's footsteps."

I suppose it made a sort of sense. There were little opportunities for women. Apart from nursing, teaching and perhaps writing, middle-class ladies were expected to do nothing. "So, sir, what is the plan?"

"The men I led today had a hard ride and I can see that your men worked hard. Tomorrow, we rest and then the day after you can take a patrol north and west and Sergeant Major Leonard will take one south and west. They will both be small patrols. If you think you need more men…"

I shook my head, "If we are just looking for signs then we do not need to go in large numbers. Better to use our resources as well as we can."

"Good man. Do you regret taking me up on my offer?"

I grinned, "Oh, no, sir, not for a moment. This is the kind of soldiering I always envisaged."

"Good. The day after your patrol you and Sergeant Major Leonard can have the day off and I will take the next patrol out."

I had a better night of sleep. Perhaps it was the exhaustion from working in the sun all day but I think the relief of knowing I was no longer in sole charge helped. With the whole troop toiling we completed the cleaning of the ditches and had embedded a few stakes.

"When you patrol tomorrow, look for more stakes as you ride. We have to be like the vultures out here and scavenge what we can."

I had with me, Cartwright, Charley Atkinson and Bill Foulkes. The trail we would be taking was better defined as it led to Siwa and had been used more recently. Even so, I took nothing for granted. I had my map and compass and stopped frequently to take bearings. We stopped at a tiny oasis just twenty-five miles from the fort. The water was barely enough for the four camels as Captain Dunn and his men had used it twice. It would refill but it would take time. That patrol was uneventful and that pleased me. No news was, in my view, good news.

Our day off meant no riding but we had work to do. We had not, as yet, had time to practise with the new rifles. They had been unpacked and cleaned but that was all. The sergeant major and I took out our men when Captain Dunn and his patrol had left. We filled empty corned beef cans with sand and used them as targets. The first range we used was one hundred and fifty paces. Nothing was wasted here in the desert. The cans could be taken back to the fort and, filled with sand, used to add protection to the walls.

I had not fired a Lee Enfield since college and that seemed a lifetime ago. As with all new weapons, it took a few shots for me to acclimatise myself to the gun. It did not need much adjustment and when I was satisfied I fired five shots at the targets. The sergeant major and I then moved the targets three hundred paces from us and we turned them around so that we had a side of the cans to aim at and they were free from previous bullet holes. As I expected the men were less accurate at that range. Three out of five struck the target. Sergeant Major Leonard was impressed that not only did all five of my shots hit the target, the grouping was close.

"Not many officers are that good, sir. Well done."

I shrugged, "It is one of the few things that come naturally, Sergeant Major. It must be an inherited trait."

Captain Dunn saw nothing on his patrol. He said when he returned, "I think we will all rest tomorrow and the day after I will lead one patrol and you another Mr Roberts." He pointed to the sky. "I know it is rare in these parts but a storm is brewing." The skies were, indeed, growing darker and there was a heavy oppressive feel to the air. "With luck, it will bring that rarest of benefits, rain but it might just bring a sandstorm. Let us not risk losing men and animals in a storm."

Captain Dunn not only knew how to navigate but also about the weather and that night the storm arrived. There was thunder and lightning. We stood to and calmed the animals. Rain did come. It was not the sort of rain we enjoyed in England. It was a short but very violent shower. The rain pounded down and looked like exploding artillery shells. The deluge showed where there were leaks, they were mainly in the stables and, as such we could ignore them. By dawn, as quickly as it had come, it had passed.

Until the sun began to heat up we had to endure a parade ground that was muddy. Sergeant Major Leonard ordered the men to stay away from it and we led the camels from the fort to the oasis. The rain had made it greener as well as filling it up and we took advantage of the gift from the skies.

"A good job you said for us not to patrol, sir."

Captain Dunn shrugged, "Luck. Still, as I once read, luck to a soldier was as valuable as a good weapon."

It was just before noon that the small caravan arrived at the fort from the direction of Siwa. There were four men and eight camels. They left their camels at the oasis and joined us in the fort. Hospitality was the rule in the desert and we fed them. They were served coffee. The garrison preferred that to the tea enjoyed by the troop. We learned, from the leader of the caravan, Ismail, that they were heading for Abu Minqar and then Mut.

"Lieutenant Roberts, I know I said you would not have to patrol today but it seems to me that it would be prudent to provide an escort for these merchants, at least as far as Abu Minqar."

"Of course, sir. The animals and men are well rested."

"It is fifty miles to the oasis. You will require two camps, outward and inward."

"That is fine, sir. I knew this day would be coming. This will be as good a time as any. With the rain, there should be less dust and the oases fuller."

"Then choose your men."

I nodded, "I will take Sergeant Shaw, Corporal Atkinson, and Troopers Cartwright, Hunter and Flynn."

"Will that be enough?"

"It should be, sir, and it means you can still take a decent-sized patrol out tomorrow."

Desert War

We knew that the nights could be cold and we took kindling for a fire. We still had some of the boxes from the rifles and ammunition. We also took our own food.

"How much ammo, sir?"

"Fifty rounds a man should be sufficient, Sergeant Shaw."

We left at two in the afternoon. We followed in the wake of the caravan. That way we could respond to danger quickly. As we rode I told the others my plans in case of an attack. "Cartwright, you will stay at the rear, Shaw, you and Hunter will cover the left flank and Atkinson and I the right. Flynn, you will ride close to Ismail at the front."

I knew, from my first patrol, that there would be no water for our first camp. We camped just five miles shy of the place where the previous caravan had been ambushed. I had told the leader of the caravan, Ismail, of the danger and he had been philosophical about the deaths. If the earlier caravan had not reached Mut then he would gain a higher price for his goods when he did reach his destination. He was a merchant.

I set sentries to keep watch. With just five of us it meant we would each have to stand a watch. All of us would lose a couple of hours of sleep but we would be safer. We rose and ate a cold breakfast. As we left we passed the graves, although only we knew where they were. The desert was claiming the bodies. Once we had passed them we were in unknown territory.

Desert War

Griff

Chapter 21

Each time I rode in the desert I learned something new. It was when we were twenty miles from Abu Minqar that I learned how the men who used the desert employed mirrors to signal. I caught the flash to the right. Cartwright said, "Sir, I just saw a flash of light from my left."

"And I saw one to the right. Sergeant Shaw, ride ahead and warn Ismail that there may be danger and the possibility of an ambush."

"Sir."

"Cartwright, guard the rear."

"Sir." He took out his Lee Enfield and loaded a magazine. He looped the strap around his pommel.

I had my rifle ready too. I knew my two pistols were loaded. My men were vigilant and the merchants were prepared. The problem we had was that we had no idea where or when the attack would come. It could come on the caravan trail or they could be waiting at the oasis, knowing that we were heading for it. Their unknown was that they had no idea there were five soldiers with the caravan. From a distance, with our keffiyeh and cloaks, we could be more merchants. The mirrors had merely warned us of danger and not its location

The signalling mirrors had done one other thing. They had made us all more alert. The attack, when it came, could have caught us out for the raiders had disguised themselves amongst the rocks that lay close to the caravan trail. They rose on both sides of us and, screaming war cries, hurled their animals at us. Had this been an unprotected caravan then the attack would have succeeded for they were close to the trail. The men leading the camels would not be able to defend themselves.

I shouted, "Open fire!"

This was the first time we had used our rifles from the backs of camels in battle. We had practised and I knew that Scheherazade would not be spooked but we were moving and that made aiming more of a lottery. I fired five bullets at the nearest rider. I thought I had missed him completely until he clutched his arm. It encouraged me. I fired the rest of the bullets and then changed the magazine. The attackers were firing as were my men; the difference was in the sounds and the smoke. There was less smoke from our more modern weapons but the ancient rifles boomed like cannons. The speed of their attack was astonishing and they rapidly closed the ground with us. One saddle had been emptied but there were still more than a dozen mounted men. I emptied my magazine. Sergeant Instructor Snoxall had called it a mad minute. My rifle sent a hail of bullets at the warriors racing at me. One fell from his saddle. I looped the rifle strap around my pommel and drew my pistol. At the closer range, it was an easier weapon to use and slightly more accurate. I aimed and squeezed just as Sergeant Instructor Snoxall had taught us. My pistol was aimed at the next warrior's chest and the bullet plucked him from his saddle. My men were having success too and before the warriors could close with the merchants and the camels we had halved the odds. The confused movement was such that I could not be certain how many men were attacking us. Atkinson and I were firing at the wave of men attacking from the right. Both Flynn and Cartwright were vulnerable at the head and rear of the caravan.

My camel had taken me close to the head of the caravan and three riders urged their camels to close with the merchant leading it. Flynn was doing his best but he had men riding at him from two different directions. It was then that they fired their guns and the merchant was hit and I saw him clutch his arm. The reins of the camel he was leading dropped. A bullet whizzed over my head. I had five bullets left and I fired all of them at the three riders. I hit one and the other two, realising, as I dropped my pistol, that I was defenceless came at me. I drew my father's Webley and sent all six bullets at the two men. Their looks of joy were wiped from their faces as my bullets ended their lives. The deaths of the three men effectively ended the attack and the survivors raced off.

"Hold fast! Sound off." I needed to know if any of my men had been hit.

"Here sir!" Sergeant Shaw had survived.

"Here sir!" Charlie waved as he shouted. He had a grin on his face.

"Here sir!" Cartwright's shaky voice came from behind me.

"Here sir!" Trooper Flynn sounded amazed that he was still alive.

"Here sir but only just!" Trooper Hunter held out his left arm to show where the bullet had made a hole in his cloak.

"Sergeant Shaw, see to the wounded. I think Ismail is hurt. Corporal Atkinson, take Hunter and Flynn and retrieve any weapons. Cartwright, reload and you and I will stand guard until we are ready to move."

A chorus of 'yes sirs' followed my commands. As my shaking hands tried to reload my three guns I reflected that I had endured my first test of leadership not to mention combat and I had survived. It had all happened in a blur. I had not had time to think. Nothing I had learned at Sandhurst had prepared me for the speed of the action. I had just reacted as had my men. I was pleased that none had suffered a wound and I knew that we had been lucky or, perhaps, it was a sign that our training had paid off. I hoped that the merchant was not seriously hurt. Even as the thought entered my head, I realised that without our presence all four men would be dead and their families impoverished. By the time I had reloaded Corporal Atkinson and the two troopers had brought a collection of ancient rifles, swords and daggers from the dead men.

"We will take them back to the fort."

Charlie shook his head, "They are old, sir, and fairly useless."

"Yes, but if we leave them here then they can be reused. Ismail's wound shows us that they are not as useless as you might think, Corporal. We deny them the ability to attack and that protects other travellers. We can destroy them at the fort if we need to."

Trooper Flynn said, "The swords would be nice souvenirs to take home, sir."

I smiled, "Something to show the children, eh?"

"Not married yet, sir. I wanted to see a bit of the world first but, it would be nice to have one hanging over the fireplace and tell my children how we were attacked in the desert."

Sergeant Shaw rode up, "Ismail is a tough old bird, sir. The bullet went through and missed the bone but it must have hurt. I have put his arm in a sling. Hunter, you lead his camel."

"Right, Sergeant."

"Move off, Sergeant. I would like to make the oasis before dark."

Abu Minqar had no fort but there were people who lived in the huddle of mud huts. It was a bigger oasis than Farafra and the recent storm had made it even greener. There were flocks of goats and, by the standards of the desert was almost a busy place. Ismail was known and he was welcomed into a house along with his men. I daresay that we would have been given a roof had we asked but I was quite happy to stay by the water. We would need to stand watch. Just because we had beaten off the attack did not mean that we were safe.

We lit a fire and put on some water to boil. When it had boiled, we made a dixie of tea and then added some dried beans and chunks of corned beef to the remaining water, along with salt and pepper to make a stew. A youth came over with a handful of freshly made flatbreads,

"Effendi, these are from my mother. She thanks you for protecting our cousin."

"Tell her thank you."

The warm bread would mop up the juices from the stew. As we ate the filling meal we spoke about the attack. "They weren't Ottomans, sir."

I nodded, "You are right, Sergeant Shaw. Regular troops would have better weapons. I think these were the same bandits who attacked the other caravan. The question is, where is their base?"

Cartwright shook his head, "This is the largest place we have seen, sir. I fail to see where they could be hiding."

Charlie lit a cigarette, the smell would deter flies, "The thing is, Paul, that they might not live out here. They could be from the west and have homes across the border. To them this might be just a business. They spend a few months plundering the caravans and take their ill-gotten gains to sell them. With the money they make they might not need to raid again for a while. It sounds like a relatively easy life. Without us those four men

Desert War

would be dead and the bandits would not have lost a man. The eight camels are valuable and the cargo would mean they could spend half a year doing nothing."

"Then will we have to escort every caravan that heads south, sir?"

I shrugged, "Perhaps, Flynn. If the corporal is right and I can see no flaws in his arguments, then if we were to keep men with the caravans for a while it would mean they might have to find somewhere else to raid. Captain Dunn told me that we are the first unit of this type. Siwa has Egyptian Camel Corps but this empty wilderness has had no protection. The Suez Canal is vital to the Empire. We won't be the last men who are sent here. We have six months to prove our worth and then we get to go home for a leave."

It was as though a penny had just dropped, "There must be men being trained to relieve us then, sir."

"Probably."

We each stood a watch but we had a quiet night. The next morning, we rose. Ismail, looking pained, came to see us off and to thank us. If nothing else we had made real friends of the merchant, his men and the people of Abu Minqar. I hoped that Captain Dunn would be pleased with our efforts.

When we passed the scene of the ambush we saw that the scavengers of the desert, the animals and birds, had already begun the process of devouring the corpses. Within a few weeks all that would be left would be the remains of bones buried beneath the shifting sands. Our defence had meant that the bandits had not died on the trail itself. We, the bandits who had survived and the men of the caravan, would be the only ones who knew where the attack had taken place. It was a sobering thought. My own end could be in just such a desolate place.

We camped in the same place we had on the way south. Without a slow-moving caravan, we made the fort well before noon and the welcoming sight of the flag flying from the tower made us all smile. It might be a little outpost in the middle of the desert but it was our home.

Captain Dunn was in the fort to welcome us. "Welcome back, Lieutenant Roberts. The sergeant major has the rest of the men heading for the dig. It has been lonely here. Come into the office and make your report."

I took off the keffiyeh and cloak. Shaking the dust from them I entered the welcoming cool of the office. Trooper Burton brought in tea and I drank deeply before I began. By the time I had finished the mug of tea was empty and Captain Dunn had transcribed my words. "At the end of the month, we shall have to send a report back to Cairo. We were sent here to deter raids from across the border. I don't think that Colonel Dickenson realised the scale of the problem. If we are to keep on top of the bandits we need more men. With your men and those with the sergeant major absent from the fort, I was left with just four men. That is not enough."

"Sir, when you send the report back to Cairo, won't that take away men from the fort?"

He nodded, "There is a new telegraph office being built at Faiyum but you are right that is still a round trip of almost five hundred miles. It is not to be undertaken lightly."

The next couple of weeks began to follow the same pattern. Every three days a long patrol would head to the dig. If a caravan came through Farafra to head south it would be escorted. There were two such caravans. There were also caravans that came to head to Faiyum. They were not escorted for the simple reason that we did not have the manpower. Captain Dunn and I added to the long report that we would send to Cairo. We were limited in what we could say in a telegram.

We learned to appreciate little things. When our clothes were washed and dried, a weekly event, it was a pleasure to put on a uniform that did not stink and was not covered in dust. When we went to practice with our rifles we occasionally managed to bring down the odd bird or two and when that was added to a stew, even though it was a small addition, the pleasure of a new taste was exciting. When we were not on long patrols Captain Dunn and I would play chess. Some of the men played dominoes while Cartwright, Burton, Higgins and Sergeant Shaw enjoyed a game of whist. They were simple pleasures but they enlivened our evenings.

It was the captain who escorted the four new archaeologists to the dig. They had with them fresh supplies for their camp. The

Desert War

water they had found at the oasis meant that they did not need to return to our fort to resupply. I felt better when the captain returned and told us that they were making progress and had found, beneath the sand, some quarried stone. Those who lived in the desert tended to use mud. Quarried stone suggested an important building. The party had not been bothered by anyone and the only people they had seen, apart from us, were the occasional merchants and their caravans.

My patrol was the only one that had caused us to use our guns in anger but that single action had shown us the drawbacks of our camels and our weapons. We practised not just shooting from a prone position but also from the back of a camel. It was not so bad when we were stationary but if we tried it when moving then it was impossible to have any sort of accuracy. Captain Dunn and I decided that if we were attacked then the order would be given to halt and fire while we were motionless. We husbanded our ammunition as we did not know when we would be getting more supplies. The Egyptian garrison said that the caravan bringing fresh supplies arrived every two months.

When the first caravan with supplies arrived it felt like Christmas. They had travelled from Faiyum and so there was nothing fresh with them but they had dried fruit as well as more flour, the inevitable bully beef and dried beans not to mention more ammunition. There were even some two month old newspapers. To the rest of the world, it might be old news but to us it would be a source of information, not to mention entertainment. Captain Dunn gave the merchant who had brought the supplies the sealed report to deliver to the officer in command of Faiyum. It would be sent by train to Cairo. Captain Dunn was sceptical about the effect the report would have in Cairo.

"The men there are pencil pushers. They will simply look at the report and see that we have lost no men. That will be a box to be ticked. Eventually, it might be sent to Alexandria and thence to London. When Lord Kitchener was the Sirdar he would have read the report and acted upon it. He is now in South Africa. We, Griff, are a forgotten outpost. Perhaps when Colonel Dickenson reads the report, he may act upon it but by then it will be about time for us to be relieved."

Desert War

It was a chastening thought. I wanted to go home. I wanted to see my family. I now understood what my father had endured in his time in Africa. It was a long way from home and while we were happy to serve Great Britain and the Empire, a taste of home was little to ask. As the caravan and the report left I realised that we would have no mail. Even though I knew my father and Aunt Sarah would have written to me any letters they sent might miss me if we were relieved on time. The outpost suddenly felt like a prison and I was not even halfway through my sentence.

Once the euphoria of fresh supplies had evaporated the mood in the fort became more depressive. Cartwright suffered more than most. One evening, after we had eaten, I found him in his room with his head in his hands. At first, I feared that he was ill. We had no doctor. Sergeant Shaw was the nearest we had to a first aider and he could treat wounds but illnesses were something we dreaded.

"Is everything alright, Paul? Are you ill?"

He shook his head, "No, sir...I am sorry, sir but this is not what I expected. What am I doing here? I was brought up to be a gentleman's gentleman. You are a gentleman, sir, and a fine officer but my talents are wasted here."

I sat on the bed next to him, "The trouble is, Paul, that you made a decision back in England. None of us could have known what this would be like. Even Sergeant Shaw, who served in Sudan, is finding it hard. I am afraid that you have to serve out your time. If you like I can recommend that you be transferred back to England. Even then you would have to serve your six months out here. Would you like me to speak to the captain about the possibility?"

He shook his head, "I don't want to fail, sir. Will you come back after your six months?"

"I will. I intend to make a career out of the army. I know I am lucky and that I am an officer but it is in my blood. You are different. You were trained to be something different. Just do your best, eh, Paul. You know you can always talk to me."

"Will this conversation be on my record, sir?"

Desert War

"Of course not. It is just two comrades having a chat about life out here. None of us finds it easy, Paul. I think others are suffering just as you are."

"Thank you, sir. I will try my best, I swear."

As I returned to my own room I realised that nothing I had experienced at Sandhurst had prepared me for this. I was learning to be an officer out here in this desert outpost. My conversation with Cartwright gave me another job. I needed to get to know the rest of the troop. There might be others feeling as low as my batman.

Griff

Chapter 22

We had a peaceful month. I was kept busy trying to get to know the men I led. Some were happy to be the subject of my questions, others let me know that they wished to be private. I honoured that request. It was my third patrol to the dig and, as we had not been asked to escort caravans for a while Captain Dunn gave me a larger number of men. It would constitute more than half of the troop. I had Sergeant Shaw and Corporal Atkinson as well as Bugler Wilson. The bugler had been promoted to Lance Corporal and that meant I had the luxury of three non-commissioned officers. Even more important was that I now felt comfortable in the desert. That is, I was as comfortable as anyone can be when the temperature was over fifty degrees and sand blew into every orifice. I think I was comfortable in terms of knowing what I had to do. The attack by the bandits had given me confidence. To give Cartwright more confidence I had taken to riding with him next to me rather than a sergeant or a corporal. He had formed a good friendship with Burton but as I rarely went on patrol with Captain Dunn the two batmen did not get to ride together. Cartwright was lonely.

When I had been to the dig the last time we had stayed overnight and I had got to chat to the professor and his people. Lucinda was a bright young woman and she enthused about what they had found. I found myself fascinated and I had told her that she could be a teacher such was her eloquence. She had not liked the suggestion. It was as though I had implied that she was better suited to a more mundane occupation. That had not been my intention. I had been complimenting her. It showed me that I had few skills when it came to talking to women apart from those in my family. I resolved to keep my mouth shut in future.

As we rode towards the dig, I was trying to formulate the words that would explain what I had meant. We camped at the usual place. It was Charlie, who had an eye for such things, that spotted the anomaly. "Sir, something odd here."

Desert War

I walked over to where he stood. He had been making water. "Yes, Corporal, what is it?"

"Someone took a dump here."

I laughed, "So? We all need to obey a call of nature."

"Sir, everyone who uses this oasis either passes through our fort on the way here or on the way back. That is fresh. It is less than twenty-four hours old. You know how quickly everything dries out here. The last caravan that arrived from Siwa was a week ago and none has gone north since the captain took the new fellows to the dig. Someone has been here and they did not come through the fort."

He was right. That was suspicious. "Everyone, search the oasis and look for signs of whoever was here last."

Once we knew what we were looking for it became more obvious. There were cigarette butts and that was not unusual but these were the Turkish cigarettes favoured by the Ottoman army. There were the signs of boots and not the kind worn by merchants. The most telling piece of evidence was the spent bullet casing. It was not a British casing. It was 7.92mm and it smelled fresh. Someone had fired a bullet in the last day. I gathered my NCOs around me.

"I think, and I am happy for you to correct me, that soldiers have been through here." No one disagreed. "That leaves us with two possibilities. Either they are on their way to the fort to cause mischief or they intend to attack someone along the caravan route. This is not Tripolitania and Cyrenaica. This is Egypt and they have no right to be here."

Stan stubbed out his cigarette, "So, sir, what do we do?"

Their faces all told me that this was an officer's decision. "We have to warn the fort but we also have a duty to the people who use this caravan trail. I will send Hunter and Flynn back to the fort, first thing in the morning. We will push on to the dig and warn them."

Stan said, "Hunter and Flynn, sir?"

"They are reliable chaps and get on well together. I can ill afford to send any of you. If there is trouble then I will need all the help I can get."

Charlie nodded, "He is right, Sergeant. I will have a word with them and give them some tips."

Desert War

We rose early and Flynn and Hunter set off at the same time as we did. They would reach the fort about the same time that we reached the dig. We were alert and vigilant as we rode. Sergeant Shaw put two men out on the flanks and ahead of us as scouts. We were on a war footing and it was better to be prepared than ride blindly into what might be an ambush. The mischief that these soldiers might wish to make could be the ambush of a British patrol.

Sound travels a long way in the desert. However, it can also be deceptive. The direction could be misleading. This time, however, when we heard the sound of gunfire, we knew whence it emanated. It was from the dig, just two miles ahead. There was no time to delay. I drew my gun. "As fast as we can, eh boys?"

My camel was the best in the troop. I had been more than lucky in her selection. She opened her legs and was soon eating up the ground and I had caught up with the two scouts in a matter of yards. The gunfire became more rapid. I heard the boom of shotguns and I heard cries. I was the first to crest the rise and I saw that there were men surrounding the dig. I also saw bodies. The defenders looked to have made a sort of improvised fort from stones and boxes.

I shouted, "Wilson, sound the charge!"

I gave the order for two reasons. Firstly, to give hope to the defenders and secondly to frighten off the attackers. We could always pursue them. I just had to stop their attack. I recognised the guns that the Turkish irregulars were using. It was the Lee Metford. It was an accurate weapon but being single shot was not a match for our Lee Enfields. The problem was that they were firing from a prone position and we were on our camels. I left the rifle looped around my pommel and drew my pistol. I urged my camel on. I knew that the Turkish soldiers would not find it easy to hit us as a camel's movement made it hard to make an accurate shot. You were more likely to hit the camel than the rider. The bullets zipped over my head and one plucked at my cloak. I opened fire when I was just forty yards from the first Turk. I heard the distinctive sound of the Lee Enfields behind me and knew that my men were firing. They might not hit anything but they would serve to make the Turks take cover. The Turkish soldier who aimed at me was close enough to guarantee a hit and I leaned to the right and sighted the gun. I squeezed the trigger of my pistol a heartbeat before he did and my bullet spun him around. The dig was surrounded but by hitting one man I had created a gap into the area defended by the archaeologists. A Turkish soldier rose from my right and I fired almost instinctively and my bullet made his face disappear. It was as the fusillade of fire increased that I realised the size of the problem. My patrol would not be enough to see off these soldiers.

I had never jumped with a camel and I would not have chosen to do so that day had not my camel been going so fast as to mean she either jumped the barrier or crashed into it. I landed and barely kept my seat. I managed to stop her and I made her sit. I dismounted and chambered a round into the rifle. I used the saddle to keep the weapon steady. My men had not been travelling as fast and they were able to step over the stone and box barrier. I saw that one of our camels was riderless. It looked to be Trooper Davis'.

"Sergeant, form a skirmish line on both sides of the dig. I will command this side." I raised my rifle and fired at the Turk who had risen from the sand and was wielding a long sword to hack at the legs of the tardy Trooper Peters, the last of my men to reach the dig. My bullet threw the Turk to the ground. I emptied my magazine in a mad minute, spraying the places the Turks were taking cover.

"Corporal, take charge on this side. We have killed some of them here but the other side of the dig is exposed."

"Right, sir, you three go with the lieutenant and reinforce Sergeant Shaw."

It was as I crossed the camp I saw Lucinda Cowley cradling her father's head. His eyes were open but he was dead. I said, "We are here now, Miss. You keep your head down, eh?" The bodies of the other new archaeologists were scattered around as though flung like rag dolls. Their bloodied bodies showed that they had each been hit more than once.

She nodded, dumbly as though she had no idea what was going on.

I reached the other side and saw that John Bannerman-Carlisle was wounded. Sergeant Shaw was putting a tourniquet around his leg. Some of the diggers had picked up the shotguns and pistols. They were not soldiers and, at best, their gunfire was annoying to the attackers. It was my men who would have to win the day.

"Thank God, you got here. They came at dawn..." he winced.

"Tell me later. You are in good hands." I raised my voice, "Right men on my command I want to make the other side of the oasis very unhealthy. Give them a mad minute."

They roared, "Yes, sir!"

I had a full magazine and I shouted, "Fire!"

With the men brought by Shaw and the three I had brought, we had eight rifles and they spat eighty bullets out. I heard cries and shouts and then the command, "Fall back!"

"Reload! Again!"

I knew that once they rose to get to their camels they would be vulnerable. I wanted to hit as many as I could. It was not out of vengeance but it was a practical decision. They would be more likely to leave if they had bled and would be reluctant to return. We fired into the smoke and the greenery of the oasis and were rewarded by the cries of men who had been hit. I saw the camels racing away and shouted, "Cease fire!"

As I reloaded my pistol I turned to Sergeant Shaw and said, "Take charge here."

"Sir!"

"Corporal."

"Sir."

"I want you and eight men to mount. Choose the best mounted. Let us chase these men as far as we can."

"Is that wise, sir?"

I smiled, "Yes, Sergeant Shaw. In my opinion, it is."

The men we were pursuing outnumbered us, hence the sergeant's warning but they would not know there were just ten of us. We had superior firepower and, I hoped confidence. The ones we had routed clearly did not.

We began to gain on them and I drew my pistol. I fired at the man at the rear of the fleeing men and I saw his arms spread as he was hit. I knew that the wound was not a killing one for when he hit the ground he was able to try to rise. His camel followed

Desert War

the others. My men risked the odd shot with their rifles and another rider fell. It was a lucky shot.

The man leading them must have realised how few we were for I saw the Turks stop at some rocks and dismount. They intended to fight. I spied a wadi just two hundred yards from their position. "Corporal, the wadi!"

"Sir."

We headed for the depression as the first bullets came in our direction. The most dangerous moments were as we slowed to descend into the wadi and it was there that Bates was struck by a bullet.

"Use your guns wisely. Our weapons are better than theirs."

"You heard the officer, now spread out."

I knelt next to Trooper Bates, "Where were you hit?" He pointed to his leg. The bullet had nicked it as he had begun to dismount.

"It's a nick, sir, I can still fight."

I took my puggaree and made a rough tourniquet above the wound. "Release it every fifteen minutes and then tighten it."

"I haven't got a watch, sir."

I smiled, "Then I shall tell you the time."

Bullets were flying in both directions as I took my place on the wadi. The Turks were hidden in the rocks and we were protected by the wadi. This would be a test of our skills as well as our weapons. I sighted the rifle and looked for a target. The enemy soldiers were well within my range. I knew, from Sandhurst, that I was a good shot. Sergeant Instructor Snoxall had called me a natural. I saw the Turkish soldier lift his head as he aimed his rifle and I fired two bullets in his direction. One must have hit him for he fell from the rocks. I saw another movement to the left of the dead man and I fired three bullets in quick succession. If nothing else our rate of fire was keeping down their heads. The advantage of our guns was that we could send two or three bullets to their one and we began to wear them down. Thanks to the supplies we had received we had plenty of ammunition. Another two Turks were hit and their rate of fire slowed and then stopped.

We heard the sound of camels and Corporal Atkinson said, "Sir, they have scarpered."

"Dixon, stay with Bates. By the way, Bates, fifteen minutes."
He grinned, "Right sir."
We crossed the open ground in skirmish order. When we reached the rocks we saw the survivors in the distance. We had killed five of them in total. I pointed to the bodies. "We had better cover them with rocks. They had been soldiers."

The rock-covered graves would be the only memorial to these men.

When they were crudely buried we headed back to the dig. We passed one of the men who had been shot in the early pursuit. He was dead and we buried him. When we reached the man I had hit with my pistol, he was still alive although his life would be measured in minutes and not hours. The pooled blood told me that. Had we reached him earlier we might have saved him. I held my water bottle to his lips.

"Soldier, what was the purpose of your attack?"

He gave a sad smile when I spoke Arabic and closed his eyes. I wondered if he was slipping away. He opened them and said, "Captain Mustapha was ordered to rid the desert of foreigners. We thought it would be easy."

"And where is your fort?"

"Al Jagbub, it is..."

He was dead and we buried him. By the time we reached the dig, it was too late to leave for the fort. I saw the line of neat graves and saw that Sergeant Shaw had organised food. Trooper Davis would not be going home. Lucinda Cowley was the nurse who was tending to the surviving archaeologist, Bannerman-Carlisle. I knelt, "How are you, sir?"

"Alive which is more than can be said for the others." He smiled at Lucinda. "And now I have the responsibility of you, eh, my dear?"

"You need not worry about me. I can look after myself."

"I am not sure that you can but your father was my friend and I shall return to England with you."

"But the dig!"

He sighed, "This is not the tomb of Alexander. All that we have found is evidence of a small Roman fort. There are hundreds of them in the desert. Your father and I knew that. At the end of the season, we would have packed up the dig and

Desert War

returned to England. I will write up what we have discovered and see if it can be published. I fear that my days as one who digs into the past are over. I shall seek a place where I can teach others."

She nodded. I stood and she did too, "I would like to thank you, Lieutenant, for coming to our aid. You came when the odds were against you and you tried to chase down the soldiers. Your sergeant thought it was foolish, I think it was gallant." She pecked me on the cheek. "I am grateful."

That night my thoughts and dreams were not of the skirmish but of Lucinda. My fantasies were not those of a warrior but one who hopes for another touch of a soft hand or the brush of lips on rough skin.

We rigged a litter between two camels as we headed back to the fort. Sergeant Shaw rode one camel and Lucinda the other. She rode a camel well. I ensured that the seven survivors of the attack, the five diggers, Bannerman-Carlisle and Lucinda, were well protected. We rode with rifles at the ready and we were vigilant. Captain Dunn and the rest of the troop met us when we were close to the oasis that we had used on our way north. That night we all camped together and I told him what had happened.

"Then we will have to seek permission to cross the border. Al Jagbub is not far from Siwa."

"That might escalate this conflict, sir."

"And that is why, Lieutenant, you will wait at Faiyum for a reply from England. We need more men and we need clearer orders. I want you to escort these survivors to Faiyum." He smiled, "You have shown that you are a brave soldier so let me take some of the risks that you have endured. I do not wish to have to send a letter back to England with bad news. You have ridden your luck enough. A couple of weeks away from this is what you need."

He would not be dissuaded. We had one night at the fort and then I left with an escort of six men. John Bannerman-Carlisle was fit enough to be able to ride and that made life easier.

I found myself next to Lucinda and we talked. She told me of her father and why she had chosen to come on the dig and I told her of my father and my time at Sandhurst.

"You are lucky, you had choices. For an educated woman, I have few. My teachers tried to steer me into becoming an educator or a librarian. Those careers are not for me."

"And what will you do now?"

"Uncle John is the only family I have left. My mother and father were only children and John is a confirmed bachelor. He has said that I can live with him. He has a home in the north, a village in Westmoreland, Grasmere. He says it is beautiful."

I nodded, "I know of it, and it is. It is a contrast to this land. As I recall it is green and verdant. Will you be happy there?"

She sighed, "As happy as I would be anywhere. But you, what about you?"

"What do you mean?"

"Is this your future? Will you spend your days here, drying out to become as desiccated as the land? Do you not wish for a family?"

I shrugged, "I have barely begun my life as a soldier and I am young. I will not spend my whole life in the desert."

"Are you granted leave?"

I nodded, "At the end of six months I get to spend a month in England."

"And then return here."

"And return here."

"I know that you will wish to visit your family but I would like to see you there too. Would you call on me at Grasmere?"

I found myself grinning like a child who had just been given the best present ever, "Of course, I would."

Her smile seemed, to me, to be just as wide. Out of tragedy came hope and I found myself hoping that the journey to Faiyum would take forever.

Desert War

Jack

Epilogue

I had written to Griff but I did not expect a letter in reply. When one came it was an unexpected pleasure and I savoured the reading of it.

May, Faiyum
Dear Father,
I am taking advantage of a sad turn of events to send a letter to you. While in the desert we had to rescue some archaeologists. This letter is being posted in England by one of the survivors, a delightful young lady called Lucinda. Her father was killed in an attack and when they return to England, will live at Grasmere. I have promised that when I am granted leave I will visit with her. She is a bright and witty young lady and I admire her spirit.
I am serving with some of your old comrades...

I read the long letter twice. I read between the lines about the various actions in which he had fought and I was proud of him. That he had lost men would change him. Bet and Sarah came in and I showed them the letter.

Bet's face lit up as she handed it to Aunt Sarah, "Well, it seems that Griff has lost his heart."

"What? I did not read that. The bulk of the letter is about the desert."

"That is for you, Jack. He begins with that which is closest to his heart, the young lady. This is a good thing, Jack."

I took the letter and read it again. Perhaps Bet was right. I thought back to my meeting with Annie, Griff's mother. That had been unexpected and had things turned out differently I might have enjoyed a life with her. Would Griff be able to enjoy a normal life? Had his decision to become a soldier been a wise one?

Sarah said, "And when he does return you can show him that it is possible to have a life outside the army."

"What?"

She held up the book which had been sent from the publisher two weeks earlier, "You are now a published author. He will be pleased."

I wondered for I knew the bonds that tied soldiers together. While Bet had read of romance in the letter I had read of courage under fire. I went to the calendar. If all went well and they were relieved, he might be home by August. That was just under two months away. I had sent away a boy but when he came back, it would be a man who walked through the door.

The End

Glossary

Bevvy - a drink (slang)
Butty (pl butties) - 19th-century slang for close friends
en banderole - worn diagonally across the body
Cataracts - rapids and rocks that impede the passage of boats
Dhobi (n) - washing (from the Indian) dhobying (v)
Fellah - an Egyptian soldier, the equivalent of a private in a British regiment
Half a crown - two shillings and sixpence (20 shillings to the pound, 12 pennies to a shilling)
Laager - an improvised fort made of wagons
Jibbah - short white blouse worn by the Mahdists
Lunger - nickname for the sword bayonet
Nabob - someone from India who has made a fortune
Peaching - informing
Puggaree - a cloth tied around a helmet
Souk - market

Desert War

Historical Background

This book is about life as soldiers, ordinary soldiers. The soldiers of the Queen did not care who they were fighting they just knew they were fighting for their Queen and country. That idea may seem a little old-fashioned now, but I am not rewriting history, I am trying to show what it might have been like to live in 19th Century Britain. The British Army saluted with their left hand until the First World War. The weapons used are, according to my research (see book list) the ones used in the period.

Anyone who has researched their family history in the nineteenth century and looked at the census records will know how even relatively well-off factory workers rented or boarded. Four and five to a bed was the norm. We take so much for granted today but even in the 1950s life was hard and had a pattern. With coal fires, no bathroom, an outside toilet, no carpets and little money for food it was closer to life in the 1870s. Offal was often on the menu and you ate what was there. Nothing was wasted. Drinking beer and smoking were not considered unhealthy pastimes. There was a teetotal movement but it was only in the latter part of the nineteenth century that the water the people drank became healthy. Until then it was small beer that was drunk.

This series will continue but unlike my British Ace Series and my WW2 one, I will not be working my way through wars. I intend to look at how British soldiers served this country and how their lives changed as Britain changed.

One reason why the attempt to relieve Khartoum failed, apart from the usual vacillations of the politicians, was that the main army travelled by boats which had to be unloaded and carried over the cataracts and the smaller, allegedly faster relief force led by General Stewart, marched in square and took ten days to cover one hundred miles.

The British NCOs who were recruited to retrain the Egyptian army were the Sergeant Whatsisnames made famous by Kipling. They did a good job. Every officer who volunteered was given the rank of major so that no Egyptian officer could give them orders.

Desert War

Berber was, indeed, without defenders. It was an irregular troop that discovered that fact. I have allowed Jack and his men to gain the glory.

George Reynolds was real and he was the one who discovered oil in Persia. He did not receive the credit he should have. He said about his time there, *"smallpox raged, bandits and warlords ruled, water was all but unavailable, and temperatures often soared past 50°C."*

The use of the border patrols is factual but I have made up the incidents. There were bandits who came from what is now Libya as well as regular and irregular Ottoman soldiers. The British presence was resented. Further south the French had similar problems. The two nations had built the canal and would do all that they could to keep it safe.

Books used in the research:

- The Oxford Illustrated History of the British Army- David Chandler
- The Thin Red Line- Fosten and Fosten
- The Zulu War- Angus McBride
- Rorke's Drift- Michael Glover
- British Forces in Zululand 1879- Knight and Scollins
- The Sudan Campaign 1881-1898 -Wilkinson-Lathom
- Onwards to Desert War- Keith Surridge
- Desert War- Donal Featherstone

Griff Hosker
March 2024

Desert War

Other books by Griff Hosker

If you enjoyed reading this book, then why not read another one by the author?

Ancient History

The Sword of Cartimandua Series
(Germania and Britannia 50 A.D. – 128 A.D.)
Ulpius Felix- Roman Warrior (prequel)
The Sword of Cartimandua
The Horse Warriors
Invasion Caledonia
Roman Retreat
Revolt of the Red Witch
Druid's Gold
Trajan's Hunters
The Last Frontier
Hero of Rome
Roman Hawk
Roman Treachery
Roman Wall
Roman Courage

The Wolf Warrior series
(Britain in the late 6th Century)
Saxon Dawn
Saxon Revenge
Saxon England
Saxon Blood
Saxon Slayer
Saxon Slaughter
Saxon Bane
Saxon Fall: Rise of the Warlord
Saxon Throne

Desert War

Saxon Sword

Medieval History

The Dragon Heart Series
Viking Slave *
Viking Warrior *
Viking Jarl *
Viking Kingdom *
Viking Wolf *
Viking War
Viking Sword
Viking Wrath
Viking Raid
Viking Legend
Viking Vengeance
Viking Dragon
Viking Treasure
Viking Enemy
Viking Witch
Viking Blood
Viking Weregeld
Viking Storm
Viking Warband
Viking Shadow
Viking Legacy
Viking Clan
Viking Bravery

The Norman Genesis Series
Hrolf the Viking *
Horseman *
The Battle for a Home *
Revenge of the Franks *
The Land of the Northmen
Ragnvald Hrolfsson

Desert War

Brothers in Blood
Lord of Rouen
Drekar in the Seine
Duke of Normandy
The Duke and the King

Danelaw
(England and Denmark in the 11th Century)
Dragon Sword *
Oathsword *
Bloodsword *
Danish Sword
The Sword of Cnut

New World Series
Blood on the Blade *
Across the Seas *
The Savage Wilderness *
The Bear and the Wolf *
Erik The Navigator *
Erik's Clan *
The Last Viking

The Vengeance Trail *

The Conquest Series
(Normandy and England 1050-1100)
Hastings
Conquest

The Aelfraed Series
(Britain and Byzantium 1050 A.D. - 1085 A.D.)
Housecarl *
Outlaw *
Varangian *

Desert War

The Reconquista Chronicles
Castilian Knight *
El Campeador *
The Lord of Valencia *

The Anarchy Series England 1120-1180
English Knight *
Knight of the Empress *
Northern Knight *
Baron of the North *
Earl *
King Henry's Champion *
The King is Dead *
Warlord of the North
Enemy at the Gate
The Fallen Crown
Warlord's War
Kingmaker
Henry II
Crusader
The Welsh Marches
Irish War
Poisonous Plots
The Princes' Revolt
Earl Marshal
The Perfect Knight

Border Knight 1182-1300
Sword for Hire *
Return of the Knight *
Baron's War *
Magna Carta *
Welsh Wars *
Henry III *

Desert War

The Bloody Border *
Baron's Crusade*
Sentinel of the North
War in the West*
Debt of Honour*
The Blood of the Warlord
The Fettered King
de Montfort's Crown
Ripples of Rebellion

Sir John Hawkwood Series
France and Italy 1339- 1387
Crécy: The Age of the Archer *
Man At Arms *
The White Company *
Leader of Men *
Tuscan Warlord *
Condottiere*

Lord Edward's Archer
Lord Edward's Archer *
King in Waiting *
An Archer's Crusade *
Targets of Treachery *
The Great Cause *
Wallace's War *
The Hunt

Struggle for a Crown
1360- 1485
Blood on the Crown *
To Murder a King *
The Throne *
King Henry IV *
The Road to Agincourt *
St Crispin's Day *

Desert War

The Battle for France *
The Last Knight *
Queen's Knight *
The Knight's Tale

Tales from the Sword I
(Short stories from the Medieval period)

Tudor Warrior series
England and Scotland in the late 15th and early 16th century
Tudor Warrior *
Tudor Spy *
Flodden*

Conquistador
England and America in the 16th Century
Conquistador *
The English Adventurer *

English Mercenary
The 30 Years War and the English Civil War
Horse and Pistol

Modern History

The Napoleonic Horseman Series
Chasseur à Cheval
Napoleon's Guard
British Light Dragoon
Soldier Spy
1808: The Road to Coruña
Talavera
The Lines of Torres Vedras
Bloody Badajoz
The Road to France

Desert War

Waterloo

The Lucky Jack American Civil War series
Rebel Raiders
Confederate Rangers
The Road to Gettysburg

Soldier of the Queen series
Soldier of the Queen*
Redcoat's Rifle*
Omdurman*
Desert War

The British Ace Series
1914
1915 Fokker Scourge
1916 Angels over the Somme
1917 Eagles Fall
1918 We will remember them
From Arctic Snow to Desert Sand
Wings over Persia

Combined Operations series
1940-1945
Commando *
Raider *
Behind Enemy Lines
Dieppe
Toehold in Europe
Sword Beach
Breakout
The Battle for Antwerp
King Tiger
Beyond the Rhine
Korea
Korean Winter

Tales from the Sword II
(Short stories from the Modern period)

Books marked thus *, are also available in the audio format.
For more information on all of the books then please visit the author's website at www.griffhosker.com where there is a link to contact him or visit his Facebook page: GriffHosker at Sword Books or follow him on Twitter: @HoskerGriff or Sword (@swordbooksltd)
If you wish to be on the mailing list then contact the author through his website.

Printed in Great Britain
by Amazon